The Mystery of Engli

英文文法
的奧秘

用聽的 探索世界*48*大神秘事件
同步學英文文法，用聽的學文法更有效！

3大篇章
基礎句型結構、字詞與常見文法錯誤、文法應用

7大主題
自然、生物、天文、地理、歷史事件、藝術、人文

Bonus
附 Good vs. NG 版文法用法

文法一看就懂！

孟瑞秋 ◎著

MP3

　　本書共分三個部分，48個章節，各章節分別搭配文法及神秘事件主題。文法內容包含句型結構、字詞文法、常見文法錯誤，以及文法應用。神秘事件的搭配主題則為神秘自然、生物、天文、地理、歷史事件及藝術、人文。

　　地球上存在著許多無法利用科學方式來解讀未知的神祕現象以及未解之謎，令人費解的現象背後所隱藏的神秘真相觸發了人們探索其中奧秘的好奇心。本書文法編排條列分明，循序漸進，可讓讀者透過閱讀神秘事件而學習英文文法。藉由對於神秘事件的好奇心來學習，不僅提高學習文法的興趣，且增進英文句型結構、字詞文法能力、探索文法錯誤，以及建立簡單寫作應用的基礎。此外，在探索神秘事件的過程中亦能獲得許多科學知識。希望透過閱讀神秘事件學習英文文法中可獲得學習英文的充實、快樂及成就。

孟瑞秋

　　《英文文法的奧秘》收錄的神秘事件版圖遍及世界各地，種類包羅萬象；為讓讀者於展讀世界48大神秘事件的同時，又能吸收英文文法，作者特別以英文文法學習為主軸，將神秘事件精心改寫作為學習上的輔助，成就了這一本超級英文文法學習書，並為英文文法添加趣味、生動的色彩，擺脫一般對英文文法生硬、制式化的印象。現在就翻開本書，邊聽故事邊用聽的記憶文法，讓英文文法、閱讀能力的進步速度突飛猛進！

編輯部

Longknife, Ann, and K.D. Sullivan. *Easy Writing Skills Step-by-Step*. New York: McGraw-Hill Education, 2012. Print.
Dutwin, Phyllis. *Easy Grammar Step-by-Step*. New York: McGraw-Hill Education, 2014. Print.
Guerrero, Angeles Gavira, Peter Frances, and Janet Mohun, eds. *History Year by Year*. London: Dorling Kindersley Ltd, 2011. Print.
ASIOS（2015）。《古文明解密，33個真相大公開！》（王美娟譯）。台北：台灣東販。
Conklin, Steven R.（2004）。《超自然的神秘世界》（黃語忻譯）。台北：亞洲圖書。
FUTABASHA（2011）。《探索古文明》（朱園園譯）。新北：人類智庫。
Keating, James T.（2004）。《英文寫作正誤範例》。（張嘉容譯）。台北：眾文圖書。
Strunk Jr., William.（2015）。《英文寫作風格的要素》。（吳煒聲譯）。台北：所以文化。
王雷（2003）。《世界歷史未解之謎》。台中：好讀。
朱崧浩（2014）。《別嚇到，千奇百怪的動植物大集合》。新北：智學堂文化。
李清課、楊欣倫（2015）。《歷史未解之謎》。新北：人類智庫。
南山宏（2011）。《未知生物之謎》（龐雪譯）。新北：人類智庫。
張鈺閎（2014）。《千奇百怪的自然與玄奇世界》。新北：智學堂文化。
陳奇勳（2013）。《聳人聽聞的離奇巧合事件：真的是巧合嗎？》。新北：學堂文化。
陳浚德（2012）。《高中英文文法與句型全功略》。新北：建興文化。
陳賢、陳重宇（2013）。《英文文法總複習講義》。新北：康熹文化。
許寶芳、郭春安、楊毓琳、薛夙娟（2014）。《英文句型與翻譯》。高雄：晟景數位文化。
黑川裕一（2013）。《英文寫作修飾手冊》。（戴偉傑譯）。新北：眾文圖書。
楊景邁、曾淵培（2003）。《東華當代英文法—上、下冊》。台北：東華書局。
圖說天下編委會（2014）。《可怕的現象》。新北：西北國際文化。
圖說天下編委會（2015）。《世界65個懸疑詭譎神秘現象》。新北：西北國際文化。
圖說天下編委會（2015）。《世界100個神秘地帶》。新北：西北國際文化。
圖說天下編委會（2015）。《全球42起驚人懸疑案件》。新北：西北國際文化。
鄭炎活（2015）。《英文文法拆招秘笈》。新北：龍騰文化。
鄭俊琪（2015）。《句型x翻譯—英語力的關鍵》。台北：希伯崙。
劉進軍（2013）。《太空探測器》。台北：旗林文化。
賴水信（1994）。《高分托福文法》。台北：眾文圖書。
霍晨昕（2014）。《不可思議的異度空間》。新北：西北國際文化。
蘇秦（2014）。《當代英語用法指南》。台中：晨星。
https://en.wikipedia.org
https://zh.wikipedia.org/zh-tw/中文維基百科
www.livescience.com
www.epicadamwildlife.com
http://paranormal.lovetoknow.com
www.world-mysteries.com
www.webmd.com
http://mysteriousuniverse.org
www.aliens-everything-you-want-to-know.com
http://www.theplanetstoday.com
www.history.com
http://www.cracked.com
https://www.quora.com
www.historytoday.com
http://adventure.howstuffworks.com
www.ancient-origins.net
http://www.exploringlifesmysteries.com
www.travelchinaguid.com
whc.unesco.org
www.worldheritagesite.org

參考書目
及
相關網站

目 次 CONTENTS

CHAPTER
2

字詞文法

搭配主題 神秘天文、地理篇

CHAPTER 3 常見文法錯誤、文法應用

搭配主題 神秘歷史事件、藝術、人文篇

CHAPTER

1

句型結構

搭配主題▶ 神秘自然、生物篇

UNIT 1

五大句型 1

The Loch Ness Monster

尼斯湖水怪

 英文依據動詞之不同類別
可區分成五大基本句型：

I. 基本句型 1：主詞＋不及物動詞（S＋Vi＋（Adv））

  1. 這類動詞，如 run, sit, rain, live, rise, shine, stand, arrive, …等，後面不用接受詞或補語便可表達完整概念，即屬於「完全不及物動詞」。

    ♦ The birds fly.　鳥飛。

    ♦ It rained.　下過雨了。

    ♦ The little girl smiles.　小女孩微笑。

  2. 完全不及物動詞後面可用副詞或副詞片語修飾。此外，完全不及物動詞後面雖不得接受詞，但是加介系詞後，則可以接受詞。

    ♦ The dog and its master run happily.
    狗和牠的主人快樂地跑。

    ♦ The sun rises in the east.
    日出於東。

II. 基本句型 2：主詞＋不及物動詞＋主詞補語（S＋Vi＋SC）

  1. 這類動詞，如 go, get, seem, become, fall, grow, turn, stay, prove, …等，因本身語意不完整，後面必須接主詞補語以表達完整

概念，屬於「不完全不及物動詞」。Be 動詞及感官動詞如 feel, look, smell, taste, sound, …等也是這類動詞。這類動詞亦被稱為「連綴動詞」（Linking Verb）。主詞補語可以是名詞或形容詞。

♦ You look happy today.
你今天看起來很開心。

♦ Edward seems energetic all the time.
愛德華似乎總是精力充沛。

2. 感官動詞後加 like，則可以接受詞，表示「像……」的意思。

♦ The man looks like a millionaire.
這個人看起來像是百萬富翁。

III. 基本句型 3：主詞＋及物動詞＋受詞（S＋Vt＋O）

1. 這類動詞，如 do, drink, read, eat, speak, understand, …等，屬於「完全及物動詞」，要接一個受詞，使其語意完整。受詞可以是名詞、動名詞或不定詞。

♦ The boy speaks fluent Spanish.
這個男孩說著流利的西班牙語。

2. 及物動詞如 mind, practice, enjoy, imagine, avoid, …等後面要接動名詞做為受詞。

♦ Martha practices playing the violin in the afternoon.
瑪莎在下午練習拉小提琴。

3. 及物動詞如 plan, hope, want, decide, promise,…等則常接不定詞做為受詞。

♦ Pam plans to go on a vacation this weekend.
潘計畫這個週末去度假。

★ The Loch Ness Monster

The Loch Ness Monster is an **aquatic** creature said to live in Loch Ness, a lake in the Scottish Highlands. The earliest mention of "Nessie," another name for it, can be dated back to AD 565. The modern legends of the Monster have started since 1933. However, it became famous only when the so-called "**Surgeon**'s Photograph," taken by a London doctor, Robert Wilson, was published in 1934. The picture was the first photo that clearly captured a dinosaur-like creature with a long "head and neck." Specialized and **amateur investigators** kept **launching expeditions**, using sonar and underwater photography to search in the deep lake and tried to explore the truth about it. Over the years, a variety of explanations have been made to account for sightings of the Monster. The giant long-necked creature could probably be an eel, a bird, an elephant, or a resident animal. Nevertheless, nothing **conclusive** was found. The famous 1934 photo was later proven to be fake, and most scientists claimed it was impossible for a dinosaur-like creature to have **survived** for millions of years. With the complicated formations of the water areas there, till today, scientists still can't be sure if the monster actually exists.

☥ 尼斯湖水怪

　　尼斯湖水怪據說是住在蘇格蘭高地尼斯湖的海洋生物。小尼斯，它的另一個名字，最早被提及的時間可追溯到西元 565 年。水怪現代的傳說則從 1933 年開始。然而，它是在由倫敦醫生羅勃・威爾遜所拍攝所謂的「外科醫生的照片」在 1934 年出版後才出名的。這個照片是第一張很清晰地顯示出具有長的頭部和頸部像恐龍般生物的照片。專業和業餘的調查學者，不停地發動探險，並使用聲納和海底攝影術到深湖去搜尋它。多年以來，有各式各樣的說明來解說被目擊到的水怪。這隻巨大的長頸生物很可能是鰻魚、鳥、大象，或是當地的生物，然而，沒有得到具體的證實。後來，1934 年著名的照片被證實是假造的，而大部分的科學家們宣稱像恐龍般的生物要存活數百萬年是不可能的。由於尼斯湖地形複雜，直到今日，科學家們仍舊無法確定水怪是否存在。

▲ 關鍵單字解密

aquatic *adj.* 水生的；水棲的

surgeon *n.* 外科醫生

amateur *adj.* 業餘的；外行的

investigator *n.* 調查者；研究者

launch *v.* 開辦；發起

expedition *n.* 遠征；探險

conclusive *adj.* 決定性的；最終的

survive *v.* 由……生還；活下來

⚓ 文法分析

分析 1. ▶

例句 | However, it became famous only when the so-called "Surgeon's Photograph," taken by a London doctor, Robert Wilson, was published in 1934.

例句 | However, it became famously only when the so-called "Surgeon's Photograph," taken by a London doctor, Robert Wilson, was published in 1934.

中譯

然而它是在由倫敦醫生羅勃‧威爾遜所拍攝所謂的「外科醫生的照片」在 1934 年出版後才出名的。

用法解析

become 屬於「不完全不及物動詞」（連綴動詞的一種），根據基本句型 2：主詞＋不及物動詞＋主詞補語（S＋Vi＋SC）的用法，因本身語意不完整，後面必須接主詞補語以表達完整概念，故此處後面應接形容詞 famous 做補語，而非接副詞 famously，故第 2 句屬於錯誤的句子。

分析 **2.** ▶

例句│Over the years, a variety of explanations have been made to account for sightings of the Monster.

例句│Over the years, a variety of explanations have been made to account sightings of the Monster.

中譯

多年以來，有各式各樣的說明來解說被目擊到的水怪。

用法解析

account 屬於「完全不及物動詞」，根據基本句型 1：主詞＋不及物動詞（S＋Vi＋（Adv））的用法，後面不接受詞或補語。完全不及物動詞後面雖不得接受詞，但是加介系詞後，是可以接受詞的。第 1 句中 account 後面接 for 是正確的，但是第 2 句中 account 未加介系詞即接受詞是錯誤的用法。

UNIT
2

五大句型 2

Horrible Haunted Houses
恐怖鬼屋

**英文依據動詞之不同類別可區分成
五大基本句型，下列為句型 4 及句型 5：**

I. 基本句型 4：主詞＋及物動詞＋間接受詞（人）＋直接受詞（物）（S
    ＋Vt＋IO＋DO）＝（B）主詞＋及物動詞＋直接受詞（物）＋介系詞
    ＋間接受詞（人）（S＋Vt＋DO＋Prep＋IO）

1. 這類動詞，如 give, bring, get, buy, send, tell, teach……等，又
    被稱為「授與動詞」。屬於「及物動詞」，需要接兩個受詞，即
    「間接受詞」，人，及「直接受詞」，事物，使其語意完整。
    ◆ Alex sends his wife roses every Valentine's Day.
      艾力克斯每年情人節都送玫瑰花給太太。

2. 在此基本句型中，上述形式可和下述情境代換，意義相同。及物動
    詞後的「間接受詞」若置於「直接受詞」後，中間則要加上一個介
    系詞。動詞如 give, bring, lend, write, teach ……等，加 to，動
    詞如 buy, get, make, find, prepare……等，加 for，動詞如
    ask，則加 of。
    ◆ Lucy gave her pet dog some food.
      = Lucy gave some food to her pet dog.

露西給狗一些食物吃。

- ◆ Mr. Jackson bought his son a new smartphone.
  = Mr. Jackson bought a new smartphone for his son.
  傑克森先生買了新款智慧型手機給兒子。

II. 基本句型 5：主詞＋及物動詞＋受詞＋受詞補語（S＋Vt＋O＋OC）

1. 這類動詞，如 find, make, keep, choose, name……等，屬於「不完全及物動詞」，接受詞後，得要再接一個受詞補語，語意才完整。

- ◆ Please keep it a secret.
  請保密。
- ◆ We found the door locked.
  我們發現門上鎖了。
- ◆ The news made everybody happy.
  這則新聞使得每個人快樂。

2. 受詞補語的部份可以是名詞，形容詞，現在分詞，或過去分詞。

- ◆ Helen finds English interesting.
  海倫覺得英文很有趣。
- ◆ You had better not keep others waiting.
  你最好不要讓別人等。
- ◆ The ghost story made the children frightened.
  鬼故事讓小孩驚嚇。
- ◆ They chose Ted their class leader.
  他們選擇泰德當他們的班長。

Parents may tell **creepy** ghost stories to young children to keep them well-behaved. And the young children may curiously ask a lot of questions of their parents concerning haunted houses. In fact, haunted houses are terrifying to most people, the old and the young alike. In America, some modern buildings and ancient houses have a reputation for being haunted by evil spirits. **Paranormal** activities are constantly reported, which may include sounds of footsteps, or door-slamming, strange blood dripping down the wall, sudden appearances and **mischievous** behaviors of ghosts, or even brutal killing scenes. All these are told to be made by previous ghost-house owners too **obsessed** to leave or victims trying to get **revenge**. The haunted houses usually have special family, regional, or historical backgrounds. **Originally**, they might be built right on or close to a cemetery, battlegrounds, or crime scenes. The reasons they were haunted could be the locations where a mass murder, battle **conflicts**, or suicides happened. Therefore, the wandering **spirits** may include mistreated slaves, witches with great grievance, ghost soldiers, or serial-killing victims. The horrible spirits and the supernatural occurrences make people afraid and wish to keep them away, for the mysterious power is way beyond humans' understanding and control.

✡ 恐怖鬼屋

　　家長們會講述驚悚的鬼故事給小孩聽，使他們安分守己，而年幼的孩童會好奇地問父母親許多關於鬼屋的問題。事實上，對大部分人來說，老年人和年輕人都一樣，鬼屋是很恐怖的。在美國，一些現代建築物及古老的房子因為被邪靈纏繞而聲名大噪。超自然活動經常被報導，包括腳步聲、開門聲、奇異的血漬沿著牆壁滴下來、鬼魂突然地出現和惡作劇，或甚至有殘酷的殺戮場景。這些都是由不願離去的前任鬼屋屋主或試圖復仇的受害者所製造出來的。鬼屋通常有著特殊家庭、區域或是歷史的背景。起初，它們可能是在公墓、戰場或是犯罪現場的正上方或者是附近被建造出來的。它們被鬼纏身的理由可能是集體謀殺、戰場上衝突或自殺事發之地。因此，鬼屋的遊魂可能是被虐待的奴隸、心懷怨恨的女巫、士兵或是連續殺人案的受害者。可怕的鬼魂和超自然事件令人們畏懼並且希望能夠離它們遠遠地，因為這股神祕的力量遠超過人們的理解及掌控。

⧖ 關鍵單字解密

creepy *adj.* 令人毛骨悚然的；不寒而慄的

paranormal *adj.* 超自然的

mischievous *adj.* 調皮的；淘氣的

obsess *v.* 著迷；煩擾

revenge *n.* 報仇；報復

originally *adv.* 起初地；原來地

conflict *n.* 衝突；鬥爭

spirit *n.* 幽靈；精靈

⚙ 文法分析

分析 1.

例句 | Parents may tell creepy ghost stories to young children.

例句 | Parents may tell creepy ghost stories for young children.

中譯

家長們會講述驚悚的鬼故事給小孩聽。

用法解析

及物動詞後的「間接受詞」若置於「直接受詞」後，中間則要加上一個介系詞。動詞 tell 後加介系詞 to，而非接 for，故第 2 句是錯誤的句子。

分析 2.

例句 | The horrible spirits and the supernatural occurrences make people afraid and wish to keep them away. ○

例句 | The horrible spirits and the supernatural occurrences make people and wish to keep them. ✕

中譯

可怕的鬼魂和超自然事件令人們畏懼並且希望能夠離他們遠遠地。

用法解析

Make 及 keep 屬於「不完全及物動詞」，接受詞 people 後，得要再接受詞補語 afraid 及 away，語意才完整。第 2 句是錯誤的，因為缺受詞補語。

時態 1

The Swarming Locusts

蝗蟲過境

英文依據動詞時態可分現在式、過去式，以及未來式。現在式的用法如下：

I. 現在簡單式（V-s / es）：

1. 用於表示現在的狀態、固定會有的習慣動作或不變的真理。
   - ◆ Peter goes to work by MRT every morning.
     彼得每天早上搭捷運上班。

2. Be 動詞之使用為 am, is, are，第一人稱單數用 am，第三人稱單數用 is，第二人稱單數及所有人稱複數則用 are。一般動詞若主詞為第三人稱單數，字尾加 s 或 es。字尾若是母音加 y，字尾直接加 s，若是子音，則去 y，加 ies。
   - ◆ Both the two cats enjoy sleeping on the sofa.
     這兩隻貓很喜愛睡在沙發上。

3. 與表示現在或習慣的副詞、副詞片語連用時，要用現在式。如 always, usually, often, seldom, every morning / afternoon / week / month / summer / year ⋯⋯等。
   - ◆ Mrs. Johnson goes to church every Sunday.
     強森太太在每個星期日上教堂。

II. 現在進行式（am / is / are＋V.ing）：

1. 用以表示現在正在進行的動作。常與下列時間副詞及副詞片語連用：now, at the moment, at the present time ……等。

   ♦ Lucy is playing volleyball in the court now.

     露西現在正在球場打排球。

2. 遇到動詞如 listen, look 等表示現在進行的動作時要用現在進行式。

   ♦ Listen! Someone is knocking on the door!

     聽！有人正在敲門！

III. 現在完成式（have / has＋p.p）：

1. 常用以表達現在已完成的動作、過去的經驗，以及從過去持續進行到現在完成的動作。

   ♦ Kenny has finally finished his report.

     肯尼終於完成他的報告。

2. 常與下列副詞及副詞片語連用、如 already, lately, recently, ever, never ……等。亦可用 for 加一段時間以及 since 加名詞或子句連用，表示動作之持續進行。

   ♦ The two brothers have watched TV for two hours.

     兩兄弟已經看了兩個小時的電視。

IV. 現在完成進行式（have / has been＋V.ing）：此時態用以表達從過去進行到現在完成的動作，並將繼續往下延伸。

   ♦ The children have been playing in the playground since ten o'clock.

     孩子們從十點鐘開始一直在操場上玩。

Locusts are mysterious and powerful destructors capable of **endangering** human beings' **livelihood** by causing great crop losses. Within a short period of time, the estimated billions of locusts gather in cohesive groups and swarm over and down the vast areas of farming lands at high speeds. They feed and rest on the ground, and then move on when the whole vegetation is **exhausted**. With food shortage being one of the global crises, the destructive locusts can be an important **contributing** factor to plaguing all plants, vegetables, and crops. Therefore, human beings take preventive measures for locust control, such as spreading pesticides, or eating them as food, since they are high in **protein**. According to researchers, the possible factors for them to fly in great swarms may be their habitual behavior and a certain locust **pheromone**, which makes them attracted to each other and fly cohesively. Due to having a strong sense of direction induced by the sun, the swarming locusts can fly a great distance. The puzzle of how they have own such unusual power still needs to be solved. Hopefully, with more secrets **unraveled**, human beings can have an excellent locust control to lessen the **impact** they bring to the world.

☥ 蝗蟲過境

　　蝗蟲是神秘且有強大力量的毀滅者，牠們能使農作物蒙受重大損害而危及到人類的生計。在極短的時間內，據估計有數十億成群的蝗蟲以高速蜂擁於廣大農田上方。牠們停留在農地上覓食，然後當所有的作物被吃光了之後，就繼續向前走。食物短缺已是全球危機之一，具毀滅性的蝗蟲，可能是禍及所有的植物、蔬菜和農作物重要的主因。因此，人類採取蝗蟲管制的預防措施，譬如噴灑殺蟲劑，或因為蝗蟲富含蛋白質而把牠們當作食物來食用。根據研究學者的說法，蝗蟲會群飛的可能因素是由於牠們的自然習性，以及因為具有特定的蝗蟲費洛蒙導致牠們彼此吸引，並且群飛。由於藉由太陽所引導出強烈的方向感，牠們能夠做長距離的飛行。牠們是如何能夠擁有如此不尋常能力的謎，仍有待揭曉。但願隨著越多祕密的揭曉，人類可以做絕佳的蝗蟲管控來減緩牠們帶給世人的衝擊。

 關鍵單字解密

endanger *v.* 危及；使遭到危險

livelihood *n.* 生活；生計

exhaust *v.* 耗盡；精疲力盡

contribute *v.* 貢獻；促成

protein *n.* 蛋白質

pheromone *n.* 費洛蒙；外荷爾蒙

unravel *v.* 闡明；解開

impact *n.* 衝擊；影響

☸ 文法分析

分析 1.

例句 | Locusts are mysterious and powerful destructors capable of endangering human beings' livelihood by causing great crop losses.

例句 | Locusts is mysterious and powerful destructors capable of endangering human beings' livelihood by causing great crop losses.

中譯

蝗蟲是神秘且有強大力量的毀滅者，牠們能使農作物蒙受重大損害而危及到人類的生計。

用法解析

現在簡單式中，be 動詞之使用為 am, is, are，第一人稱單數用 am，第三人稱單數用 is，第二人稱單數及所有人稱的複數則用 are。Locusts 是第三人稱複數要用 are。

分析 2.

例句 | The possible factors for them to fly in great swarms may be their habitual behavior and a certain locust pheromone, which makes them attracted to each other and fly cohesively.

例句 | The possible factors for them to fly in great swarms may be their habitual behavior and a certain locust pheromone, which make them attracted to each other and fly cohesively.

中譯

蝗蟲會群飛的可能因素是由於牠們的自然習性，以及因為具有特定的蝗蟲費洛蒙導致牠們彼此吸引，並且群飛。

用法解析

非限定子句 make 的主詞是逗點前全部的子句，為第三人稱單數，make 字尾應要加 s 才對。故第 2 句是錯誤的。

UNIT 4

時態 2
The Yeti
大雪怪

 英文動詞時態中過去式的分類及使用如下：

I. 過去簡單式（V-ed）：常用以表示過去的習慣、動作，或狀態。常與下列表示過去時間的副詞及副詞片語連用，如：yesterday, just now, this morning, two days / several months / three years ago, last week / month / winter / year……等。
   ♦ Why didn't you attend the party last night?
   你昨晚怎麼沒有參加派對？

II. 過去進行式（were / was＋V.ing）：常用以表達過去某一定點正在進行的動作，或過去某一動作發生時，另一個正在進行的動作。
   ♦ The baby was sleeping soundly at three o'clock yesterday afternoon.
   小嬰兒昨天下午三點整正熟睡著。

III. 過去完成式（had＋p.p.）：
   1. 過去完成式常用以表達過去時間某一定點前，已完成的動作。或過去的兩個動作，先發生者用過去完成式，動作晚發生者則用簡單過去式。

- ◆ I believe I had seen that movie two years before.

  我確信兩年前我看過那部電影。

- ◆ The storm had stopped at nine o'clock last night.

  暴風雨在昨晚九點鐘停止。

2. 過去完成式也可用以表示過去未能實現的期盼、計劃，或原來打算要做的事。

- ◆ Sam had intended to go abroad last year but his father suddenly fell sick.

  山姆本來打算在去年出國，但是他的父親突然生病。

- ◆ We had planned to go shopping yesterday but it kept raining hard then.

  我們昨天原來計畫去逛街，但是當時大雨下個不停。

- ◆ The couple had expected to get married last month but had canceled it because of a big fight.

  這對情侶原來打算上個月結婚，但是因為大吵一架而取消了。

IV. 過去完成進行式（had been＋V.ing）：用以強調過去完成並持續進行的情境。

- ◆ Peggy had been working hard before she finally got the scholarship.

  佩姬在她終於得到獎學金前，一直努力用功。

- ◆ Mr. White was exhausted last night because he had been jogging all afternoon yesterday.

  懷特先生昨晚累壞了，因為他昨天整個下午都在慢跑。

- ◆ I was told that Sean had been trying to reach his brother for two hours then but in vain.

  有人告訴我西恩當時找他的哥哥找了兩個鐘頭，但是沒有找到。

The Yeti, also known as the **Abominable** Snowman, is a mysterious human-like beast spotted in the beautifully bleak and frozen Himalayan regions of Nepal and Tibet. Since the 19th century, the Yeti has been mentioned by the **indigenous** Himalayan people, and the Sherpa guides along with mountain-climbers from all over the world. Till the present day, a large number of reports and accounts sighting the Yeti have been **released**. Most of them described the Yeti as a tall, big, and fearful creature, weighing 200 to 400 pounds and covered with long, dark hair. It walked upright, roared **fiercely**, carried a large stone as a weapon, and always left big footprints on the snowy ground. However, some of the seemingly convincing accounts and photos were later **suspected** as untrue and unreliable evidence from **hoaxers** with a view to boosting the **tourism** in the poor region. In fact, the Yeti is probably only an indigenous gorilla or bear. Since there is little physical evidence concerning it, the scientific **community** generally regards the Yeti as a mere legend. So, the Yeti, as a mysterious creature always raising in people great fear and terror, remains to be a great myth waiting for us to explore.

⚱ 大雪怪

　　大雪怪，又被稱為喜馬拉雅山雪人，是在美麗荒涼冰凍的尼泊爾和西藏喜馬拉雅山區被發現神秘似人的野獸。自從 19 世紀以來，大雪怪一直被當地的喜馬拉雅人和西藏導遊連同來自世界各地的登山客所提及。到目前為止，有關目擊大雪怪大量的報導和文獻已被公諸於世。大部分的報導及文獻把大雪怪描述為重 200~400 磅，全身覆蓋著長且黑的毛髮，高大且嚇人的生物。它直立行走，大聲怒吼，隨身帶著一顆巨大的石塊作為武器，並且總是在雪地上留下巨大的足跡。但是，有些表面上看似可信的文章和照片，後來被懷疑是來自於欺騙者不實且不可靠的證據，目的是要振興當地窮困地區的觀光業。事實上，大雪怪很可能只是當地的一隻大猩猩或者是一頭熊。由於有關於大雪怪的實質證據非常少，科學界一般只把大雪怪視為一個傳奇罷了。所以，大雪怪，身為一個總是造成民眾極大畏懼和恐怖的神祕生物，依舊是有待我們去探索的。

 關鍵單字解密

abominable *adj.* 令人憎惡的；極其討厭的

indigenous *adj.* 土著的；本地的

release *v.* 釋放；發行

fiercely *adv.* 兇猛地；強烈地

suspect *v.* 懷疑；料想

hoaxer *n.* 騙子

tourism *n.* 觀光；旅遊業

community *n.* 社區；團體

⚙ 文法分析

例句 | Till the present day, a large number of reports and accounts sighting the Yeti have been released.

例句 | Till the present day, a large number of reports and accounts sighting the Yeti had been released.

中譯

到目前為止，有關目擊大雪怪大量的報導和文獻已被公諸於世。

用法解析

過去完成式（had＋p.p.）用以表達過去時間某一定點前，已完成的動作。但此句指的是到目前為止已完成的動作，應用現在完成式。

分析 2.

例句 | Most of them <u>described</u> the Yeti as a tall, big, and fearful creature, weighing 200 to 400 pounds and covered with long, dark hair.

例句 | Most of them <u>was describing</u> the Yeti as a tall, big, and fearful creature, weighing 200 to 400 pounds and covered with long, dark hair.

中譯

大部分的報導及文獻把大雪怪描述為重 200~400 磅，全身覆蓋著長且黑的毛髮，高大且嚇人的生物。

用法解析

過去進行式（were / was＋V-ing）用以表達過去某一定點正在進行的動作，過去簡單式（V-ed）則用以表示過去的事實。此句敘述的是過去的事實，故第 2 句是錯誤的句子。

UNIT 5

時態 3

Mermaids
美人魚

**英文動詞時態中，
未來式的分類及使用如下：**

I. 未來簡單式（will＋VR）：

1. 表示未來即將發生的情境，常與副詞及副詞片語，如 tonight, tomorrow ~ , next ~ 及 in ~ 連用，表示未來式。

   ◆ Kathy will be twenty years old next month.
   凱西下個月將滿 20 歲。

   ◆ The waiter will come to our service in five minutes.
   服務生將會在 5 分鐘後來為我們服務。

   ◆ There will be a sales meeting tomorrow morning.
   明天早上將會有一場業務會議。

2. 除了 will＋VR 外，表示即將發生的 be going to＋VR, be about to＋VR 及 be V-ing 與表示未來的時間副詞及副詞片語連用時，亦可表達未來式。

   ◆ Jill is about to finish reading her book soon.
   吉兒即將讀完她的書。

   ◆ How are you going to celebrate your birthday tonight?
   今晚你打算如何慶祝你的生日？

II. 未來進行式（will be＋V-ing）：用以表示未來某一定點將會進行的某一動作。

- ◆ All his fans will be waiting for him at the airport at this time tomorrow.
  明日此時，所有他的粉絲將會在機場等他。

III. 未來完成式（will have＋p.p.）：用以表示直至未來某一定點即將完成的動作。

- ◆ By next October, Mr. Parker will have worked here for thirty years.
  明年十月，派克先生在此工作將屆滿 30 年。

- ◆ Tomorrow afternoon when you come here, I will have finished reading the novel.
  明天下午當你抵達這裡時，我將閱讀完這本小說。

- ◆ Nancy will have graduated from college by this time next year.
  明年此時，南西將會從大學畢業。

IV. 未來完成進行式（will have been＋V.ing）：強調在未來某一定點即將完成的動作以外，將繼續往下進行的動作。

- ◆ By the end of this year, Oscar will have been working in the same company for seven years.
  今年年底，奧斯卡在同一家公司工作將屆滿 7 年。

- ◆ The two friends will have been quarreling for three days if they don't stop tomorrow.
  這兩個朋友明天若不停止吵架，他們就連續吵三天架了。

Images of **surpassing** beauty and strong determination will flash into one's mind when mermaids are mentioned. They are mysterious marine figures taking the form of a female human above the waist and the tail of a fish below. Mermaids are rich in **symbolism** in all kinds of depictions about them. In fact, when reading British folklore, you will be surprised to find that they have been deemed as unlucky **omens**. They are believed to be able to foretell or even **deliberately** create disasters and bring mariners terrible misfortunes and tragic death. However, on the other hand, they have been praised for courageously seeking ways to realize their wishes. Among the **fascinating** legendary works, Hans Anderson's fairy tale, *The Little Mermaid*, published in 1873, enjoys the greatest popularity. In the tale, the Mermaid bravely pursues her true love at the cost of her life. Though she fails **eventually** and ends up dissolving into foam, the tragic yet romantic love story has greatly touched and inspired readers worldwide. In 1913, a statue of the Little Mermaid was set up in Copenhagen, Denmark. Till today, countless fans go to visit her and **admire** her persistence in seeking eternal love and at the same time, **lament** over her tragic doom.

☥ 美人魚

當美人魚被提及的時候,絕佳的美貌和堅定意志的形象會在人們的心中浮現。它們是神祕的海洋生物,腰部以上是女性的外貌,腰部以下則呈現魚尾的樣貌。美人魚在各式各樣有關於它們的描述中有豐富的意象。事實上,當閱讀英國民間故事時,你會很驚訝於發現它們一向被視為不吉利的象徵。人們相信它們可以預測或甚至故意地製造災難,帶給水手可怕的厄運及悲劇般的死亡。但是,從另一方面來說,它們在實現心願當中所表現出來的勇氣常被讚美。在所有令人嚮往的傳奇性作品當中,漢斯‧安徒生 1873 年出版的童話故事,「小美人魚」,最受到歡迎。故事當中,小美人魚在犧牲自己性命的代價下,勇敢追求它的真愛。雖然終究失敗並幻化成泡沫,這悲劇卻浪漫的愛情故事大大地感動且啟發全世界的讀者。在 1913 年,以安徒生童話故事為基礎,小美人魚的雕像在丹麥哥本哈根被設立。至今,無數的美人魚迷會去拜訪它,仰慕它尋求永恆真愛的毅力並且同時感慨它悲劇般的命運。

 關鍵單字解密

surpassing *adj.* 出眾的;非凡的

symbolism *n.* 象徵性;象徵主義

omen *n.* 預兆;預告

deliberately *adv.* 故意地;慎重地

fascinating *adj.* 迷人的;極好的

eventually *adv.* 最後;終於

admire *v.* 欽佩;欣賞

lament *v.* 悲痛;痛惜

 **文法分析**

分析 1.

例句 | Images of surpassing beauty and strong determination <u>will flash</u> into one's mind when mermaids are mentioned.

例句 | Images of surpassing beauty and strong determination <u>were to flash</u> into one's mind when mermaids are mentioned.

中譯

當美人魚被提及的時候，絕佳的美貌和堅定意志的形象會在人們的心中浮現。

用法解析

主要子句中表示未來即將發生的情境，應用未來式 will＋VR，而非過去式 were to flash 來表達。故第 2 句屬於錯誤的句子。

分析 2.

例句 | Among the fascinating legendary works, Hans Anderson's fairy tale, The Little Mermaid, published in 1873, enjoys the greatest popularity

例句 | Among the fascinating legendary works, Hans Anderson's fairy tale, The Little Mermaid, will be published in 1873, enjoys the greatest popularity.

中譯

在所有令人嚮往的傳奇性作品當中，漢斯‧安徒生 1873 年出版的童話故事，「小美人魚」，最受到歡迎。

用法解析

1873 年發生的事已屬過去發生的事，要用過去分詞 published 來補充説明，而非用未來被動語態 will be published 來表達。

UNIT 6

主動式與被動式 1
Crop Circles
麥田圈

 英文句子中，主動語態與被動語態的類別及互換如下：

I. 簡單式主動語態變為被動語態時，主詞與受詞交換位置，動詞部分改為 be 動詞加上過去分詞（be v.＋p.p. by＋受詞）。

1. 現在被動：S＋am / is / are＋p.p.＋by O
2. 過去被動：S＋was / were＋p.p.＋by O
3. 未來被動：S＋will be＋p.p.＋by O

   ♦ Sally does her homework in the afternoon.（主動）

   莎莉下午做她的作業。

   →Sally's homework is done by her in the afternoon.（被動）

   ♦ Tom painted the wall yesterday.

   湯姆昨天漆牆壁。

   →The wall was painted by Tom yesterday.

II. 進行式主動語態變為被動語態時，主詞與受詞交換位置，動詞部分 be 動詞與過去分詞間要加入 be 動詞的現在分詞 being 表示進行的意味。

1. 現在進行被動：S＋am / is / are＋being＋p.p.＋by O
2. 過去進行被動：S＋was / were＋being＋p.p.＋by O

♦ The constructors are building a house now.（主動）
施工人員正在建造房屋。

→ A house is being built by the constructors now.（被動）
房子現在正由施工工人所建造。

♦ Mrs. Johnson was washing the dishes at seven last night.
強生太太昨晚七點鐘正在洗碗盤。

→ The dishes were being washed by Mrs. Johnson at seven last night.

III. 完成式主動語態變為被動語態時，主詞與受詞交換位置，動詞部分 have 或 has 與過去分詞中間要加入 be 動詞的過去分詞 been，表示被動語態。

1. 現在完成被動：S＋have / has＋been＋p.p.＋by O
2. 過去完成被動：S＋had＋been＋p.p.＋by O
3. 未來完成被動：S＋will have＋been＋p.p.＋by O

♦ Researches on GM food have been made for quite a long time.
基改食物的相關研究已進行一段時間了。

♦ The house had been burned down before the fire was put out.
火災撲滅前，房子已經被燒光。

♦ The novel will have been returned by the time you want to borrow it tomorrow.
明天你想借這本小說之前，它將已被歸還。

Each year, when the first crops ripen, crop circle **enthusiasts**, including researchers, artists, and tourists can't wait to visit the crop fields in England to **appreciate** and research into the **diverse** and mysterious crop circles. Since the first crop circles were sighted and reported in England in the 17th century, they have **aroused** worldwide attention. Recently, the refined and complicated designs of the flattened crop formations have increased in size and amount attracting even more public interest. As to the causes of crop circles, it is still open to **dispute**. In the 1960s, many reports of UFO sightings described farmers' witnessing saucer-shaped crafts, implying that the crop circles were made by aliens overnight. In the meantime, scientists doing research have come up with all kinds of scientific theories about the **phenomena** without good evidence. However, in 1991, Bower and Chorley made headline claims that they, inspired by the **extraterrestrial** explanations, made all the circles during the 1978-1991 with simple tools. Whether all the **amazing** crop circles were created by a natural phenomenon or by human hands still puzzles the world. Before solving the mystery, we may as well appreciate the beautiful crop circles as public art.

☥ 麥田圈

　　每一年，當第一批農作物成熟時，麥田圈的狂熱分子，包括研究者、藝術家，以及觀光客，等不及要到英國去探望麥田來欣賞並且研究多變化而且神秘的麥田圈。自從 17 世紀第一批麥田圈在英國被發現並被報導之後，他們已經引起全世界的矚目。最近，精緻而且複雜的平坦麥田圈的圖案，在大小和數量上大大地增加，並且引起更多民眾的興趣。至於麥田圈形成的原因，目前仍是眾說紛紜。在 1960 年代，許多目擊不明飛行物體的報導，描述農夫親眼目睹到飛碟外觀的太空船，暗示著麥田圈是在一夜之間被外星人所製造出來的。在此同時，做研究的科學家們有提出各種關於此現象的科學理論，卻沒有實質的證據。然而，在 1991 年，鮑爾和柯里做出頭條新聞的宣稱說，他們受到外星人說法的啟發，用簡單的工具在 1978 到 1991 年之間創造出所有的圈圈。所有驚人的麥田圈究竟是由自然現象還是藉由人類之手所創造來的仍舊困惑著整個世界。在謎底揭曉前，我們不妨把美麗的麥田圈當作公共藝術來欣賞。

 ## 關鍵單字解密

enthusiast *n.* 熱心者；狂熱份子

appreciate *v.* 欣賞；感謝

diverse *adj.* 多種多樣的；多變化的

arouse *v.* 喚起；使奮發

dispute *n.* 爭論；爭執

phenomenon *n.* 現象；稀有的事

extraterrestrial *adj.* 地球外的；外星球的

amazing *adj.* 驚奇的；驚人的

⚙ 文法分析

例句 | Since the first crop circles <u>were sighted and reported</u> in England in the 17th century, they have aroused worldwide attention.

例句 | Since the first crop circles <u>had been sighted and reported</u> in England in the 17th century, they have aroused worldwide attention.

中譯

自從 17 世紀第一批麥田圈在英國被發現並被報導之後,他們已經引起全世界的矚目。

用法解析

附屬子句講述過去事實,用過去簡單式被動語態(be v.＋p.p.)即可。不須用到過去完成式被動語態,故第 2 句是錯誤的句子。

分析 **2.**

例句 | Recently, the refined and complicated designs of the flattened crop formations <u>have increased</u> in size and amount.

例句 | Recently, the refined and complicated designs of the flattened crop formations <u>have been increased</u> in size and amount.

中譯

最近，精緻而且複雜的平坦麥田圈的圖案，在大小和數量上大大地增加。

用法解析

講述現在完成的情境，語態用現在完成主動語態 have increased，而非現在完成被動語態 have been increased。

UNIT 7

主動式與被動式 2

Whales' Mass Suicide
鯨魚集體自殺

 英文一般時態以外的
主動語態及被動語態的變換如下：

I. 主詞後有語氣助動詞，如 can, may, will, must, could, might, would, should……等，主動改為被動時，原助動詞仍要保留，助動詞後接 be 動詞之原形動詞（be），加上過去分詞（p.p.），再加上 by ＋受詞。

♦ All the students can answer the easy question.（主動）
所有學生都能回答這個簡單的問題。

→ The easy question can be answered by all the students.（被動）

II. 感官動詞，如 see, hear, watch, notice, …等的被動語態是主詞加 be 動詞後加上感官動詞的過去分詞，接不定詞 to＋原形動詞，再加上 by＋受詞。即 S＋be v.＋seen / heard / watched / noticed＋to VR＋by O。

♦ Sharon saw Peter enter the main gate of the library.（主動）
雪倫看到彼得從圖書館門口走進去。

→ Peter was seen to enter the main gate of the library by Sharon.（被動）

III. 使役動詞，如 make 的被動式是主詞加 be 動詞以及 make 的過去分詞 made 加上不定詞 to，接原形動詞，再加上 by 受詞。（即：S be v.＋made to VR＋by O）。使役動詞 let 的被動式則是主詞加 let 加受詞後加 be 動詞以及過去分詞，再加上 by 受詞。（即：S let O＋be v.＋p.p.＋by O）

◆ I made the boy do errands for me.（主動）
我命令這個男孩為我跑腿。

→ The boy was made to do errands for me.（被動）

IV. 含介系詞的動詞片語改為被動語態時，原有的介系詞不可省略。

◆ The naughty boys made fun of the beggar.（主動）
這些頑皮的男孩捉弄乞丐。

→ The beggar was made fun of by the naughty boys.（被動）

◆ The servant waited on Mrs. Smith in the restaurant.
服務生在餐廳服務史密斯太太。

→ Mrs. Smith was waited on in the restaurant by the servant.

V. 表示客觀的說法，常使用下列固定的句型：It is said / believed / reported / supposed / suggested / expected 加上 that 名詞子句。

◆ It is generally believed that the Earth is round.
一般人認為地球是圓的。

◆ It is always expected that there will be a day off when a violent typhoon comes.
人們總是期盼強烈颱風來臨時會放颱風假。

★ Whales' Mass Suicide

Once in a while, there are reports about **suicidal** behaviors of animals. Among them, cases of whales' mass suicidal behaviors are the most alarming and tragic. It is **supposed** that as the largest creature in the ocean, whales' lives aren't easily **threatened** by other marine life. However, quite a few cases have been reported recently. Groups of whales, about 100 whales or so, would swim on shore together, get **stranded** on the beach and die due to lack of water. With such weight and body shape, whales, once on shore, are hard to be **rescued**, and die eventually. Researchers have given several possible reasons for the causes. One is the leading whales' losing their sense of hearing and misleading the direction. Another is that they want to save their partners. Others may include their getting **diseases** from certain parasites, being terrified by violent thunderstorms, or simply their being influenced by the power of **magnetic** fields. All these uncertain factors may need to be studied and **verified**. Hopefully, after realizing the reasons, human beings will offer help to save their lives.

☥ 鯨魚集體自殺

　　偶爾，我們會聽聞到有關於動物自殺行為的報導。這些報導中，鯨魚集體自殺的行為是最令人震驚且最悲慘的。一般人認為，身為海洋中最巨大的生物，鯨魚的生命並不容易被其他海洋生物所威脅。然而，最近有相當多的個案被報導出來。將近一百條的成群鯨魚會集體游上岸，在沙灘上擱淺並因缺乏水分而死亡。鯨魚有著極重的重量和龐大的體型，一旦上岸便難以拯救，終究會死亡。研究學者們對於這樣的現象提出數項可能的解釋。一個原因是說領頭的鯨魚失去了聽覺，所以誤導方向，另一個原因是牠們想要拯救牠們的夥伴。還有其他可能的原因是有某些寄生蟲導致鯨魚罹患疾病，另或被強烈的暴風雨所嚇到，或是僅僅是因為被磁場的力量所影響。這些不確定的因素也許有待研究與釐清。但願人們在了解原因後能夠提供幫助以拯救牠們的生命。

關鍵單字解密

suicidal *adj.* 自殺的；自我毀滅的

supposed *adj.* 根據推測的；據稱的

threaten *v.* 威脅；恐嚇

strand *v.* 擱淺；處於困境

rescue *v.* 援救；挽救

disease *n.* 疾病

magnetic *adj.* 磁鐵的；有磁性的

verify *v.* 核對；證實

⚙ 文法分析

例句 | It is supposed that as the largest creature in the ocean, whales' lives aren't easily threatened by other marine life.

例句 | It is supposedly that as the largest creature in the ocean, whales' lives aren't easily threatened by other marine life.

中譯

一般人認為，身為海洋中最巨大的生物，鯨魚的生命並不容易被其他海洋生物所威脅。

用法解析

表示客觀的說法，常使用下列固定的句型：It is said / believed / reported / supposed / suggested / expected 加上 that 名詞子句。「假設；認為」，在 It is 後面應該要用形容詞 supposed，而非副詞 supposedly。

分析 **2.** ▶

例句 | However, quite a few cases have been reported recently.

○

✕

例句 | However, quite a few cases have reported recently

中譯

然而，最近有相當多的個案被報導出來。

用法解析

此句中出現副詞 recently，所以應用現在完成式，cases 是被報導的，所以要用現在完成被動語態 have been reported，而非主動的 have reported，故第 2 句屬於錯誤的句子。

UNIT 8

比較句 1

Vampires

吸血鬼

英文中，形容詞的比較類別及基本句型如下：

I. 使用原級形容詞做同等比較時用 as...as 來表達，as...as 中間置放的形容詞必用原級，即形容詞原始的字。S＋as＋形容詞原級＋as...，用於肯定句。S＋not as / not so＋形容詞原級＋as...，則用於否定句，表示較劣等的情境。

- ◆ This novel is as interesting as that one.
  這本小說跟那本小說一樣有趣。
- ◆ The watch cost as much money as that one.
  這隻手錶跟那隻手錶一樣貴。

II. 使用比較級形容詞比較時，優等比較中，形容詞是單音節字的句型是主詞加比較級（~er）＋than⋯，形容詞是多音節字時是 more＋形容詞原級＋than⋯。劣等比較則是主詞加 less＋形容詞原級＋than⋯。

- ◆ The apartment is smaller than the mansion.
  這座公寓比那棟豪宅小。
- ◆ Bill is more intelligent than Tim.
  比爾比提姆聰明。

III. 表示「逐漸…」的比較，常用 –er / more and –er / more。表示「比例」的比較，則常用 the＋形容詞比較級 …, the＋形容詞比較級 …。

  ◆ More and more people are not satisfied with the traffic jam downtown.
    越來越多人不滿於市區的塞車。
  ◆ Fewer and fewer students are seen to hang around in this cyber café.
    越來越少的學生被看見在這座網咖流連。

IV. 形容詞最高級比較時則用主詞加動詞＋定冠詞 the，後接最高級，加上介系詞 of 或 in 再加上某一範圍的片語。

  ◆ Mary is the tallest girl in her class.
    瑪莉是班上最高的女生。
  ◆ The Nile is the longest river in the world.
    尼羅河是全世界最長的河流。
  ◆ To Willy, English is the most important subject of all.
    對威力來說，英文是所有科目當中最重要的。

V. 修飾形容詞比較級的副詞及副詞片語可以是 much, far, even, still, a little, a lot, a great / good deal……等。

  ◆ Your hair is much longer than Susan's.
    你的頭髮比蘇珊的頭髮長多了。
  ◆ The Wangs are now living a life much more comfortable than before.
    王家人目前過的生活比以往舒服多了。

A vampire is a mysterious being who feeds on the blood of living creatures to **sustain** its life. Since the early 19th century, frightful vampires **roaming** streets at midnight have been recorded in legends. They were depicted as pale-faced evils in a black cape, obsessed with drinking blood. They feared the sunlight, so they came out after midnight and went back to their **coffin** before dawn. They drank fresh blood from human victims for **immortality**. According to vampire hunters, the best time to **permanently** end a vampire's life is in the daytime. And the best way to kill it is to penetrate its heart by a **sharpened** stick. Besides, by holding garlic and crosses in hand, one can also keep vampires away. In the past, among all the vampire figures created in fictional stories, Count Dracula was probably the most famous of all time. However, nowadays, the vampires in the recently released *Twilight* movie series seem to be more widely known and the vampires in the movies tend to be comparatively powerful. Garlic, holy crosses, and sunlight can harm them no more. And the young vampire characters attract even more young **audiences** than the old Count Dracula. With the thriving adaptations of vampire myths, it seems that the related images of such mysterious creatures will remain vivid among the public.

☥ 吸血鬼

　　吸血鬼是一種神祕的生物，它仰賴生物的血液來延續生命。自從 19 世紀早期以來，嚇人的吸血鬼在傳說中就有被描述到半夜在街頭遊走。它們被描述成蒼白、邪惡、吸血，並且穿著黑色的斗篷。它們畏懼陽光，所以在午夜後才出來，並在天亮之前回到棺木中。它們為了求得永生，吸取來自人類受害者身上的鮮血。根據吸血鬼獵人的說法，永遠終止吸血鬼生命最好的時機是在白天，而殺死它最好的辦法是利用銳利的木棍插入其心臟。此外，藉由手中握著蒜頭以及十字架，人們可以使得吸血鬼遠離。在過去，在所有創造出來的吸血鬼人物之中，德古拉伯爵很可能是所有時期以來最著名的。但是，今日來說，在最近放映的「暮光之城」電影系列中的吸血鬼似乎更有名，力量也更為強大。蒜頭、神聖十字架以及陽光皆再也無法傷害它們。而年輕的吸血鬼角色比老德古拉伯爵吸引更多的年輕觀眾。吸血鬼的改編傳說如此盛行，看來對於大眾來說，這種神祕生物延伸出來的相關形象依然生動不已。

 關鍵單字解密

sustain *v.* 維持；支撐

roam *v.* 漫步；漫遊

coffin *n.* 棺材；靈柩

immortality *n.* 不朽；不滅

permanently *adv.* 永久地；長期不變地

sharpen *v.* 削尖；使尖銳

twilight *n.* 薄暮；暮光

audience *n.* 觀眾；聽眾

 **文法分析**

分析 **1.**

例句 According to vampire hunters, the best time to permanently end a vampire's life is in the daytime.

例句 According to vampire hunters, best time to permanently end a vampire's life is in the daytime.

中譯

根據吸血鬼獵人的說法，永遠終止吸血鬼生命最好的時機是在白天。

用法解析

形容詞最高級比較時用定冠詞 the，後接最高級 best time。第 2 句中 best time 前少了定冠詞 the，故第 2 句屬於錯誤的句子。

分析 **2.** ▶

例句 │ And the young vampire characters attract even more young audiences than the old Count Dracula.

例句 │ And the young vampire characters attract very more young audiences than the old Count Dracula.

中譯

而年輕的吸血鬼角色比老德古拉伯爵吸引更多的年輕觀眾。

用法解析

修飾形容詞比較級的副詞及副詞片語可以是 much, far, even, still, a little, a lot, a great / good deal…… 等。修飾最高級的副詞及副詞片語常用 very 或 by far，表示語氣的加強。原句是比較級的句子，more 前應用 much，而非修飾最高級的 very。

UNIT
9

比較句 2
Human Electricity Generators
人體發電機

英文中，
副詞的比較類別及基本句型如下：

I. 使用原級副詞做同等比較時用 as…as 來表達，as…as 中間置放的副詞必用原級，即副詞之原始的字。S as＋副詞原級＋as…，用於肯定句。S not as / not so＋副詞原級＋as…，則用於否定句，表示較劣等的情境。

- ◆ Jerry finished his work as soon as possible.
  傑瑞盡快完成了他的工作。
- ◆ Girls can do physical work as well as boys.
  女孩可以和男孩一樣把體能工作做好。
- ◆ You should study as diligently as your sister.
  你應該像你姊姊一樣用功。
- ◆ Sharon can't speak English as / so fluently as Andy.
  雪倫無法像安迪一樣流利地說英文。

II. 使用比較級副詞比較時，優等比較中，副詞是單音節字的句型是：主詞加比較級（~er）＋than…，副詞是多音節字時是：more＋副詞原級＋than…。劣等比較則是主詞加 less＋副詞原級＋than…。

- ◆ Can pigeons fly higher than eagles?
  鴿子可以飛得比老鷹高嗎？

♦ Mike answered the question more promptly than Janice.

麥克比珍妮絲更快地回答問題。

♦ The boy played the piano less beautifully than the girl.

這個男孩演奏鋼琴不如那個女孩演奏的美。

III. 表示「逐漸……」的比較，常用 –er / more and –er / more，表示「比例」的比較，則常用 the＋副詞比較級 …, the＋副詞比較級 …. 。

♦ The truck is moving on faster and faster.

卡車行駛的越來越快。

♦ New urban cities are changing more and more rapidly.

新興的都市改變地越來越快速。

IV. 副詞最高級比較時則用主詞加動詞＋定冠詞 the，後接最高級，加上介系詞 of , in, 或 among 再加上某一範圍的片語。定冠詞 the 在副詞最高級使用中，除非要特別強調，否則也可省略不用。

♦ Bill ran the fastest of the three athletes.

比爾是三名運動員中跑最快的。

♦ Simon arrived at school the earliest in class.

賽門是班上最早到校的。

V. 修飾副詞最高級的副詞及副詞片語常用 very, much, 或 by far，表示語氣的加強，但是位置不同。

♦ Max is the very best student in his class.

麥克斯是他班上最好的學生。

♦ Glory is much / by far the cutest dog among all.

葛洛莉是所有的狗當中最可愛的。

☪ Human Electricity Generators

Human electricity generators refer to people who **possess** the special ability to generate electricity. They are by far the most **extraordinary** and the most amazing people to the general public. Some seem to have higher **voltage** of electricity than normal people and can suddenly send off strong electric currents. They were said to electrify the fish in the tank to death or damage electric appliances, and the electric from them was so powerful that it even once knocked down people nearby. However, one interesting thing about them is that they could easily light a bulb or a **flashlight**, which is considered supernatural power when performed in a show or a **competition**. On the other hand, some extraordinary people can touch high voltage of electricity with their bare hands without being shocked by electricity. Among all ordinary people, they can endure high voltage of electric currents the best. Probably it's because they have rougher or drier skin than others, functioning as an insulating mechanism. And, according to scientists, that is why some people could **escape** from being hurt though stricken by some violent **lightning**. As to the true reasons why the human electricity generators can have such extraordinary power, it still calls for scientists' **persistent** working to find out.

☥ 人體發電機

　　人體發電機指的是某些擁有特殊能力可以產生電的人。就一般大眾而言，他們是最獨特而且是最驚人的。他們之中有些人似乎比一般正常人擁有更高的電量並且能突然發送強烈的電流。他們曾經被傳聞電死水族箱中的魚，損壞電器設備，而且他們身上散發出的電流是如此的強烈以至於附近的人遭電擊而暈倒。然而，有一件有趣的事是他們可以輕易地點燃燈泡或手電筒，而這種能力在表演場或競賽場中被視為是一種超能力。從另一方面來說，有些具有超能力的人可以直接用手去觸摸高壓電而不會被電到。在所有平常人中，他們最能忍受高電壓的電流。那或許是因為他們比別人擁有更粗糙或更乾燥的皮膚以充當絕緣的作用。根據科學家的說法，那也是有些人縱使被雷電擊中仍然可以免於受到傷害的原因。至於為什麼人體發電機能夠擁有如此超能力的真實原因，仍有待科學家持續努力地去尋找。

⧉ 關鍵單字解密

possess *v.* 擁有；具有

extraordinary *adv.* 非凡的；令人驚奇的

voltage *n.* 電壓；伏特數

flashlight *n.* 手電筒

competition *n.* 競爭；競賽

escape *v.* 逃跑；擺脫

lightning *n.* 閃電

persistent *adj.* 執著的；堅持不懈的

 文法分析

分析 1.

例句 | They are by far the most extraordinary and the most amazing people to the general public.

例句 | They are by far the more extraordinary and the more amazing people to the general public.

中譯

就一般大眾而言,他們是最獨特而且是最驚人的。

用法解析

修飾副詞最高級的副詞及副詞片語常用 very, much, 或 by far,表示語氣的加強,第 2 句誤用為比較級,因此是錯誤的句子。

分析 2.

例句 | Probably it's because they have <u>rougher or drier skin than others</u>, functioning as insulating mechanism.

例句 | Probably it's because they have <u>roughest or driest skin than others</u>, functioning as insulating mechanism.

中譯

那或許是因他們比別人擁有更粗糙或更乾燥的皮膚以充當絕緣的作用。

用法解析

此句應用比較級 **rougher or drier**，非最高級 **roughest or driest** 來修飾名詞 **skin**，故第 2 句是錯誤的用法。

UNIT 10

分詞構句 1

Ghost Ships

幽靈船

動詞可有延伸的用法，即現在分詞以及過去分詞，現在分詞表示主動意味，過去分詞代表被動含意。現在分詞構句及過去分詞構句是由對等子句或副詞子句簡化而來的結構。由對等子句簡化而來的的分詞構句常用以表附帶的狀況。而表示條件、時間、原因或讓步……等的副詞子句亦可簡化成分詞構句。簡化後的分詞，若是現在分詞，表示主動意味，或是過去分詞，則表示被動含意。

I. 對等子句中，前後子句主詞相同，則可簡化為分詞構句，表附帶的狀況。此分詞結構常置於後半段。

   ◆ Mr. Brown went home early but he found that nobody was home yet.

   → Mr. Brown went home early, finding that nobody was home yet.　布朗先生提早回家，但是發現尚未有人返家。

   ◆ Philip sat on the bench and he waited for his girlfriend patiently.

   → Philip sat on the bench, waiting for his girlfriend patiently.　菲利浦坐在長凳上很有耐心地等待女朋友。

II. 附屬子句的類別及變化如下：

   1. 表條件

♦ If you get up early in the morning, you will not be late for school.

→ Getting up early in the morning, you will not be late for school.　如果早上早起，你上學就不會遲到。

2. 表時間

♦ When Rebecca knew that her English was flunked, she cried loudly.

→ Knowing that her English was flunked, Rebecca cried loudly.　當蕾貝嘉知道她的英文被當，她放聲大哭。

3. 表原因

♦ Because Ed has much homework to do, he can't play video games after school.

→ Having much homework to do, Ed can't play video games after school.　因為愛德有許多功課要做，他放學後不能打電動。

4. 表讓步

♦ Though Rick had a serious cold, he still went to work.

→ Having a serious cold, Rick still went to work.　雖然瑞克感冒很嚴重，他仍舊去上班。

III. 原附屬子句中，若有完成式的時態，簡化為分詞構句時使用「完成」分詞，having＋p.p. 以敘述在主要子句動詞的時間之前先完成的動作。

♦ Because George had spent a lot of money buying the expensive sports car, he got scolded by his parents.

→ Having spent a lot of money buying the expensive sports car, George got scolded by his parents.　因為喬治花很多錢買昂貴的跑車，他被他的雙親責罵。

For centuries, ghost ships, spotted constantly in vast oceans, are **heated** subjects for **adventurous** explorers to discover and make research into. Ghost ships, also named "Phantom Ships," are ships **drifting** endlessly in the enormous ocean with no passengers or crew aboard, who might be previously missing or killed for unknown reasons. The possible causes, according to researchers, could be bad weather, **malfunction** of the mechanism, getting lost in the sea, or some human-caused reasons, such as piracy, **mutiny**, murdering or poisoning. Some even **attribute** the tragic occurrences to alien abductions, which of course need to be proven. For the past few hundred years, ghost ships have attracted the world's attention, a phenomenon created by **literary** fictions and horror films. Those artistic works portray the mystically unknown causes of the ship's getting lost in the sea and crew members disappearing overnight. The mysterious settings and tragic happenings truly catch readers' and the audience's eye. With the unanswered questions related to those **abandoned** and forgotten ships, ghost ships remain the center of focus of public attention.

♀ 幽靈船

　　許多世紀以來，經常在廣大海域被發現到的幽靈船提供熱門的話題給富冒險精神的探險家去發現並研究。鬼船又名幽靈船，是無止盡地在廣大海域上漂流的船隻，船上並沒有乘客或是船員，他們很可能是因不知名的原因而失蹤或被謀殺。根據研究學者的說法，可能的原因是不良的天候、機械故障、在海上迷失方向，或者是其他人為的因素，例如海盜、叛艦、謀殺或毒殺。有些人甚至把這些悲劇的發生歸因於外星人綁架，然而這一點當然有待證實。過去數百年來，由於文學小說以及恐怖電影的推波助瀾之下，幽靈船吸引了世人的注意。那些藝術作品描述在一夜之間，船隻以及船員神秘失蹤的可能原因。這些神秘的背景和悲慘的事件，確實吸引了讀者及觀眾的注意。在解決那些遭遺棄且遭人遺忘船隻的事件前，幽靈船仍是眾人矚目的焦點。

關鍵單字解密

heated *adj.* 激烈的；激動的

adventurous *adj.* 冒險的；大膽的

drift *v.* 漂流；漂泊

malfunction *n.* 失常；出現故障

mutiny *n.* 反叛；叛亂

attribute *v.* 歸因於……；歸咎於……

literary *adj.* 文學的；文藝的

abandon *v.* 遺棄；捨棄

 文法分析

分析 **1.**

例句 | For centuries, ghost ships, spotted constantly in vast oceans, are heated subjects for adventurous explorers to discover and make research into.

例句 | For centuries, ghost ships, spotting constantly in vast oceans, are heating subjects for adventurous explorers to discover and make research into.

中譯

許多世紀以來,經常在廣大海域被發現到的幽靈船提供熱門的話題給富冒險精神的探險家去發現並研究。

用法解析

動詞可有延伸的用法,即現在分詞以及過去分詞,現在分詞表示主動意味,過去分詞代表被動含意。第 2 句中,被發現應用過去分詞 spotted 非現在分詞 spotting,被炒熱的主題應用過去分詞 heated subjects 非現在分詞 heating subjects。

分析 2. ▶

例句 │ With the <u>unanswered</u> questions <u>related</u> to those abandoned and forgotten ships, ghost ships remain the center of focus of public attention.

例句 │ With the <u>unanswering</u> questions <u>relate</u> to those abandoned and forgotten ships, ghost ships remain the center of focus of public attention.

中譯

在解決那些遭遺棄且遭人遺忘船隻的事件前，幽靈船仍是眾人矚目的焦點。

用法解析

動詞可有延伸的用法，即現在分詞以及過去分詞，現在分詞表示主動意味，過去分詞代表被動含意。第 2 句中，未被回答應用過去分詞 unanswered 非現在分詞 unanswering，與…相關，應用過去分詞 related 非原形動詞 relate，故第 2 句屬於錯誤的句子。

分詞構句 2

UNIT 11

The Mothman
天蛾人

I. 分詞構句的語意否定時，要在分詞前加上 not 或 never，否定分詞片語可置句首或句末。

- ◆ Not having enough money, Lisa had to give up buying the beautiful doll.
  因為沒有足夠的錢，麗莎必須放棄購買那個美麗的洋娃娃。
- ◆ Never making contact with his old classmates, Ted had very little information about them.
  由於從不和老同學聯絡，泰德對他們的了解非常少。

II. 獨立分詞構句：一般的分詞構句是在原前後對等或附屬子句中主詞相同時，才可以簡化。若前後主詞不同時，保留原主詞簡化子句時，便形成所謂的「獨立分詞構句」。

- ◆ The weather being fine, Mr. and Mrs. Smith went on a picnic. 由於天氣很好，史密斯夫婦去野餐。
- ◆ Annie is riding a bike now, her long hair blowing in the wind. 安妮現在正騎著腳踏車，她的長髮在風中飄揚著。

III. 獨立分詞構句所延伸出來的句型：…, with＋N＋Ving / p.p。with 後面的受詞補語，表示主動含意時用現在分詞，被動含意時則用過去分詞。另外也可用一般形容詞修飾。分詞片語部份可置句首或句末。

◆ With tears rolling down her face, Mary ran out of the classroom.　瑪莉淚流滿面地跑出教室。

◆ The old man sat in front of the fireplace, with his eyes closed.　老先生坐在火爐前，雙眼緊閉著。

IV. 若附屬作用的副詞子句中主詞和主要子句的主詞相同，可簡化成連接詞加分詞構句，即保留附屬連接詞，如附屬連接詞 before, after, when, 及 while 等後可接分詞構句。before V-ing 即是副詞子句 before＋S＋V 簡化後的分詞構句。

◆ After taking a painkiller, Nancy felt better.
吃了止痛藥後，南西覺得好多了。

◆ When walking along the street, Helen found a man following her.
走在街道上時，海倫發現有人跟蹤她。

V. 無人稱的獨立分詞構句：獨立分詞構句的意義主詞，若為人稱代名詞常予以省略而形成獨立分詞片語，如 generally / frankly / strictly speaking, judging from …, speaking of …, based on………等等。

◆ Frankly speaking, I don't like his attitude.
坦白說，我不喜歡他的態度。

◆ Judging from the evidence, the victim was murdered.
依證據看來，受害者是被謀殺的。

◆ Speaking of music, what is your favorite kind?
論到音樂，你最喜歡哪一種？

◆ Based on a true story, the movie made a great hit.
因為是根據真實故事改編的，這部電影很賣座。

The Mothman is a moth-like creature, about seven feet tall with large flying wings and **glowing** red eyes. It first appeared in the Point Pleasant Area, West Virginia, from 1966 to 1977. In November, 1966, different **witnesses** separately claimed to have seen the huge, gray, human-like creature, saying that it **attempted** to fly close to them and chase after them. Frightened by the evil-looking monster, local **residents** were in great panic. Rumors had it that it was probably the product of a government experiment that went wrong or a bird **poisoned** by chemical waste from an industrial plant and became mutated. With its **bizarre**, transformed looks, it was even believed to be a kind of alien from outer space, since the places where it was witnessed were also famous for sighting UFOs. In addition, it was an omen of bad luck, for some people making contact with it died for unknown reasons. Also, in December, 1967, right after it appeared, the Silver Bridge suddenly **collapsed**, with 46 people tragically dead. These unexplained incidents **triggered** people's firm belief that it brought about disasters. Therefore, when watching the exciting and horrifying movie, *the Mothman*, we can't help wondering about the true identity and the myth about it.

天蛾人

天蛾人是一個長得像飛蛾的生物，大約七英尺高，有著巨大的飛行翅膀及閃閃發亮的紅眼睛。它是從 1966 到 1977 年間，在西維吉尼亞州的歡樂城附近首度出現。在 1966 年 11 月，不同的目擊者分別宣稱曾經看過這隻巨大灰白色似人類的生物，提及它企圖飛近他們並追逐他們。受到邪惡長相怪物的驚嚇，當地居民極度地恐慌。謠傳它可能是政府實驗失敗的產物，或是一種被來自工業工廠化學廢棄物毒害而變種的鳥。它帶著奇異變形的外貌，因為它被目擊的地點平時是以常見 UFO 的地點為名，所以它甚至被認為是來自於外太空的外星人。此外，因為有些和它做過接觸的人們因不明原因身亡，導致它被視為一個厄運的徵兆。在 1967 年 12 月，就在它出現之後，銀橋（Silver Bridge）突然塌陷，造成 46 人死亡的悲劇。這些無法解說的事件，導致人們堅信天蛾人會帶來災難。因此，當我們觀賞刺激嚇人的天蛾人電影時，我們不得不懷疑有關天蛾人的真實身分及傳說。

關鍵單字解密

glowing *adj.* 發光的；強烈的

witness *n.* 目擊者；見證人

attempt *v.* 企圖；嘗試

resident *n.* 居民；住戶

poison *v.* 中毒

bizarre *adj.* 奇異的；異乎尋常的

collapse *v.* 倒塌；崩潰

trigger *v.* 發動；引起

 **文法分析**

分析 **1.**

例句 │ The Mothman is a moth-like creature, about seven feet tall with large flying wings and glowing red eyes.

例句 │ The Mothman is a moth-like creature, about seven feet tall with large flown wings and glowed red eyes.

中譯

天蛾人是一個長得像飛蛾的生物，大約七英尺高，有著巨大的飛行翅膀及閃閃發亮的紅眼睛。

用法解析

動詞可有延伸的用法，即現在分詞以及過去分詞，現在分詞表示主動意味，過去分詞代表被動含意。「翅膀」wings 應用現在分詞 flying，「紅眼睛」應用現在分詞 glowing 修飾，而非過去分詞 flown 及 glowed 修飾，故第 2 句屬於錯誤的句子。

分析 2.

例句 | Therefore, when <u>watching</u> the exciting and horrifying movie, *the Mothman*, we can't help wondering about the true identity and the myth about it.

例句 | Therefore, when <u>watched</u> the exciting and horrifying movie, *the Mothman*, we can't help wondering about the true identity and the myth about it.

中譯

因此，當我們觀賞刺激嚇人的天蛾人電影時，我們不得不懷疑有關天蛾人的真實身分及傳說。

用法解析

若附屬作用的副詞子句中主詞和主要子句的主詞相同，可簡化成連接詞加分詞構句，即保留附屬連接詞，如附屬連接詞 before, after, when, 及 while 等後可接分詞構句。When V-ing 即是副詞子句 When＋S＋V 簡化後的分詞構句。第 1 句中 When＋V-ing⋯是正確的，但是第 2 句中 When＋V-ed⋯則是錯誤的用法。

假設語氣 1

Kappa, the Japanese River Child

日本河童

英文假設語氣有與「現在事實相反」的假設語氣，與「過去事實相反」的假設語氣以及與「未來事實相反」的假設語氣。

I. 與「現在事實相反」的假設語氣： if 子句即條件句，動詞遇到 be 動詞，不管人稱，一律用 were，一般動詞則變成過去式的動詞，結果子句則要用表示假設的語氣助動詞 would, could, should, 或 might，後面加上原形動詞。

- If I were you, I might do the same.
  如果我是你，我也會這麼做。

II. 與「過去事實相反」的假設語氣： 條件子句 if 子句中動詞部分用過去完成式，結果子句則 would, could, should 或 might 加上現在完成式。

- If Ernie had been more careful then, he would not have fallen into the river.
  假使恩尼當時小心一點，他不會掉落河中。
- If you had behaved well in class yesterday, the teacher would not have punished you.
  假使你昨天在班上表現良好，老師不會處罰你。

III. 與「未來事實相反」的假設語氣：

1. 有可能發生，用一般表條件的副詞子句用法即可，即用普通的直敘語氣：if 子句可用現在式取代未來，主要子句要用主詞後用助動詞 will 加原形動詞。

   ♦ If it rains tomorrow, they will cancel the trip.
   假使明天下雨，他們將取消旅程。

   ♦ If Wendy comes to our new house this afternoon, we will show her around.
   假使溫蒂今天下午來我們的新房子，我們將會帶她四處參觀。

2. 對於未來表示懷疑，則是 if 條件句中主詞加 should＋原形動詞，結果子句則是主詞加 will（表有可能發生）或 would（表不太有可能發生）再加原形動詞。

   ♦ If Mary should be here, I will walk her home.
   萬一瑪莉來了，我會送她回家。

   ♦ If Austin should be late for work again, he would be fired.
   萬一奧斯丁再度上班遲到，他會被解僱。

3. 若要對未來表示極高度的懷疑，非常不可能發生，則是 if 子句主詞加上 were to 加原形動詞，結果子句是主詞加 would 再加上原形動詞。

   ♦ If the sun were to rise in the west, you could pass all the tests.
   要是太陽從西邊升起，你就可以通過所有的考試。

   ♦ If anybody were to see a tiger on the street, he would be too scared to utter a word.
   要是任何人在街上看見老虎，他會嚇到說不出話來。

Kappa in Japanese folklore is an elf in the water. The name is a **combination** of "kawa," meaning "river," and "wappa," meaning "child." According to legends, the river child **resembles** the giant amphibian, the salamander. It lives in the ponds and rivers, about the size of a child with a beak, a turtle-like shell and webbed hands and feet. It has scaly skin with different colors. In addition, there is a bowl-like plate on the top of its head. If the plate were full of water, it would be powerful. However, if the plate ever dried out, the Kappa would lose its power and might even die. The Kappa sometimes acts as if it were a cute little **troublemaker**, hiding under the river surface and playing tricks on people who fall in the river. But it also has a bad **reputation** for killing horses, cows, **kidnapping** children, and **suffocating** people who fall into water. And that is why the Kappa has long been used to warn children of the **potential** danger from the river. However, the Kappa isn't always bad. It is sometimes helpful and brings good fortune to local people. Some Japanese shrines worship it as the River God. So, the mysterious Kappa surely has great **influence** on the Japanese culture.

☥ 日本河童

　　「河童」在日本民間傳說中是水中的精靈。這個名字是由表示「河流」的 *kawa* 以及表示「孩童」的 *wappa* 所結合而成的。根據傳說，河童類似於巨大的兩棲生物—蠑螈。牠居住在池塘和河流中，體型和孩童類似，身上有著鳥嘴、龜殼以及有蹼的手和腳。牠的鱗皮可以有各種不同的顏色。此外，牠的頭頂有著碗狀的托盤。假使這個托盤是滿水狀態時，牠便會力大無窮。相反地，假使這個托盤乾涸了，河童便會失去力量，甚至死亡。河童有時表現地宛如只是一個俏皮的小麻煩製造者，牠會躲在河裡捉弄落入河中的人。但是，牠也具有不好的名聲是因為牠會殺死馬和牛、綁架孩童，並且會將墜入水中的人們悶死。這也就是為什麼「河童」長久以來被用來警告孩童要去注意潛伏在河流中的危險。但事實上，河童並不總是那麼糟糕，有時牠也樂於助人，並且會為當地人帶來好運，有些日本寺廟將它尊奉為「河神」。所以神秘的河童確實為日本文化帶來極大的影響。

 關鍵單字解密

combination	*n.* 結合；聯合
resemble	*v.* 相像；類似
troublemaker	*n.* 惹麻煩的人；鬧事者
reputation	*n.* 名譽；名聲
kidnap	*v.* 劫持；綁架
suffocate	*v.* 窒息；悶死
potential	*adj.* 潛在的；可能的
influence	*n.* 影響；作用

⚙ 文法分析

分析 1.

例句 | If the plate were full of water, it would be powerful.

○

例句 | If the plate was full of water, it would is powerful.

✗

中譯

假使這個托盤是滿水狀態時，祂便會力大無窮。

用法解析

與「現在事實相反」的假設語氣中，if 子句即條件句，動詞遇到 be 動詞，不管人稱，一律用 were，結果子句用表示語氣助動詞 would, could, should, 或 might，後加原形動詞。講述日本一般傳說中「河童」的情境，用現在式的時態來表達。第 2 句的假設句屬於錯誤的句子，因為 was 應該用 were，而助動詞 would 後應接原形動詞 be。

分析 **2.**

例句 | Kappa sometimes acts <u>as if it were</u> a cute little troublemaker, hiding under the river surface and playing tricks on people who fall in the river.

○

例句 | Kappa sometimes acts <u>as if it had been</u> a cute little troublemaker, hiding under the river surface and playing tricks on people who fall in the river.

✕

中譯

河童有時表現地宛如只是一個俏皮的小麻煩製造者，牠會躲在河裡捉弄落入河中的人。

用法解析

中文解釋為「宛如」、「好像」的假設語氣使用 as if / as though， 同於 I wish 的用法一樣，即與現在事實相反時，後接 S＋were 或 v-ed，與過去事實相反時，則用過去完成式，即 S＋had＋p.p.。講述日本一般傳說中「河童」的情境，用現在式的時態來表達。第 2 句的假設句屬於錯誤的句子，因為 as if 後 it had been 應該用 it were。

UNIT 13

假設語氣 2
Reincarnation
輪迴轉世

I. 表示不可能實現的願望時，常用 S＋wish＋過去式（were 或 v-ed）表示與現在事實相反。或用 S＋wish＋過去完成式（had＋p.p）表示與過去事實相反。中文解釋為「但願……」。

 ♦ I wish I were young again.
   但願我能再度年輕。

 ♦ I wish I had time to travel around the world.
   但願我有時間環遊世界。

 ♦ Pam wishes she had taken the job last month.
   潘祈願上個月她有接下那份工作。

II. 中文解釋為「宛如」、「好像」的假設語氣使用 as if / as though，同於 I wish 的用法一樣，即與現在事實相反時，後接 S＋were 或 v-ed，與過去事實相反時，則用過去完成式，即 S＋had＋p.p.。

 ♦ The boy talks as if / though he were an adult.
   這個男孩說話宛如是個大人。

 ♦ I feel as if / though I were going to faint.
   我覺得好像快昏倒了。

 ♦ The man acts as if / though he knew the secret.
   這個男人的表現好像他知道這個秘密。

 ♦ Henry speaks Spanish as if / though he had lived in Spain

for long.

亨利說西班牙文宛如曾在西班牙久住。

III. 遇到表示強烈命令、建議、堅持、請求語意的動詞，如 command, suggest, insist, request, demand……等時，後面子句部分要用假設語氣，即 S＋should＋原形動詞，而助動詞 should 經常可以省略。

♦ The doctor suggested that Larry（should）stop smoking for his health's sake.

醫生建議賴瑞為了健康著想應該戒菸。

♦ The wife insisted that her husband（should）pay all the bills.

這名妻子堅持她的丈夫應該付所有的帳單。

♦ The teacher requested that Philip（should）hand in his assignment before noon.

老師要求飛利浦中午之前繳交作業。

IV. 表示「某人早該做某事」的句型「It is time that…」中，也常用假設語氣，表示預期未能實現。用與現在事實相反的假設語氣，即後接 S＋were 或 v-ed。

♦ Your hair is too long. It is time that you had a haircut.

你的頭髮太長了。你早就該剪頭髮了。

♦ It is high time that little Johnny went to bed.

小強尼早就該上床睡覺了。

♦ It is about time that Vivian stopped gossiping and concentrated on her studies.

薇薇安早就該停止八卦並且專心於課業。

Reincarnation is the natural process of birth, death, and rebirth. A human being's soul or spirit, after death, can begin a new life in a new body. In Buddhism, we human beings are the true masters of our own fate. What you did yesterday makes what you are today. If you did good **deeds** in the previous life, you would enjoy the fruitful taste in this life. On the contrary, if you were **immoral** then, you would **suffer** now. Seeing life from this point of view, we should think that it is high time that we worked hard to **discipline** ourselves and performed **charities** to have a better life in both this life and the next life.

The notions of reincarnation in religion may differ from culture to culture, while most scientists and researchers hold **skeptical** attitudes toward them. Those who **oppose** hold the idea that ordinary people do not remember previous lives and it is impossible for them to survive death and enter another body. Nevertheless, with more and more cases of reincarnation reported all over the world, they have started to accept the possibility of its **existence**. For the future to come, reincarnation will still remain a magical mystery that needs to be explored.

☥ 輪迴轉世

輪迴轉世是出生，死亡而再生的過程。人類的靈魂或鬼魂在死亡後能夠藉由一個新的軀體開始一個新的生命。就佛教而言，我們人類是我們自己命運的真實主宰者。昨天你的所作所為造就今日的你，如果你前世做好事，今生你將享受美果。相反地，假使你當時不道德，你現在將會受折磨。從這個角度看人生，我們應該想到我們早就該努力規範自己並且做善事，好讓我們今生與來生都會有一個比較好的人生。

宗教轉世輪迴的觀念可能因文化而異，然而大部分科學家和調查員對轉世輪迴抱持著懷疑的態度。反對者認為一般人不記得前世，他們也不可能規避死亡並且進入另一個軀體。然而，隨著全世界有越來越多關於輪迴轉世的報導，他們也開始接受輪迴轉世確實存在的可能性。就未來的歲月來說，輪迴轉世將持續保持是需要被探索的魔幻之謎。

⛰ 關鍵單字解密

deed *n.* 行為；功績

immoral *adj.* 不道德的；邪惡的

suffer *v.* 受苦；患病

discipline *v.* 訓練；有紀律

charity *n.* 慈悲；慈善事業

skeptical *adj.* 懷疑的；多疑的

oppose *v.* 反對；反抗

existence *n.* 存在；生存

文法分析

分析 1.

例句 | If you did good deeds in the previous life, you would enjoy the fruitful taste in this life.

例句 | If you do good deeds in the previous life, you would have enjoyed the fruitful taste in this life.

中譯

如果你前世做好事，今生你將享受美果。

用法解析

與「現在事實相反」的假設語氣中，if 子句即條件句，動詞遇到一般動詞則變成過去式的動詞，結果子句用表示語氣助動詞 would, could, should, 或 might，後加原形動詞。第 2 句與「現在事實相反」的假設句屬於錯誤的句子，因為 If you 後應該用 did，而助動詞 would 後應接原形動詞 enjoy，而非 have enjoyed。

分析 2. ▶

例句 | Seeing life from this point of view, we should think that <u>it is high time that we worked</u> hard to discipline ourselves and <u>performed charities</u> to have a better life in both this life and the next life.

例句 | Seeing life from this point of view, we should think that <u>it is high time that we will work</u> hard to discipline ourselves and <u>will perform charities</u> to have a better life in both this life and the next life.

中譯

從這個角度看人生，我們應該想到我們早就該努力規範自己並且做善事，好讓我們今生與來生都會有一個比較好的人生。

用法解析

表示「某人早該做某事」的句型 "It is time that…" 中，用假設語氣，表示預期未能實現。用與現在事實相反的假設語氣，即後接 S +were 或 v-ed。第 2 句與「現在事實相反」的假設句屬於錯誤的句子，因為 it is high time 後應該用 that we worked…and performed charities…，而非用 that we will work… and will perform charities …。

UNIT 14

對等子句與附屬子句
Pica Eating Disorder
異食癖

I. 對等連接詞，如 and, but, or, for, …等，用以連接兩個語意同等重要且同等結構的「對等子句」。連接的兩個子句要用對等時態，如兩句都用「現在式」或都用「過去式」，以求對等。

- ♦ You should tell no more lies, or you will hurt others.
  你應該不要再說謊了，否則你會傷害到別人。
- ♦ The young salesman seems honest, but I don't trust him.
  這個年輕的業務員似乎很誠實，但是我不信任他。
- ♦ Rachel took an umbrella with her, for it was raining hard then.
  瑞秋隨身帶著一把傘，因為當時正下著大雨。

II. 附屬連接詞，如 who, which, that, if, though, when, where, because, after, before ……等引導的子句稱為「附屬子句」，表示附帶的語意，另一句則為「主要子句」，表示主要的語意內容。附屬連接詞依用法及語意可有不同類別。

- ♦ It matters not who you are but what you are.
  你是誰並不重要，重要的是你的內涵。
- ♦ If you are late tomorrow, we will have to leave without you.
  假使你明天遲到，我們就必須先離開。

♦ After Emma graduated from college, she became an assistant.

艾瑪大學畢業後，成為一名助理。

1. 引導「名詞子句」的附屬連接詞，有 what, that, who, how, why, whether ……等。此名詞子句常充當主詞、受詞，或補語。

♦ What you said is unbelievable.

你說的話並不可信。

♦ We wonder how the bird managed to escape from the cage.

我們懷疑這隻鳥如何設法從鳥籠逃離的。

2. 引導「形容詞子句」的附屬連接詞則常用 who, which, that, when, where ……等。

♦ The speaker who made an admirable speech is my uncle.

那位發表令人欽佩演說的演講者是我的叔叔。

♦ The purse which was dropped on the ground belonged to Judy.

掉在地上的錢包是茱蒂的。

3. 引導「副詞子句」的附屬連接詞則常用 when, before, after ……等表示「時間」，because, since ……等表示「原因」，if 表示「條件」，though 表示「讓步」， while 則可表示「對比」。

♦ Before you leave the house, remember to turn all the lights off.

出門前，記得把所有的燈關掉。

♦ Though Mr. Smith is over seventy years old, he is still active and energetic.

雖然史密斯先生已經超過70歲了，他仍舊是活耀且精力充沛。

★ Pica Eating Disorder

When it's time to enjoy a great meal, people think of **delicious** fish, meat, vegetables, and fruits. However, to people suffering from Pica, they will have a totally different menu. Pica is an **abnormal** craving or appetite for nonfood substances, such as soil, clay, glass, or metal. In fact, eating soil in certain African regions that lack **sufficient** food is a common practice. To people there, especially to pregnant women, the underground soil is rich in different minerals, from which they can **supplement** nutrition. However, medically speaking, a Pica patient may get seriously sick because of lead-poisoning, **malnutrition**, parasite infection, intestinal obstruction, or tearing in the stomach. Some Pica patients may have certain mental disorders, while others may simply want to **relieve** the stress from their family or the society. As for the healing solutions, besides taking medication, **psychological** treatments, family guidance, and reinforcement of social communication skills are recommended. Though it's hard to imagine eating odd stuff, from dirt, glass, to even bikes, or TV sets, most of them claim that they will feel sick if **forbidden** to eat the nonfood they like. Aren't patients who suffer from Pica eating disorder mysterious kinds of people? They are truly worth further research and exploration.

☥ 異食癖

　　享受大餐時，人們會想到美味的魚，肉，蔬菜，和水果。然而，對罹患異食癖的人來說，他們菜單上的菜色卻是大大的不同。異食癖是對非食物的物質，譬如像土壤，黏土，玻璃，或金屬，產生一種不正常的熱愛或食慾。事實上，在某些缺乏足夠糧食的非洲地區，吃土壤是司空見慣的。對那裡的人來說，地下土壤富含礦物質，他們，尤其是孕婦，可以從地下土壤補充營養。但是就醫學而言，有異食癖的病患可能會因為鉛中毒、營養不足、寄生蟲感染、腸阻塞、或腸胃撕裂而病重。某些異食癖病患也許有特定的精神異常狀況，而有些可能只是想要舒緩來自於家庭或社會的壓力。至於治療的解決方法，除了吃藥之外，心理治療、家庭指導以及社交溝通技能的強化是被推薦的。雖然人們很難想像去吃像泥土、玻璃，甚至是腳踏車或電視機這樣古怪的東西，大部分異食癖患者卻宣稱，假使他們被禁止吃他們喜愛吃的非食物，他們反而會生病。異食癖患者是不是很神秘的人物呢？他們確實值得進一步研究並探索。

 關鍵單字解密

delicious *adj.* 美味的；好吃的

abnormal *adj.* 不正常的；反常的

sufficient *adj.* 足夠的；充分的

supplement *v.* 補充；補給

malnutrition *n.* 營養不良；營養失調

relieve *v.* 減輕；寬慰

psychological *adj.* 心理學的；精神的

forbidden *adj.* 禁止的；被禁止的

 文法分析

分析 1.

例句 In fact, eating soil in certain African regions that lack sufficient food is a common practice.

例句 In fact, eating soil in certain African regions if lack sufficient food is a common practice.

中譯

事實上，在某些缺乏足夠糧食的非洲地區，吃土壤是司空見慣的。

用法解析

附屬連接詞，如 who, which, that, if, though, when, where, because, after, before ……等引導的子句稱為「附屬子句」，表示附帶的語意，另一句則為「主要子句」，表示主要的語意內容。附屬連接詞依用法及語意可有不同類別。引導「形容詞子句」的附屬連接詞則可用 who, which, that, when, where ……等，但不可用表示「假設」的連接詞 if，故第 2 句屬於錯誤的句子。

分析 2.

例句 | Some Pica patients may have certain mental disorders, while others may simply want to relieve the stress from their family or the society.

例句 | Some Pica patients may have certain mental disorders, that others may simply want to relieve the stress from their family or the society.

中譯

某些異食癖病患也許有特定的精神異常狀況， 然而有些可能只是想要舒緩來自於家庭或社會的壓力。

用法解析

附屬連接詞，如 who, which, that, if, though, when, where, because, after, before ……等引導的子句稱為「附屬子句」，表示附帶的語意，另一句則為「主要子句」，表示主要的語意內容。附屬連接詞依用法及語意可有不同類別。引導「副詞子句」的附屬連接詞則常用 when, before, after, …等表示「時間」，because, since ……等表示「原因」，if 表示「條件」，though 表示「讓步」，while 則可表示「對比」。此句表示「對比」，但是第 2 句中未用 while 而用 that 是錯誤的用法。

UNIT
15

直接問句與間接問句
The Elephants' Graveyard
大象墓園

I. 「直接問句」有下列三種常見的類型：

1. 帶有 be 動詞，一般動詞以及助動詞的問句，肯定時用 Yes ，否定
時用 No 回答。Yes-no 問句要把句中主詞和動詞的字序顛倒而
得。

   ♦ Is John a scholar?　約翰是名學者嗎？

   → Yes, he is.　是的，他是。

   ♦ Did they have a happy weekend?

   他們週末過得愉快嗎？

   → No, they didn't.　不，他們過得不快樂。

   ♦ Will you do me a favor?　幫我一個忙好嗎？

   → Yes, of course.　是的，當然。

2. 帶有疑問詞 who, which, what, when ……等的問句，稱為 Wh-
問句。直接問句中，這些疑問詞要置於句首，問的時候，先接動
詞，再接主詞。回答時直接依實際內容回答，而不用 Yes 或 No 。

   ♦ Who can play the cello?　誰會拉大提琴？

   ♦ What did May wish to have for her birthday?

   梅想要什麼生日禮物？

   ♦ When was the table available then?

   那麼何時會有空位呢？

3. 附加問句,即在敘述句後面加上的問句。前面為肯定句,後面附加部分要用否定。前面為否定句,後面附加部分則要用肯定。

♦ Sherry is from Canada, isn't she?

雪莉來自加拿大,不是嗎?

♦ They just won't stop arguing, will they?

他們就是吵個不停,不是嗎?

♦ Rex and Jenny have finished their homework, haven't they?

雷克斯和珍妮功課做完了,不是嗎?

II. 直接問句在語意上,變成是如 know, ask, tell, wonder, doubt, …等及物動詞或介系詞的受詞時,則形成「間接問句」。字序要變成:疑問詞＋主詞＋動詞(＋介系詞)之肯定敘述的樣式,而非「直接問句」,動詞在主詞前的樣式。

♦ Who did Lisa go to the movies with?

麗莎和誰去看電影?

→ We want to know who Lisa went to the movies with.

我們想知道麗莎和誰去看電影。

♦ What can they do to solve the problem?

他們如何解決問題?

→ Most of the people doubt what they can do to solve the problem.

大部份人懷疑他們如何解決問題。

♦ When will you start your new job?

你何時開始你的新工作?

→ I wonder when you will start your new job.

我想知道你何時開始你的新工作。

☾ ★ The Elephants' Graveyard

In Africa, there's a **legendary** myth that when elephants get old and sense their upcoming death, they would walk a long distance to the "Elephants' Graveyard" and die there alone. However, till now, we still haven't had the slightest idea about where the burial grounds are. Elephant tusks can be made into **ivories** that are highly valuable, so greedy hunters are always searching for the graveyard. To them, they must be full of precious ivory tusks. Strange to say, their wishful thinking has never been **fulfilled**. Most hunters and explorers had difficulty finding it, though some local tribal chiefs claimed to have seen one. But, here comes the question: Why couldn't they find the graveyard? In fact, whether the graveyard exits or not still remain doubtful. Besides, the causes of elephants' death vary. Researchers **maintain** that some seemingly tusk-piled locations cannot be sure to be the graveyard where elephants choose to complete the process to death, for water floods may have resulted in the **accumulation** of large piles of the tusks. And, great numbers of elephants may have died there shortly after some great food or water shortage. Besides, other natural **disasters** may have caused their death, too. Still another supposition is that cruel and **notorious poachers** might deliberately trap and kill them to get ivory tusks. With all the reasons above, it's no wonder that it's no easy task to locate the whereabouts of graveyards.

☥ 大象墓園

　　在非洲，有一個流傳的神秘說法：當大象年紀大了，並且意識到即將死亡，牠們會單獨走很長一段路去到「大象墓園」，並且獨自在那兒死亡。但是至今我們仍不知「大象墓園」在那裡。大象的牙齒可以製造成高價值的象牙，所以貪婪的獵人一直在搜尋墓園。對他們來說，墓園裡必定充滿著珍貴的象牙。說也奇怪，他們的心願從來沒有實現過。雖然曾有當地土著酋長宣稱曾經看過墓園，大部分的獵人和探險家找不到它。但，問題是：為什麼他們找不到墓園呢？事實上，墓園是否真的存在仍令人懷疑。此外，大象死亡的原因不一。研究學者們主張，某些看起來似乎堆滿了象牙的地方無法確定就是大象選擇結束生命過程的墓園，因為大洪水可能導致大量的象牙成堆地累積。而且，在某個重大的食物或飲水短缺之後不久，大量的大象有可能死於墓園內。此外，其他天然災害也有可能導致牠們的死亡。另一個假設是說，殘忍且聲名狼藉的盜獵者有可能蓄意地設陷阱捕殺牠們取得象牙。由上述所有的原因看來，難怪找尋墓園所在地並非容易之事。

⚠ 關鍵單字解密

legendary *adj.* 傳奇的；傳說的

ivory *n.* 象牙；象牙製品

fulfill *v.* 完成；實現

maintain *v.* 維持；堅持意見

accumulation *n.* 累積；積聚

disaster *n.* 災害；災難

notorious *adj.* 惡名昭彰的；聲名狼藉的

poacher *n.* 偷獵者；盜獵者

 **文法分析**

分析 1.

例句 | However, till now, we still haven't had the slightest idea about where the burial grounds are. ⭕

例句 | However, till now, we still haven't had the slightest idea about where are the burial grounds. ❌

中譯

但是至今我們仍不知「大象墓園」在那裡。

用法解析

直接問句在語意上，變成是如 know, ask, tell, wonder, doubt, …等及物動詞或介系詞的受詞時，則形成「間接問句」。字序要變成：疑問詞＋主詞＋動詞（＋介系詞）之肯定敘述的樣式，而非「直接問句」，動詞在主詞前的樣式。第 2 句中 where 後應接間接問句子句，而非直接問句子句。

分析 2. ▶

例句 | But, here comes the question: Why couldn't they find the graveyard?

例句 | But, here comes the question: Why they couldn't find the graveyard.

中譯

但，問題是：為何他們找不到墓園呢？

用法解析

帶有疑問詞 who, which, what, when ……等的問句，稱為 Wh- 問句。直接問句中，這些疑問詞要置於句首，問的時候，先接動詞，再接主詞。第 2 句中 where 後應接直接問句，而非間接問句子句，並應打問號，故屬於錯誤的句子。

UNIT 16 否定句

The Disaster-Predicting Dreams

災難預知夢

I. be 動詞的否定形式，直接在 be 動詞後加上 not，一般動詞要利用助動詞 do, does 或 did，有助動詞 may, can, should, must ……等時，直接後接 not，完成式則是 have, has 或 had 後加上 not 而形成否定句。

- ◆ Sam is not going to the party tonight.
  山姆今晚不打算去參加派對。
- ◆ You should not cheat in the exam.
  你考試不該作弊。
- ◆ We have not heard from Jason for a long time.
  我們已經很久沒有傑森的消息。

II. 英文中的否定句也可以在字的前面加上代表否定的字首而構成否定意義，如 un-, dis-, in-, im-, mis- ……等。

- ◆ All the students disliked the new substitute teacher.
  所有的學生都不喜歡新來的代課老師。
- ◆ Please don't misunderstand me.
  請不要誤會我。

III. not 可接在動詞 think, suppose, expect, believe, be afraid, …等後面單獨表示否定的敘述。

♦ A: Are you coming to the party tonight?

今晚要來參加派對嗎？

B: I'm afraid not.

恐怕不行喔。

♦ A: Will you vote for Mr. Anderson?

你會投票給安德森先生嗎？

B: I suppose not.

我應該不會。

IV. no, few, little, nobody, nothing, never, neither, none 等代表否定意味的副詞置於句中即具否定的含意。

♦ Few students were absent today.

今天只有少數的學生缺席。

♦ It's a pity that we have never been to Germany.

真可惜我們從未去過德國。

♦ None of the staff members can open the locked door.

職員中沒有一個人可以打開上鎖的門。

V. 否定副詞及副詞片語 seldom, rarely, hardly, scarcely, by no means, under no circumstances ⋯⋯等亦可構成否定含意。

♦ Nick seldom takes any traffic means; he always walks.

尼克很少搭乘任何交通工具；他總是走路。

♦ We had hardly arrived at the train station when the train left.

我們一到達火車站，火車就走了。

♦ John is by no means selfish; he always offers his help.

約翰一點也不自私；他總是熱心助人。

☪ ★ Disaster-Predicting Dreams

🎧 Track 16

Most of us spend about one third of our lives sleeping, and what we dream about while sleeping can have great **significance**. It's a long known mystery that some people claim to have disaster-predicting dreams. They seem to have a special sixth sense and, without having related **knowledge** in advance, can have dreams **predicting** the future incidents, either the natural disasters or the human-caused accidents. The natural disasters may include floods, earthquakes, tornadoes, tsunamis, or hurricanes, such as the **devastating** Hurricane Katrina. On the other hand, dreams predicting the human-caused accidents may be about the shooting incidents, plane crashes, or the **shipwrecks**, such as the tragic sinking of the dubbed "Unsinkable" Titanic. From researchers' point of view, what these predictors claimed can hardly be real. In their opinion, these foretold disaster dreams are nothing but responses to events in the dreamers' personal life, and the dreams may probably be just **coincidences**. However, with the **vivid**, detailed, and exact descriptions of those dreamers, we can't help wondering how the disasters they dream about can actually happen in the real world. Therefore, we believe there is still a long way to go to explore humans' **subconscious** minds and dreams.

☥ 災難預知夢

　　我們大多數人一生中有三分之一的時間在睡覺，而睡覺時作的夢具有極大的意義。這是一個人們長久以來聽聞的現象，即有些人宣稱能夠預先夢見災難。他們似乎擁有特別的第六感，事前並不知道任何相關的訊息，但是竟然能夠作預告未來事件的夢，不管是天然災害，或者是人為的意外事故。天然災害可能包含有水災、地震、龍捲風、海嘯，或者是颶風，譬如像極具災難性的卡翠納颶風。另一方面，預見人為意外事件的夢境則可能是搶擊事件、飛機墜機，或者是船難，譬如像號稱「永不沉沒」的鐵達尼號悲慘沉沒的事件。從研究學者的觀點來說，預測者所宣稱的夢境不可能是真實的。依他們之見，這些預知災難的夢境只是作夢者個人生活事件的反應，可能只是巧合罷了。但是，隨著那些作夢者生動詳細而且確切的描述，我們不得不納悶他們夢到的災難如何能夠確切地在真實事件中發生。所以，我們相信探索人類潛意識的心靈和夢境仍然有長遠的路要走。

⟁ 關鍵單字解密

significance *n.* 意義；重要

knowledge *n.* 知識；學識

predict *v.* 預料；預報

devastating *adj.* 毀滅性的；驚人的

shipwreck *n.* 海難；船舶失事

coincidence *n.* 巧合；巧事

vivid *adj.* 清晰的；生動的

subconscious *adj.* 潛意識的

文法分析

分析 1.

例句 | Dreams predicting the human-made accidents may be about the shooting incidents, plane crashes, or the shipwrecks, such as the tragic sinking of the dubbed "Unsinkable" Titanic.

例句 | Dreams predicting the human-made accidents may be about the shooting incidents, plane crashes, or the shipwrecks, such as the tragic sinking of the dubbed "Sinkable" Titanic.

中譯

預見人為意外事件的夢境則可能是槍擊事件、飛機墜機,或者是船難,譬如像號稱「永不沉沒」的鐵達尼號悲慘沉沒的事件。

用法解析

英文中的否定句可以在字的前面加上代表否定的字首而構成否定意義,如 un-, dis-, in-, im-, mis- ……等。「永不沉沒」,只要在「沉沒的」 sinkable 前加上 un-,即可表達出否定含意。第 2 句語意上應用 "Unsinkable" 非用 "Sinkable"。

分析 **2.** ▶

例句 | From researchers' point of view, what these predictors claimed <u>can hardly be real.</u> ○

例句 | From researchers' point of view, what these predictors claimed <u>can hard be real.</u> ✕

中譯

從研究學者的觀點來説，預測者所宣稱的夢境不可能是真實的。

用法解析

否定副詞及副詞片語 seldom, rarely, hardly, scarcely, by no means, under no circumstances ……等亦可構成否定含意。第 2 句 hard 應用 hardly，故屬於錯誤的句子。

倒裝句 1
The Mysterious Holy Water
神秘聖水

 英文句子中常使用「倒裝句」
以達加強語氣的作用：

I. 為強調「地方副詞」或「方向副詞」，可將之置於句首。表示位置的介
副詞，如 up, out, away, down, over, inside ……等，在一般敘述句
的句子中，可將介副詞往前提而構成倒裝句。主詞是名詞時，動詞應倒
裝到主詞之前，主詞是代名詞時，動詞則不用倒裝。地點副詞，如
here, there 等，為加強語氣，亦可往前提，形成倒裝句。置於句首
時，也是同樣的原則使用倒裝。

♦ The mansion Mr. Jackson bought was near the lake.
→ Near the lake was the mansion Mr. Jackson bought.
傑克森先生買的豪宅靠近湖邊。

♦ The birds flew away.
→ Away flew the birds.
鳥飛走了。

II. 表示「也…」的肯定附和句，可用下列兩句型來表達肯定附和句
「也…」：S＋be 動詞…, and so＋be 動詞＋S 及 S＋助動詞＋一般
動詞…, and so＋助動詞＋S。否定附和句後半段附和部分要倒裝時亦
同，只是肯定及否定要互換。

♦ Kyle is excited about going to college, and Annie is, too.

→ Kyle is excited about going to college, and so is Annie.

凱爾對於上大學感到興奮，而安妮也是。

III. 主詞補語倒裝可以加強語氣。句子正常的字序是「S＋V＋主詞補語」，有時為了強調主詞補語，會將補語往前提，而與主詞交換位置，形成倒裝的句型，形成「主詞補語＋V＋S」。補語置於前形成倒裝句，也可以表示強調的語意，如表示「結果」的子句，常把 so 往前提。

- ◆ The audience were so amazed that they could not speak a word.

  → So amazed were the audience that they could not speak a word.

  觀眾是如此的驚訝，以至於他們啞口無言。

- ◆ Those who are content are happy.

  → Happy are those who are content.

  知足常樂。

IV. 否定副詞 no, not, little, never, seldom, hardly, rarely, scarcely, …等及副詞片語 no longer, not a word, under no circumstances, …等，可置於句首，後接倒裝句構，即動詞與主詞互換，或另藉助動詞等方式構成倒裝句，以加強語氣。

- ◆ Rarely does Tom take a taxi home.

  湯姆很少坐計程車回家。

- ◆ Hardly had the police officer come when the robber ran away.

  警官一到達現場搶匪就跑走了。

Inside the sanctuary at Lourdes, France, is a famous place of pilgrimage providing holy water that creates **miracle** cures. Never did the local residents come up with the idea that the **sacred** water should bring great changes to them. It's said that the holy water never stopped **springing** out and possessed curing effects for illnesses. In fact, the discovery of the holy water was full of mythical origins. During the 19th century, a poor girl named Bernadette Soubirous **accidentally** found a cave and met a smiling noble lady, whom the townspeople thought to be the Virgin Mary later. She told Bernadette to dig into a cave for a spring, drink it and wash herself there. Bernadette followed her **instructions** and created a well there. People tried drinking the water and surprisingly found their sicknesses relieved or healed. So appreciative of the miracles made by the Virgin Mary were the cured people that they built churches for her. Since then, the holy water had become famous. The **pious** Catholic pilgrims and tourists would visit the place either to get their illnesses cured or to witness the miracle. After lining up for hours, they would usually light up **candles**, say prayers, drink the holy water, and bathe in it for curing or **purification**. However, where the endless holy water comes from and why it has such great healing properties are still mysteries to the world.

神秘聖水

　　在法國盧德的聖殿裡，有一處提供奇蹟療效聖水而著名的朝聖地。當地居民從未想到這聖水竟帶給他們極大的改變。據說這聖水從不停止噴湧出來，並有療病的效果。事實上，聖水的發現充滿神秘的起源。在 19 世紀期間，有一個叫做 Bernadette Soubirous 的貧窮女孩，無意間發現一個洞穴並且遇見一位面帶微笑的高貴女士，這位女士後來被居民認為是聖母瑪利亞。她告訴 Bernadette 去挖洞穴中泉水，喝泉水，並洗滌。Bernadette 遵循她的指示，並在那兒鑿出了一口井。居民試著去喝這個水，並很驚訝於發現他們的疾病症狀減緩，甚至治癒了。被治癒的民眾是如此地感激聖母瑪利亞所創造的神蹟以致於在那裡為她建造。從那時起，聖水變出名了。虔誠的天主教朝聖者以及觀光客會來參觀這個地方，也許是要為自己治療疾病，或者是要見證奇蹟。在排隊排上好幾個小時後，他們一般會點燃蠟燭，祈禱，喝聖水，並浸泡在聖水中來取得治療或淨化的作用。然而，永無止盡的聖水來自於何處，以及它為何具有如此大的治療功效，對世人來說仍舊是謎。

關鍵單字解密

miracle *n.* 奇蹟；神奇的事例

sacred *adj.* 神聖的；莊嚴的

spring *n. / v.* 源泉；根源；噴湧

accidentally *adv.* 意外地；偶然地

instruction *n.* 教導；指示

pious *adj.* 虔誠的；敬神的

candle *n.* 蠟燭；燭光

purification *n.* 洗淨；淨化

 **文法分析**

分析 1.

例句 | Inside the sanctuary at Lourdes, France, is a famous place of pilgrimage providing holy water that creates miracle cures.

⭕

例句 | Inside the sanctuary at Lourdes, France, a famous place is of pilgrimage providing holy water that creates miracle cures.

❌

中譯

在法國盧德的聖殿裡，有一處提供奇蹟療效聖水而著名的朝聖地。

用法解析

為強調「地方副詞」或「方向副詞」，可將之置於句首。表示位置的介副詞，如 up, out, away, down, over, inside ……等，在一般敘述句的句子中，可將介副詞往前提而構成倒裝句。第 2 句屬於錯誤的句子，因 be 動詞 is 未置於前，形成倒裝。

分析 2.

例句 | So appreciative of the miracles made by the Virgin Mary were the cured people that they built churches for her there.

例句 | So appreciative of the miracles made by the Virgin Mary was the cured people that they built churches for her there.

中譯

被治癒的民眾是如此地感激聖母瑪利亞所創造的神蹟以致於在那裡為她建造教堂。

用法解析

主詞補語倒裝可以加強語氣。句子正常的字序是「S＋V＋主詞補語」，有時為了強調主詞補語，會將補語往前提，而與主詞交換位置，形成倒裝的句型，形成「主詞補語＋V＋S」。補語置於前形成倒裝句，也可以表示強調的語意，如表示「結果」的子句，常把 so 往前提。第 2 句屬於錯誤的句子，因此句真正的主詞是置於後的 people，所以 be 動詞應用複數的 were，非單數的 was。

UNIT 18

倒裝句 2

Pythons That Swallow Large Animals
蟒蛇吞巨物

 一般的副詞及副詞片語常可以轉換成倒裝句，以加強語氣：

I. 副詞 only 常置於句首形成倒裝句。

   ♦ One realizes the importance of health only when he loses it.

   → Only when one loses health does he realize the importance of it. 人唯有在失去健康時，才體會到它的重要。

II. 否定副詞 no, not, little, never, seldom, hardly, rarely, scarcely ……等及副詞片語 no longer, not a word, under no circumstances ……等，可置於句首，後接倒裝句構，即動詞與主詞互換，或另藉助動詞等方式構成倒裝句，以加強語氣。

   ♦ Hardly had the police officer come when the robber ran away. 警官一到達現場搶匪就跑走了。

   ♦ No longer will Nancy shop in that mall after the unpleasant experience. 經過那次不愉快的經驗後，南西再也不會在那家購物中心購物了。

III. 含 not…until 表示「直到 …… 才……」的句型，常倒裝以加強語氣。Not until…＋助動詞＋S＋V…。not 常與 until 連用，until 可以是連接詞或介系詞。Not 置於句首時，後面的子句要倒裝，以加強語氣。

   ♦ Bill didn't meet his bosom friend until he entered college.

   → Not until Bill entered college did he meet his bosom

friend. 比爾直到上大學才遇到知己好友。

IV. not only… but also … 表示「不僅 …… 而且……」為一連接詞式的
片語，以及含 no sooner…than…表示「一 …… 就 ……」的句型，
亦常倒裝以加強語氣。

♦ The Wilsons invited not only Luke but also his pet dog to
the party.
→ Not only Luke but also his pet dog was invited to the
party by the Wilsons. 威爾森家不僅邀請路克並且邀請他的狗
來參加派對。

V. 引導讓步子句的連接詞 though, as 表示「雖然；儘管 ……」表讓
步，亦可形成倒裝句：此句型可將形容詞、副詞與名詞置於句首，接附
屬連接詞 though 或 as，但不用 although，再加附屬子句。這種倒
裝句法的讓步子句，放在句首的若為名詞，不可加冠詞。

♦ Boy as / though Max is, he is capable of doing an adult's
job. 麥克斯雖然是孩子，他能夠做大人做的事。
♦ Rich as / though Mrs. Davidson is, she is not happy at all.
雖然戴維森太太很富有，但是她一點也不快樂。
♦ Diligently as / though Ed worked, he couldn't afford to buy
a house of his own. 雖然艾德勤勉地工作，他買不起自己的房
子。

VI. 假設語氣中，省略 if 後亦常倒裝以加強語氣。

♦ Were I you, I might do the same. 假使我是你，我可能會做
同樣的事。
♦ Had Tom enough money, he would buy the mansion for
his family. 假使湯姆有足夠的錢，他會為家人買豪宅。
♦ Had Ernie been more careful then, he would not have
fallen into the river. 假使恩尼當時更小心一點，他就不會掉入
河中。

☪★ Pythons That Swallow Large Animals

Though non-venomous and often kept as pets, pythons are fierce and brutal predators when hungry. Sometimes, so hungry are some pythons that they eat whatever they see, though the **prey** may be huge. Horrifying incidents as such are frequently reported worldwide, especially in Africa and Australia. Some **ferocious** pythons can swallow huge-sized animals, such as sheep, deer, and cows. They also eat alligators, kangaroos, and even young children. Once hungry, little do they **hesitate** to ambush and swallow the animal they spot even though they are huge. With a certain **unique** method, they **consume** the innocent creature. First, they constrict it to death, and then gorge it in just one bite. In one or two gulps, the poor victim is **devoured**. Once the pythons begin to devour, seldom do they stop. Afterwards, though painful with a **swollen** stomach, they can digest the prey with their special feeding mechanism. In South Africa, no sooner had a ten-year-old boy run fast to get away from a python that moved **silently** and fast than he got swallowed and consumed within minutes. How terrible! So, next time, when planning to keep a python as a pet, one may as well give it a second thought!

☥ 蟒蛇吞巨物

　　雖然蟒蛇沒有毒性且常被飼養為寵物，饑餓時，牠們是兇猛殘暴的獵食者。有時候，某些蟒蛇是如此地飢餓以致於牠們看到甚麼都吃，儘管這個獵物可能是很大型的。像這樣恐怖的事件，經常在全世界被報導，尤其是在非洲和澳洲。有些兇猛的蟒蛇，能夠吞下像綿羊、鹿，和牛這樣大型的動物。牠們也吃鱷魚、袋鼠，甚至是孩童。一旦餓了，牠們毫不遲疑於突襲並且吞噬牠們所看見的動物，儘管牠們體型龐大。牠們會用獨特的方式把無辜的生物吞噬。首先，牠們把牠絞死，接著一口咬住，可憐的受害者一兩口就被吞下肚了。一旦蟒蛇開始吞噬，牠們很少稍作停留。稍後，雖然因腫脹的肚子而感到痛苦，牠們會以特殊的餵食機制來消化獵物。在南非，有一個 10 歲大的小男孩一快跑以逃離無聲無息且快速前行的蟒蛇，卻馬上就被吞噬而且幾分鐘內就被吃進肚了。真可怕！所以，下一次，當人們計畫要養蟒蛇做寵物時，最好能三思！

 關鍵單字解密

prey *n.* 被捕食的動物；犧牲者

ferocious *adj.* 兇猛的；殘忍的

hesitate *v.* 猶豫；有疑慮

unique *adj.* 獨特的；特有的

consume *v.* 吃完；耗費

devour *v.* 吃光；吞沒

swollen *adj.* 膨脹的；誇大的

silently *adv.* 寂靜地；沉默地

🎡 文法分析

分析 1.

例句 | Sometimes, <u>so hungry are some pythons that</u> they eat whatever they see, though the prey may be huge.

例句 | Sometimes, <u>so hungry some pythons are that</u> they eat whatever they see, though the prey may be huge.

中譯

有時候，某些蟒蛇是如此地飢餓以致於牠們看到甚麼都吃，儘管這個獵物可能是很大型的。

用法解析

主詞補語倒裝可以加強語氣。句子正常的字序是「S＋V＋主詞補語」，有時為了強調主詞補語，會將補語往前提，而與主詞交換位置，形成倒裝的句型，形成「主詞補語＋V＋S」。補語置於前形成倒裝句，也可以表示強調的語意，如表示「結果」的子句，常把 so 往前提。第 2 句屬於錯誤的句子，因 be 動詞 are 倒裝時應置於主詞 some pythons 的前面。

1
句型結構
CHAPTER

2
字詞文法
CHAPTER

3
常見文法錯誤、文法應用
CHAPTER

分析 **2.**

例句 | Once hungry, little do they hesitate to ambush and swallow the animal they spot, even though they are huge.

例句 | Once hungry, little they hesitate to ambush and swallow the animal they spot, even though they are huge.

中譯

一旦餓了，牠們毫不遲疑於突襲並且吞嚥牠們所看見的動物，儘管牠們體型龐大。

用法解析

否定副詞 no, not, little, never, seldom, hardly, rarely, scarcely ……等及副詞片語 no longer, not a word, under no circumstances, …等，可置於句首，後接倒裝句構，即動詞與主詞互換，或另藉助動詞等方式構成倒裝句，以加強語氣。第 2 句屬於錯誤的句子，因 little 置於句首時應借助動詞 do，挪至主詞 they 前才正確。

CHAPTER **2**

字詞文法

搭配主題▶ 神秘天文、地理篇

動詞 1

The Mysterious Bermuda Triangle

神秘的百慕達三角

 ## 英文動詞的類別以及使用原則：

I. 動詞基本類別可分為 be 動詞與一般動詞。

1. be 動詞包含有指現在式的 am / is / are 或過去式的 was / were，
未來式則用助動詞 will / shall＋原形 be 動詞。另外，**be** 動詞也可
充當助動詞使用於「進行式」或「被動語態」中。

   ♦ Sherry and Frank are competent teachers.　雪莉和法蘭克
   是稱職的老師。

   ♦ Yesterday was a rainy day.　昨天是下雨天。

   ♦ Soon Richard will be a senior high student.　很快地，理查
   將會是高中生。

   ♦ Oscar is making progress in English conversation.　奧斯
   卡的英文會話正在進步中。

   ♦ Protests were made against the building of nuclear power
   plants.　人們抗議核能電廠的興建。

2. 一般動詞，如 come, go, buy, see, leave, return, purchase,
achieve,…等都有現在式，過去式，未來式，過去分詞（p.p）及
現在分詞（V.ing），…等等的變化。現在式中，當主詞為第三人稱
單數時，一般動詞字尾要加「s」，「es」，或變化成「ies」。過
去式時，動詞變化則有分規則變化，字尾加「ed」或變化成
「ied」，及不規則的動詞變化。

- ◆ Janet studies in the library when the mid-term exam comes. 期中考來臨時，珍妮特在圖書館讀書。
- ◆ Mr. White polishes his shoes every morning. 懷特先生每天早上擦亮他的皮鞋。
- ◆ The boat drifted quickly downstream. 這艘船快速地沿著下游漂流。
- ◆ Jimmy tore the paper into pieces angrily. 吉米憤怒地把紙張撕成碎片。

II. 一般動詞分為及物動詞與不及物動詞。及物動詞必須接一個受詞，受詞可以是名詞、動名詞，或是名詞子句。如果是授與動詞，則要接兩個受詞，即人與事物。不及物動詞不接受詞，但可以用副詞或副詞片語修飾。

- ◆ Lily accepted Mike's suggestion and made some changes. 莉莉接受麥克的建議，並且作了一些改變。
- ◆ On Valentine's Day, Kevin bought a bunch of roses for his girlfriend. 情人節時，凱文為女友買了一束玫瑰花。
- ◆ A terrible explosion happened in the subway station yesterday morning. 昨天早上地鐵車站發生了一起恐怖的爆炸事件。

III. 不完全的動詞必須接補語，使語意完整。不完全及物動詞接受詞補語來補充說明受詞，不完全不及物動詞則得接主詞補語，以補充說明主詞。

- ◆ We found the movie interesting and exciting. 我們發現這部電影既有趣又刺激。
- ◆ Please keep the windows open. 請保持窗戶是開著的。
- ◆ The travelers seemed very tired. 旅客們似乎非常疲倦。
- ◆ Martin wishes that one day his dream will come true. 馬丁希望有一天他的夢想能夠實現。

☪★ The Mysterious **Bermuda Triangle**

Within the Bermuda Islands, the Bermuda Triangle is a region **bounded** by Florida, Bermuda, and Puerto Rico in the Atlantic Ocean. Ever since the American reporter, Edward Jones, first **published** the article about the ship missing incident in the Bermuda Triangle in 1950, it has been misted with a mysterious veil. Dozens of ships and planes, due to the alleged supernatural powers such as the UFOs or the extraterrestrials, have **disappeared** for no reason, which made the region haunted and extremely mysterious, and was thus even nicknamed "Devil's Triangle." Scientists and specialists tried to investigate and **analyze** the possible reasons for the mishaps, among which, the missing of the US navy bombers, Flight 19, in 1945 and the passenger-carrying aircraft, Star Tiger, in 1948 were the most notable. Possible factors might be human errors in violent weather, influences of the Mexican Gulf stream, compass **deviations** due to the physical magnetic power, and so on. Nevertheless, with all these scientific explanations, the Bermuda Triangle remains to be mysterious because of the **prevalent** legends of fake and **exaggerations** made by people awed by the tragic and mystical incidents. Still, the mystery is absolutely **worth** our efforts to solve.

☥ 神秘的百慕達三角

　　身處於百慕達群島裡，百慕達三角是大西洋中由佛羅里達、百慕達和波多黎各所形成的一個區域。自從美國記者，愛德華·瓊斯在1950年首度出版了有關於在百慕達三角船隻失蹤事件的文章後，這個地方就被一層神秘的面紗所籠罩著。成打的船隻和飛機，由於傳說中的超自然力量，例如：幽浮或外星人，無緣無故地失蹤了，使得這個區域鬼影幢幢，且相當地神秘，甚至因此得到「魔鬼三角」的綽號。科學家和專家們試圖去調查並分析這些不幸事件發生的可能原因。在這些不幸事件當中，1945年的美國海軍轟炸機"19號機隊"，以及1948年的民航客機「星虎號」的失蹤案件最為著名。結論指出，失蹤的可能的原因，包含劇烈天候狀況下人為的疏失、墨西哥海灣洋流的影響、物理磁力導致羅盤的變化，…等等。但是，即使有這些科學的說明，人們對這些悲劇且神秘的事件仍深感敬畏而捏造出廣泛流傳的杜撰且誇張的傳說，使得百慕達三角依舊是充滿神秘的。儘管如此，這謎題絕對值得我們努力去解開。

◬ 關鍵單字解密

bound *v.* 與……接界；限制

publish *v.* 出版；發行

disappear *v.* 消失；不見

analyze *v.* 分析；解析

deviation *n.* 偏差

prevalent *adj.* 流行的；普遍的

exaggeration *n.* 誇張；誇大

worth *adj.* 值……；值得（去）……

文法分析

分析 1.

例句 | Ever since the American reporter, Edward Jones, first published the article about the ship missing incident in the Bermuda Triangle in 1950, it has been misted with a mysterious veil.

例句 | Ever since the American reporter, Edward Jones, first published about the ship missing incident in the Bermuda Triangle in 1950, it has been misted with a mysterious veil.

中譯

自從美國記者，愛德華・瓊斯在 1950 年首度出版了有關於在百慕達三角船隻失蹤事件的文章後，這個地方就被一層神秘的面紗所籠罩著。

用法解析

一般動詞分為及物動詞與不及物動詞。及物動詞必須接一個受詞，受詞可以是名詞，動名詞，或是名詞子句。第 2 句屬於錯誤的句子，因為及物動詞 published 後缺受詞 the article。

分析 **2.**

例句 | Nevertheless, with all these scientific explanations, the Bermuda Triangle remains to be mysterious because of the prevalent legends of fake and exaggerations.

例句 | Nevertheless, with all these scientific explanations, the Bermuda Triangle remains to be mysteriously because of the prevalent legends of fake and exaggerations.

中譯

但是，即使有這些科學的說明，廣泛流傳的杜撰且誇張的傳說，使得百慕達三角依舊是充滿神祕的。

用法解析

不完全的動詞必須接補語，使語意完整。不完全及物動詞接受詞補語來補充說明受詞，不完全不及物動詞則得接主詞補語，以補充說明主詞。但是第 2 句中，不完全不及物動詞 remain 應接形容詞 mysterious 做主詞補語，而非副詞 mysteriously，所以是錯誤的句子。

UNIT 2 動詞 2

Alien Abduction　外星人綁架案

 使用動詞時要注意正確之使用：

I. 連綴動詞，如 come, go, fall, seem, appear, keep, stand, lie, grow, turn, remain, prove ……等，屬於不完全不及物動詞，語意不完整，所以後面常接名詞，形容詞或分詞當作主詞補語，以說明某種狀態。

- ◆ Kevin remained a bachelor all his life.　凱文終生未結婚。
- ◆ Leaves turn yellow when fall comes.　秋天來臨時樹葉轉黃。
- ◆ Mr. Hardy seems disappointed and upset today; we'd better leave him alone.　哈迪先生今天看起來失望且生氣；我們最好不要惹他。

II. 感官動詞，如 feel, look, hear, smell, taste, sound ……等，常用形容詞作主格補語，或後接受詞，再接原形動詞表事實的敘述，也可接現在分詞表示當時正在進行的動作來補充說明受詞的情境。

- ◆ The soup tastes delicious.　湯很美味。
- ◆ Simon sounds（to be）in a good mood today.　賽門今天聽起來心情不錯。
- ◆ We heard Peter hum / humming an old English song.　我們聽見彼得哼英文老歌。

III. 使役動詞，如 make, have, let, …等，接受詞後，要接原形動詞，或接可充當受詞補語的字，如形容詞、現在分詞、過去分詞，……等。

- ♦ The funny clown made everybody laugh.　滑稽的小丑使得每個人大笑。
- ♦ Steven had his car fixed in the garage.　史帝芬把車送到車行修理。
- ♦ Don't let trifles bother you.　不要為瑣事煩惱。

IV. 有些動詞常用被動的形式，表達的卻是主動的意味，如 determine, prepare, oppose, convince, incline, persuade ……等。

- ♦ I am determined to get into college.　我下定決心要上大學。
- ♦ Are you prepared for the meeting?　準備好開會了嗎？
- ♦ John is convinced that he is the right person for the job. 約翰相信自己是這份工作的最佳人選。

V. 動詞 rob, cure, inform, accuse, relieve, remind, deprive, …等接受詞後，必須要加介系詞 of 後才能接受詞。通常使用的句型如下： S rob＋人＋of＋O。

- ♦ The medicine can cure you of your headache.　這個藥可以治療你的頭疼。
- ♦ Max robbed the old woman of her bag and was arrested. 麥克斯搶奪老婦人的皮包並且被逮捕。
- ♦ Please remind me of our appointment by calling me tonight.　晚上請打個電話給我提醒我們的約會。

Quite a few cases of alien **abduction** have been heard in America during the 20th century. Theories concerning the high **intelligence** of aliens are a lot, from creating highly evolved **civilization** on earth to making contact with earth people. However, the most horrible are the reported cases of abduction done by them. Since the appearances of UFOs in 1940s', aliens have been heard to kidnap humans for unknown reasons, probably for research, **experiments**, or even reproduction. The first widely **publicized** case was the Betty and Barney Hill Abduction in 1961. After being attacked by some UFO at night, Mr. and Mrs. Hill seemed to have missed a large span of time and couldn't **recall** anything. And then, they painfully suffered from mental disorder until a hypnotherapist cured them of their sickness through hypnosis. As they remembered, the short, gray aliens, with arms and legs, a small mouth but no nose, looked quite different from humans. The Hills were then terrified and were made some experiments on. Other similar victims were also **convinced** that they were kidnapped by aliens. Nevertheless, some of the alleged happenings were later proved merely deceptive. There's no knowing the true **motives** behind alien abduction; hopefully, convincing conclusions will come out in the future.

☥ 外星人綁架案

　　20 世紀時，在美國有傳聞相當多的外星人綁架事件。有關於高智慧外星人的理論相當多，從創造地球高度演化文明直到跟地球人做接觸。但是，最可怕的是報導傳聞由它們所做的綁架案件。自從 1940 年代幽浮出現之後，傳說外星人為了一些不知名的理由綁架人類，很可能是要做研究、做實驗，或者是繁殖。第一宗廣為宣稱的案子是 1961 年貝蒂和巴尼‧希爾夫婦的綁架案。某一個夜晚在被幽浮攻擊過後，希爾夫婦似乎有一大段時間的記憶是空白的，而且他們無法回憶起任何事情。然而，之後，他們痛苦地蒙受精神失調的疾病，一直到有一位催眠治療師透過催眠術治癒了他們的疾病。在他們的記憶中，矮小、灰色、有手腳、小嘴巴，但是沒有鼻子的外星人，看起來和人類大不相同。希爾夫婦在當時感到害怕，同時外星人有在他們身上做了些實驗。其他類似的受害者也相信他們自己曾被外星人綁架。然而，事後有些據稱的事件被證實只是詐騙。外星人綁架人類背後的動機無從得知，但是，人們期盼可信的結論將會在未來出現。

 關鍵單字解密

abduction *n.* 綁架；劫持	
intelligence *n.* 智慧；理解力	
civilization *n.* 文明；文明社會	
experiment *n.* 實驗；試驗	
publicize *v.* 宣傳；公佈	
recall *v.* 回想；回憶	
convince *v.* 使確信；說服	
motive *n.* 動機；目的	

 文法分析

分析 1.

例句 | And then, they painfully suffered from mental disorder until a hypnotherapist cured them of their sickness through hypothesis.

例句 | And then, they painfully suffered from mental disorder until a hypnotherapist cured them their sickness through hypothesis.

中譯

然而，之後，他們痛苦地蒙受精神失調的疾病，一直到有一位催眠治療師透過催眠術治癒了他們的疾病。

用法解析

動詞 rob, cure, inform, accuse, relieve, remind, deprive ……等接受詞後，必須要加介系詞 of 後才能接受詞。通常使用的句型如下： S rob ＋人＋of＋O。第 2 句屬於錯誤的句子，因 cured them 後漏加介系詞 of。

1 句型結構
CHAPTER

2 字詞文法
CHAPTER

3 常見文法錯誤、文法應用
CHAPTER

分析 **2.**

例句｜As they remembered, the short, gray aliens, with arms and legs, a small mouth but no nose, <u>looked quite different</u> from humans.

例句｜As they remembered, the short, gray aliens, with arms and legs, a small mouth but no nose, <u>looked quite differently</u> from humans.

中譯

在他們的記憶中，矮小、灰色、有手腳、小嘴巴，但是沒有鼻子的外星人，看起來和人類大不相同。

用法解析

感官動詞，如 feel, look, hear, smell, taste, sound ⋯⋯等，常用形容詞作主格補語，或後接受詞，再接原形動詞表事實的敘述，也可接現在分詞表示當時正在進行的動作來補充說明受詞的情境。第 2 句屬於錯誤的句子，因感官動詞 looked 所接的修飾語，應該是形容詞 different，非副詞 differently。

UNIT 3

動詞 3
The Mystery of UFOs
幽浮之謎

 使用動詞時要注意正確之使用：

I. 不及物動詞加上介系詞或介副詞後，可成為「雙字動詞片語」或「三字動詞片語」，有特定含意，並且可以接受詞。「雙字動詞片語」如 put off（延後），look at（注視），depend on（依賴）……等，「三字動詞片語」如 take care of（照顧），look up to（尊敬），put up with（忍受）……等。

II. 動詞及動詞片語如 regard, view, describe, recognize, think of, look on, refer to ……等，接受詞後要接介系詞 as 才能接另一受詞。consider 後面則不須加 as。

- ◆ Miss Cooper regards Ernie as a trouble-maker. 庫柏小姐把恩尼視為麻煩製造者。
- ◆ We all recognized Mother Teresa as the most admirable person in the world. 我們公認德蕾莎修女是全世界最值得欽佩的人。
- ◆ Fanny considered the plan（to be）impracticable. 芬妮認為這個計畫不可行。

III. 有些動詞及動詞片語必用主動式，而無被動式，如 happen, occur, cost, remain, belong to, break out, consist of, take place ……等。

- The plane crash happened / occurred / took place last Friday.　墜機事件在上星期五發生。
- The committee consists of seven people.　委員會由7個人組成。
- World War II broke out in 1939.　第二次世界大戰在1939年爆發。

IV. 下列動詞，如表示存在的 be, own, have, belong,…等，表示情感的 want, like, hate, love ……等，表示感覺的 see, smell, hear, sound,…等，以及表示認知的 know, believe, understand, remember ……等，表達的是內心的感受，並非實際的動作，通常不用進行式。

- The house is belonging to me.（×）
  The house belongs to me.（○）　這個房子屬於我的。
- Nancy is wanting to go home.（×）
  Nancy wants to go home.（○）　南西想要回家。
- Eddie is knowing how to drive.（×）
  Eddie knows how to drive.（○）　艾迪知道如何開車。

V. 主詞與動詞的一致：使用連接詞或連接詞式的片語時，主詞與動詞要能一致。用 both…and…連接兩個主詞，動詞用複數動詞。用 either…or…或 neither… nor…平行並用時，動詞與最靠近它的主詞一致。兩個主詞用 as well as 連接時，與第一個主詞一致。若用 not only…but also…，則要與第二個主詞一致。

- Either you or Lisa has to accept the job.　不是你就是麗莎必須接受這個工作。
- Neither Steven nor his parents know about the bad news.　史蒂芬不知道而他的雙親也不知道這個壞消息。

For centuries, people have believed we are not alone in the universe. Aliens taking the UFO, short for **Unidentified** Flying Objects, often visit us on earth. Many sightings of UFOs were reported worldwide, and a great percentage of Americans claimed to have either witnessed or made contact with them. Among those incidents, the 1947 Rosewell Incident was the most **noticeable**, in which a flying saucer supposedly crashed in New Mexico. However, the US Air Force tried to cover up the whole incident. The US government was believed to not only take over the wreckage of the spaceship but examine the four or five aliens' dead bodies **recovered** from the site. Afterwards, the army tried to hide the truth from the public in panic to lessen the **impact** by announcing the seemingly crashed aircraft was only a weather balloon. Still, sightings of UFOs were reported one after another by both military pilots and **civilians**. Terrified people might take them for real, while skeptical investigators regard them only as people's imaginations, hoaxes or **misinterpretation** of known objects, such as balloons, meteors, or solar **reflections**. Nevertheless, it's hard to rule out the possibility of extraterrestrial phenomena, which still remains an unsolved mystery.

☥ 幽浮之謎

　　數個世紀以來，人們相信我們在宇宙中並不是孤單的。乘坐幽浮（不明飛行物體的簡稱）的外星人經常到地球來探望我們。全世界都有許多看見幽浮的報導。極大比例的美國人宣稱曾經目擊或者是跟外星人接觸過。這些事件中，1947 年羅斯威爾事件是最引人注目的。在這事件中，有一部飛碟據說在新墨西哥州墜毀。但是，美國空軍試圖遮掩整個事件。一般人相信美國政府不僅接收了太空船的殘骸，同時檢驗了在失事現場所找尋到的 4~5 具外星人屍體。稍後，軍方藉由宣布看起來似乎是墜毀的太空船只是一個觀測天氣的氣球來遮掩事實以減緩民眾的恐慌。然而，軍方的飛行員和一般百姓接而連三地通報目睹到幽浮。驚慌的民眾可能信以為真，但是懷疑的調查人員僅把它們視為人們的想像、欺騙，或是對於已知的物件，譬如像氣球、流星，或是太陽反射的誤解。然而，要排除外星人現象的可能性是很困難的，而這也將保持是一個未解的謎。

⚠ 關鍵單字解密

universe *n.* 宇宙；全世界

unidentified *adj.* 未辨別出的；身分不明的

noticeable *adj.* 顯著的；值得注意的

recover *v.* 恢復；重新找到

impact *n.* 衝擊；影響

civilian *n.* 平民；百姓

misinterpretation *n.* 誤解；誤釋

reflection *n.* 反射；反映

1 句型結構 CHAPTER

2 字詞文法 CHAPTER

3 常見文法錯誤、文法應用 CHAPTER

 **文法分析**

分析 **1.**

例句 | Terrified people might take them for real, while skeptical investigators regard them only as people's imaginations, hoaxes or misinterpretation of known objects, such as balloons, meteors, or solar reflections.

例句 | Terrified people might take them for real, while skeptical investigators regard them only people's imaginations, hoaxes or misinterpretation of known objects, such as balloons, meteors, or solar reflections.

中譯

驚慌的民眾可能信以為真，但是懷疑的調查人員僅把它們視為人們的想像、欺騙，或是對於已知的物件，譬如像氣球、流星，或是太陽反射的誤解。

用法解析

動詞及動詞片語如 regard, view, describe, recognize, think of, look on, refer to ⋯⋯等，接受詞後要接介系詞 as 才能接另一受詞。consider 後面則不須加 as。第 2 句中 regard 未加介系詞 as 即接受詞是錯誤的用法。

分析 **2.**

例句｜Nevertheless, it's hard to rule out the possibility of extraterrestrial phenomena, which <u>still remains</u> an unsolved mystery.

例句｜Nevertheless, it's hard to rule out the possibility of extraterrestrial phenomena, which <u>still is remained</u> an unsolved mystery.

中譯

然而，要排除外星人現象的可能性是很困難的，而這也將保持是一個未解的謎。

用法解析

有些動詞及動詞片語必用主動式，而無被動式，如 happen, occur, cost, remain, belong to, break out, consist of, take place,…等。動詞 remain 必用主動式，無被動式，因此第 2 句中被動式 still is remained 是錯誤的用法。

助動詞 1

The Suicide Forest

自殺森林

 助動詞指的是「語氣助動詞」，可根據語意及用法幫助動詞呈現出不同的語意。

I. be 動詞充當助動詞的用法：be 動詞現在式時是 am, is, are, 過去式則是 was 及 were。可和現在分詞搭配成為進行式，和過去分詞搭配成為被動語態。

- ◆ Bob is drawing while Nancy is doing her homework.　包柏正在畫畫，而南西正在做功課。
- ◆ All the invitation cards were written by Susan.　所有的邀請卡都是蘇珊所寫的。

II. 動詞 do 充當助動詞的用法：do, does, did 充當助動詞時，可用來造疑問句、否定句，加強語氣的功用及用於倒裝句中。後面都得接原形動詞。

- ◆ A: Did you work part-time before? B: No, I didn't.　你以前打工過嗎？不，我沒有。
- ◆ Please do join us for dinner.　請務必參加我們的晚餐。
- ◆ Little does Nick think for others.　尼克一點也不為別人設想。

III. 動詞 have 充當助動詞的用法：have, has, had 可和過去分詞搭配形成完成式。had better 表示「最好……」。

- ◆ Have you been to Korea before?　你去過韓國嗎？

- Jenny had spent two hours watching TV movies before she went to bed.　珍妮睡覺前看了兩個小時電視影片。
- Marvin had better tell the truth.　馬文最好要說實話。

IV. shall / should 的用法：

1. 助動詞 shall / should 後面動詞要用原形動詞。shall 可用於第一人稱，表示純粹的未來，will 則常表意志或決心。shall 常可用 will 來取代。表示邀請時，用 Shall I / we。shall 若與其他人稱合用，則有表示「強制要……」含意。

   - I shall / will graduate from college soon.　我很快即將要大學畢業。
   - Let's have lunch together, shall we?　咱們共進午餐，好嗎？
   - You shall not go there anymore!　你絕對不能再去那裡了！

2. should 是 shall 的過去式，表示「應該」，可以用 ought to 代換，不論人稱，都搭配原形動詞。它也可用於假設語氣中。

   - You should / ought to follow the traffic rules.　你應該遵守交通規則。
   - If it should rain again, I would stay home.　萬一再下雨，我將會待在家裡。

V. will / would 的用法：助動詞 will / would 後面動詞要用原形動詞。will 用於未來式中，表示未來的動作。would 用於過去式，表示過去的習慣。「would rather…than…」表示「寧願……也不願……」。

   - If Larry talks too much in class, Miss Brown will punish him.　如果賴瑞上課說太多話，布朗老師會處罰他。
   - Lisa would rather go shopping than watch TV.　麗莎寧願逛街也不願看電視。

Aokigahara, a forest **situated** at the northwest base of Mt. Fuji, is a well-known suicide location. Each year, the forest attracts not only **tourists** to appreciate its natural beauty but people **determined** to end their lives there. Since 1960, after the publication of a popular novel describing the main character's suicide there, even more people ended their lives there. It has become a common but horrible **trend**. In fact, entering the dense black forest with the sunlight blocked makes hikers afraid. Due to the magnetic iron deposits in the **volcanic** soil, compasses cannot work and hikers will easily get lost. Furthermore, the forest allegedly used to be a place, in ancient times, where the sick and the old were **abandoned**, so it's full of vengeful spirits. That's why the forest seems to be veiled in black mystery of **grievance**, sadness, and death, which might trigger travelers' desire to commit suicide there. With the worsening global economy, the suicide cases have increased rapidly. Therefore, the signs advising hikers that they should **cherish** their lives and should not commit suicide there are even put up at the entrance of the forest. The mystery of the suicide forest truly needs to be solved before the happening of more tragedies.

☥ 自殺森林

　　位於富士山西北山腳下的青木原是一個知名的自殺地點。每一年，這座森林吸引的不僅是要欣賞它天然美景的觀光客，也吸引了執意要在此地結束生命的民眾。1960 年以來，就在一本描述主角在此地自殺的暢銷小說出版後，更多人去到青木原結束生命。這已經成為一個普遍且可怕的流行趨勢。事實上，健行者進入這座被陽光遮蔽的茂密黑森林時，會感到害怕。由於火山土壤含磁鐵的沉積物，使得羅盤無法作用而常導致健行者迷失方向。此外，據稱這座森林在古代是一個患病者和老年者被遺棄的地方，所以森林充滿著怨恨的冤魂。這也是為何這座森林似乎是籠罩在怨恨、悲傷和死亡的黑色神秘之中，因而可能引發旅客想在此地自殺的念頭。隨著全球經濟惡化，自殺事件快速地增加。因此，勸導登山者應該要珍惜生命，不應該自殺的標語，甚至被設立於森林入口處。自殺森林之謎在更多的悲劇發生之前確實應該被解開。

⧆ 關鍵單字解密

situate *v.* 位於；處於

tourist *n.* 旅遊者；觀光者

determined *adj.* 堅定的；決然的

trend *n.* 時尚；趨勢

volcanic *adj.* 火山的；爆裂的

abandon *v.* 丟棄；遺棄

grievance *n.* 不滿；怨言

cherish *v.* 珍惜；愛護

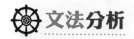 **文法分析**

分析 1.

例句 | It has become a common but horrible trend.

○

例句 | It have become a common but horrible trend.

✕

中譯

這已經成為一個普遍且可怕的流行趨勢。

用法解析

動詞 have 充當助動詞的用法：have, has, had 可和過去分詞搭配形成完成式。第 2 句屬於錯誤的句子，因現在完成式 have become 的主詞 it 是第三人稱單數，助動詞 have 要用 has，非 have。

1
句型結構
CHAPTER

2
字詞文法
CHAPTER

3
常見文法錯誤、文法應用
CHAPTER

分析 2.

例句 | Due to the magnetic iron deposits in the volcanic soil, compasses cannot work and hikers <u>will easily get lost</u>.

例句 | Due to the magnetic iron deposits in the volcanic soil, compasses cannot work and hikers <u>will easily got lost</u>.

中譯

由於火山土壤含磁鐵的沉積物，使得羅盤無法作用而常導致健行者迷失方向。

用法解析

will / would 的用法：will 用於未來式中，表示未來的動作。would 用於過去式，表示過去的習慣。「would rather…than…」表示「寧願……也不願……」。第 2 句屬於錯誤的句子，因 will 助動詞後面動詞要用原形動詞 get，而非過去式 got。

助動詞 2

The Nasca Lines

納斯卡線

 常見的助動詞及助動詞片語使用如下：

I. can / could 的用法：

1. can 用以表示技能上的能力，及許可。用於疑問句及否定句，另可表示懷疑。

   ♦ Jeremy can play basketball well. 傑瑞米籃球打得很好。

   ♦ You can watch TV after you finish the homework. 功課做完後你可以看電視。

2. could 是 can 的過去式，可用以表示過去的情境，此外，could＋現在完成式 have＋p.p.，表示過去應可以做到，但未能做到的情形。couldn't＋現在完成式 have＋p.p. 則表示對過去強烈的懷疑。

   ♦ When young, the old man could swim fast. 年輕時，這名老人游泳游得很快。

   ♦ Simon could have finished reading the novel, but then something came up. 賽門原本可以把小說閱讀完的，但是後來發生了一點事。

II. may / might 及 must 的用法：

1. may 表示可能性，也可表示許可及祝福。might 是 may 的過去式，語意較弱，較客氣，表示過去的情境外，might＋have＋p.p.可表示對於過去的推測。若 may＋have＋p.p.，指的是可能性較大，而 might＋have＋p.p.可能性則較小。

♦ A typhoon may come in a few days. 過幾天可能會有一個颱風。

♦ A: May I come in? 我可以進來嗎？ B: Yes, you may. 是的，你可以。

♦ Happy birthday! May you have a long life! 生日快樂！祝你長命百歲！

♦ Rebecca may have returned home, for I can't find her anywhere. 蕾貝嘉可能回家了，因為我四處找不到她。

♦ Mr. Baker might have forgotten the meeting because he didn't show up today. 貝克先生很可能忘記要開會，因為他今天並沒有出現。

2. must 解釋為「必須」，可代換成 have to, 過去式則是 had to。
must 另可加現在完成式 have＋p.p.表示對於過去肯定的推測。

♦ You must / have to clean the house, for we're going to have a visitor tonight. 你一定要打掃房子，因為我們今晚將有一名訪客。

♦ May had to leave home early this morning because there was a quiz in school. 梅今天早上必須提早出門，因為學校有小考。

♦ It must have rained yesterday, for the ground was wet this morning. 昨天一定下過雨了，因為今天早上地面是濕的。

III. used to / be used to 的用法：used to＋原形動詞，表示過去的習慣，to 此處為不定詞，後接原形動詞。be used to＋動名詞，be 動詞為現在式，表示現在的習慣，be 動詞為過去式，則表示過去的習慣。to 此處為介系詞，後接動名詞。

♦ Before Nick found his new job, he used to jog early in the morning. 尼克在找到新工作前，他習慣在一大清早慢跑。

♦ Philip was used to walking his dog at night. 飛利浦習慣在晚上遛狗。

The Nasca Lines are a series of straight lines cut into the surface of the Nasca Desert in southeastern Peru. Covering 450 square kilometers, the Nasca Lines have been called the biggest drawing ever created. They consist of thousands of geometric shapes and hundreds of **complex** figures from both the natural world and the human imagination. They include the hummingbird, spider, pelican, lizard, monkeys, plants and human figures. **Scholars** believe that the Lines were created by the Nasca culture between 500 BC and 500 AD. The complexity of the Lines proves that the **remarkable** Nascan people used to have highly **developed** surveying skills. Besides, the designed patterns can be clearly identified only from the sky, which shows Nascan Indians could fly in the sky, probably in balloons. It's also very likely that aliens with high intelligence from outer space might have **instructed** them to accomplish the masterpiece. Other **speculations** are that the Lines might have **functioned** for religious purposes, or for water **irrigation**, since water is vital but rare in the desert. And surprisingly, the Lines are even believed to have been used as landing areas for alien spaceships. All in all, the mystery of Nasca Lines still calls for the archaeologists nowadays to explore.

納斯卡線

　　納斯卡線是一系列被雕刻於祕魯東南方納斯卡沙漠的直線。納斯卡線面積有 450 平方公里，號稱是有史以來最大的一幅畫作。它們有上千個幾何圖形以及上百個來自於自然界和人類想像複雜的圖案。它們包含有蜂鳥、蜘蛛、鵜鶘、蜥蜴、猿猴、植物，以及人類的圖騰。學者們相信納斯卡線是在西元前 500 年至西元 500 年之間被納斯卡文化創造出來的。納斯卡線的複雜度證實了不起的納斯卡人過去曾有高度發展的測量技能。此外，這些設計圖案僅能夠從高處清楚的被看見，這表示納斯卡印地安人可能當時能夠乘坐氣球在空中飛行。因此，來自於外太空具有高度智慧的外星人可能當時曾指導他們完成這幅巨作。其他的推測則是納斯卡線可能是有著宗教的目的或者是因為沙漠地區水很重要但缺乏而做為水源灌溉的用途。令人驚訝的是，納斯卡線一度被認為是給外星人太空船降落的地點。總而言之，納斯卡線之謎仍有待今日的考古學家來探索。

關鍵單字解密

complex *adj.* 複雜的；難懂的

scholar *n.* 學者；有學問的人

remarkable *adj.* 非凡的；卓超的

developed *adj.* 發達的；先進的

instruct *v.* 指導；指示

speculation *n.* 推測；投機

function *v.* 起作用；工作

irrigation *n.* 灌溉；沖洗

 **文法分析**

分析 1.

例句 | The complexity of the Lines proves that the remarkable Nascan people <u>used to have</u> highly developed surveying skills.

例句 | The complexity of the Lines proves that the remarkable Nascan people <u>used to having</u> highly developed surveying skills.

中譯

納斯卡線的複雜度證實了不起的納斯卡人過去曾有高度發展的測量技能。

用法解析

used to / be used to 的用法：used to＋原形動詞，表示過去的習慣，to 此處為不定詞，後接原形動詞。be used to＋動名詞，be 動詞為現在式，表示現在的習慣，be 動詞為過去式，則表示過去的習慣。to 此處為介系詞，後接動名詞。第 2 句屬於錯誤的句子，因此處 used to 的 to 為不定詞，後應接原形動詞 have，非介係詞，不應接動名詞 having。

分析 **2.** ▶

例句 | It's also very likely that aliens with high intelligence from outer space might have instructed them to accomplish the masterpiece.

例句 | It's also very likely that aliens with high intelligence from outer space might instruct them to accomplish the masterpiece.

中譯

極有可能來自於外太空具有高度智慧的外星人當時曾指導他們完成這幅巨作。

用法解析

may 表示可能性，也可表示許可及祝福。might 是 may 的過去式，語意較弱，較客氣，表示過去的情境外，might＋have＋p.p.可表示對於過去的推測。若 may＋have＋p.p.，指的是可能性較大，而 might＋have＋p.p. 可能性則較小。第 2 句是錯誤的用法，因本句表示對於過去的推測，應用 might have instructed，而非表示對於現在的推測 might instruct。

動名詞 1

The Dinosaur Park

恐龍公園

 動名詞是動詞加 ing 後形成的，用法如下：

I. 動名詞仍具有動詞的意味和性質，故後面要接受詞或另有副詞修飾它。

- ♦ Receiving a reward in public is an honor.　公開獲頒獎賞是一項榮譽。
- ♦ It's good for health taking regular exercise.　規律地運動對健康有幫助。

II. 動名詞或它所引導的片語可充當名詞，作為句子中的主詞及動詞或介系詞的受詞。

- ♦ Getting up early is good for making use of the time in the morning.　早起對於利用早上的時間是有幫助的。
- ♦ Mrs. Jones loves dancing with Mr. Jones.　瓊斯太太喜歡跟瓊斯先生跳舞。

III. 動名詞有充當形容詞的功用。動名詞形容名詞時，在說明該名詞的功用或特性，並非強調它的動作。動名詞片語如：smoking room（吸煙室）, swimming pool（游泳池）, dancing hall（舞廳）, sleeping car（臥車）……等，屬於此種用法。

♦ A swimming pool is a pool where you can swim. 游泳池是可以游泳的水池。

IV. 動名詞可有充當主詞補語以及同位語的功用。

♦ Seeing is believing. 百聞不如一見。

♦ What you did is violating the traffic rules. 你的所作所為違反交通規則。

V. 及物動詞如 mind, finish, avoid, enjoy, practice, keep, imagine, help, resist ……等後面一定要接動名詞做受詞用。

♦ Do you mind my smoking here? 你介意我在這裡抽菸嗎？

♦ After a whole year's work, William enjoyed taking his vacation in Europe. 經過一年的工作，威廉在歐洲享受他的假期。

VI. 動詞如 begin, start, like, dislike, love, hate, plan, attempt, neglect ……等後面可接動名詞亦可接不定詞做為受詞，語意相同。

♦ The poet started reciting / to recite the poems out loud to the audience. 這名詩人開始對觀眾大聲朗讀詩。

♦ Nancy loves going / to go shopping on Friday nights. 南西喜歡在星期五晚上逛街。

The Dinosaur Park, located near Brooks, the Province of Alberta, Canada, has always been a popular tourists' attraction. After its grand opening in 1955, the park has become well known for both being given the honor of UNESCO World Heritage Site in 1979 and one of the most **abundant** dinosaur fossil locations in the world. About forty dinosaur species have been **discovered** there, which attracts floods of researchers and dinosaur lovers. Inside the Park Center, visitors can enjoy appreciating the exhibits about dinosaurs, fossils, the geological structures and the natural history of the park. In addition, it has unique scenery, and diverse formations of the **landscape**. Dinosaur experts can find different kinds of plant and dinosaur fossils there and usually the discoveries made will be shipped to museums worldwide for scientific **analysis** and **exhibition**. When dinosaur fans **stroll** in the park feeling sorry for the **extinction** of the dinosaurs, they can't help wondering what had exactly happened sixty-five million years ago. Why should the dinosaurs, once the master of the world, though probably got killed either by the hit of an asteroid or comet, or by the sudden freezing cold climate, completely disappear from the earth? And the wondering **definitely** leaves us the mystery and fantasy of dinosaurs' existence and extinction.

☥ 恐龍公園

　　位於加拿大艾伯塔省布魯克斯附近的恐龍公園一向是熱門的觀光景點。在1955年盛大開幕後，這座公園因為在1979年獲頒「聯合國教育科學暨文化組織」認定為世界遺產的殊榮以及號稱為全世界恐龍化石蘊藏量最大的地點之一而著名。在那兒曾發現大約有40種的恐龍品種，因而吸引大量研究者及恐龍愛好者前來。在公園中心內，訪客可以欣賞到恐龍、化石、地質情況，以及公園天然歷史等的展覽。此外，它有獨特的風景以及多變化的地質景觀。恐龍專家們可以在那兒找到各種不同的植物及恐龍的化石，而且一般在那兒的發現會被運送到全世界的博物館做科學分析以及展覽。當恐龍迷在公園漫步，為恐龍的滅絕感到遺憾時，他們不得不懷疑6500萬年前究竟發生了什麼事，為什麼一度是世界主宰者的恐龍，雖然很可能喪命於小流星或慧星的衝擊，或全球氣候的驟降，竟然會完全地從地球消失了？而這懷疑絕對會遺留給我們對於恐龍的存在和滅絕的謎題以及想像。

 關鍵單字解密

abundant *adj.* 豐富的；充足的

discover *v.* 發現；找到

landscape *n.* 風景；景色

analysis *n.* 分析；分解

exhibition *n.* 展覽；展示會

stroll *v.* 散步；閒逛

extinction *n.* 滅絕；消滅

definitely *adv.* 明確地；肯定地

 **文法分析**

分析 **1.**

例句 | After its grand opening in 1955, the park has become well known for both being given the honor of UNESCO World Heritage Site in 1979 and one of the most abundant dinosaur fossil locations in the world.

例句 | After its grand opening in 1955, the park has become well known for both be given the honor of UNESCO World Heritage Site in 1979 and one of the most abundant dinosaur fossil locations in the world.

中譯

在 1955 年盛大開幕後，這座公園因為在 1979 年獲頒「聯合國教育科學暨文化組織」認定為世界遺產的殊榮以及號稱為全世界恐龍化石蘊藏量最大的地點之一而著名。

用法解析

動名詞或它所引導的片語可充當名詞，作為句子中的主詞及動詞或介系詞的受詞。作為句子中的主詞時要視為第三人稱單數，接單數動詞。第 2 句屬於錯誤的句子，因介系詞 for 後應加動名詞 being 做受詞，而非原形動詞 be。

分析 **2.**

例句 | When dinosaur fans stroll in the park feeling sorry for the extinction of the dinosaurs, they can't help wondering what had exactly happened sixty-five million years ago.

例句 | When dinosaur fans stroll in the park feeling sorry for the extinction of the dinosaurs, they can't help wonder what had exactly happened sixty-five million years ago.

中譯

當恐龍迷在公園漫步，為恐龍的滅絕感到遺憾時，他們不得不懷疑 6500 萬年前究竟發生了什麼事。

用法解析

及物動詞如 mind, finish, avoid, enjoy, practice, keep, imagine, help, resist ……等後面一定要接動名詞做受詞用。第 2 句屬於錯誤的句子，因 help 後面應該接動名詞 wondering，並非接原形動詞 wonder 做受詞。

UNIT 7

動名詞 2

The Amazing Dead Sea

神奇的死海

 動名詞其他要注意的用法如下：

I. 在介系詞後，遇到動詞要改成動名詞。同名詞的用法，動名詞前可加上所有格。

 ◆ The liar tricked Mary into giving him five hundred dollars.
  這個騙子哄騙瑪莉給他五百元。

II. 動名詞有充當形容詞的功用。動名詞形容名詞時，在說明該名詞的功用或特性，並非強調它的動作。動名詞片語如：smoking room（吸煙室）, swimming pool（游泳池）, dancing hall（舞廳）, sleeping car（臥車）, bathing area（浸泡區）……等，屬於此種用法。

 ◆ A swimming pool is a pool where you can swim.
  游泳池是你可以在裡面游泳的水池。

III. to 若是不定詞 to，後面得接原形動詞，但若 to 是介系詞 to，則要接動名詞。下列片語的 to 為介系詞，後面要接動名詞：apply to ~ 應用於~ be accustomed to ~ 習慣於~ be opposed to ~ 反對 ~ be devoted / dedicated to ~ 奉獻於~ look forward to ~ 期盼~ object to ~ 反對~ with a view to ~ 為了要~ when it comes to ~ 論及到 ~

◆ Mrs. Smith is accustomed to getting up early.

史密斯太太習慣於早起。

◆ I am looking forward to seeing you all.

我期盼看到你們大家。

◆ The neighbors objected to the building of an incinerator here.

鄰居們反對在這裡建造焚化爐。

◆ When it comes to playing basketball, Jeremy is second to none.

論到打籃球，傑瑞米是最棒的。

IV. 動詞如 try, stop / cease, forget, regret, remember ……等，後面可接動名詞，也可接不定詞做為受詞，但語意不同。try＋v.ing 試著…、try＋to VR 盡力去…、 stop/cease＋v.ing 停止（原動作）、stop/cease＋to VR 停下來（去做另一動作）、forget＋v.ing 忘了（做過…）、forget＋to VR 忘記（去做另一動作）、regret＋v.ing 後悔（做了…）、regret＋to VR 遺憾（去做另一動作）、remember＋v.ing 記得（曾經…） remember＋to V 記得要（去做另一動作）、

◆ Please stop talking.（停止說話）

◆ Please stop to take a rest.（停下來休息一下）

◆ Kevin regretted playing too much computer.（後悔打電腦打太久）

◆ I regret to tell you the bad news.（遺憾將告訴你壞消息）

◆ Remember to mail the package on your way to the office.（記得要去寄包裹）

◆ I remember telling Bill the address, but he said I didn't.（記得曾經告訴過他）

The Dead Sea is a salt lake located between Jordan and Israel. Being about 400 meters deep, it is the deepest **landlocked** lake with the highest **concentration** of salt in the world. The high salinity prevents any life forms from surviving in the lake, the reason for its being called a "Dead" Sea. However, one thing interesting about it is that the high salinity of it **enables** people to float on the surface without **worrying** about sinking down, and many vacationers look forward to doing that. Isn't that amazing?

Nowadays, the Dead Sea has become a popular health **resort**. Tourists can visit some purely historic spots, enjoy the breathtaking natural scenery, and enjoy the seawater in the bathing areas. In addition, visitors come here for its unique products of both **healing** properties, such as beauty cosmetics. The composition of the salts and minerals in the water can be used to cure people of **chronic** diseases, such as arthritis and the deposits of the black mud from the sea can be materials for cosmetic products.

With these amazing **characteristics**, no wonder it has become such a popular tourists' attraction. Will the mysterious "Dead Sea" cease "living" one day? The answer definitely is "No!"

☥ 神奇的死海

死海是位於約旦和以色列間的鹹水湖。死海大約四百公尺深，是全世界鹽度最高且最深的內陸湖。高鹽度使得所有的生物都無法在湖裡生存，所以它被稱為「死」海。然而有趣的是，死海的高鹽度可以讓人們無憂於下沉而在海面上漂浮，許多遊客也很期盼於這麼做。那不是很神奇嗎？

今日而言，死海已成為一個受歡迎的健康度假中心。觀光客可以參觀正統的歷史景點，享受令人屏息的天然美景，並且享受浸泡區的海水此外，訪客是為了具治療藥效及美妝品的獨特產品而來到這裡。海水中鹽及礦物質的合成物能用來治療人們，譬如像關節炎的慢性疾病，而且來自大海黑泥的沉澱物可作為製造化妝品的材料。

有這些驚人的特色，難怪它成為如此受歡迎的觀光景點。神秘的死海有一天將停止「生存」嗎？答案是「絕對不可能」！

⛰ 關鍵單字解密

landlocked *adj.* 內陸的；閉合水域的

concentration *n.* 專心；濃度

enable *v.* 使能夠；使成為可能

worry *v.* 擔心；憂慮

resort *n.* 休閒度假之處；名勝

healing *adj.* 有治療功用的；康復中的

chronic *adj.* 慢性的；長期的

characteristic *n.* 特徵；特色

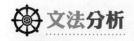

文法分析

分析 1.

例句 | However, one thing interesting about it is that the high salinity of it enables people to float on the surface without worrying about sinking down, and many vacationers look forward to doing that.

例句 | However, one thing interesting about it is that the high salinity of it enables people to float on the surface without worry about sink down, and many vacationers look forward to do that.

中譯

然而有趣的是，死海的高鹽度可以讓人們無憂於下沉而在海面上漂浮，許多遊客也很期盼於這麼做。

用法解析

在介系詞後，遇到動詞要改成動名詞。在介系詞 without 及 about 後，動詞 worry 及 sink 要改成動名詞，而非原形動詞。to 若是不定詞 to，後面得接原形動詞，但若 to 是介系詞 to，則要接動名詞。片語 look forward to ~ 期盼~ 的 to 為介系詞，而非不定詞 to，後面要接動名詞 doing 而非原形動詞 do，故第 2 句屬於錯誤的句子。

分析 **2.** ▶

例句│Will the mysterious "Dead Sea" cease "living" one day? The answer is definitely "No!"

例句│Will the mysterious "Dead Sea" cease "to live" one day? The answer is definitely "No!"

中譯

神秘的死海有一天將停止「生存」嗎？答案是「絕對不可能」！

用法解析

動詞 stop / cease，後面可接動名詞，也可接不定詞做為受詞，但語意不同。stop/cease＋v.ing 停止（原動作）；stop/cease＋to VR 停下來（去做另一動作），但是第 2 句中 cease 後面應用動名詞，表示停止原動作，「生存」，非用不定詞 to＋原形動詞 live，所以第 2 句是錯誤的用法。

UNIT 8 不定詞 1

Area 51
51 區

 一般動詞前加 to 即形成不定詞 to VR，用法如下：

I. 不定詞 to 後的動詞必定是原形動詞。

  ◆ To know is one thing. To do is another. 知道是一回事，做又是另一回事。

  ◆ Jack wanted to go home to take a rest. 傑克想回家休息。

II. 不定詞引導的片語 to VR，具名詞作用，可作句子的主詞或及物動詞的受詞。

  ◆ To master a foreign language takes time and patience.
    精通外國語言需要時間和耐心。

  ◆ Simon has decided to lose weight. 賽門決定要減肥。

III. 不定詞片語 to VR 可作主詞補語或名詞的同位語。

  ◆ To see is to believe. 百聞不如一見。

  ◆ Mrs. Wang's everyday work is to clean the house. 王太太每天例行的工作是打掃房子。

IV. 不定詞片語 to VR 可當作形容詞，修飾補充說明置於前的主詞、受詞。

◆ Jane is very shy. She doesn't have many friends to talk to. 珍很害羞。她沒有很多可以聊天的朋友。

◆ Max is always the first person to enter our office in the morning. 麥克斯總是第一個早上進入我們辦公室的人。

V. 及物動詞如 try, plan, hope, learn, decide, determine, promise, refuse, manage, pretend ⋯⋯等後面常接不定詞片語 to VR 做為受詞。

◆ Richard is planning to go on a vacation this weekend. 理查計畫這個周末去度假。

◆ The suspect refused to accept the charge against him. 這名嫌疑犯拒絕接受對於他的指控。

VI. 不定詞 to 可與疑問詞 what, who, which, when, how, where,⋯等連用，充當名詞作用。此結構原來是一個子句的縮短樣式，兩者的動作執行者是同一主詞。

◆ Larry forgot which way to go.
→Larry forgot which way he should go. 賴瑞忘記（應該）走哪一條路。

◆ Not knowing what to do, Sally turned to her teacher for help.
→Not knowing what she should do, Sally turned to her teacher for help. 不知（應該）怎麼做，莎莉向老師請求幫助。

The famous US Air Force **facility**, commonly known as Area 51, is located in Nevada, the western United States. It is estimated that probably the main **purpose** of the large military airfield is to test and develop the experimental aircraft and weapons systems. Nevertheless, what is done there is in fact a generally held secret from the public, which adds a certain mysterious **atmosphere** to the area. One of the most common rumors has it that inside the base, there are crashed alien spacecrafts. And, also, the researches of the **manufacture** of the alien aircraft and the aliens, both living and dead, are done there. Therefore, Area 51 has always attracted UFO fans all over the world and they all hope to visit the public areas **surrounding** it. It was not until July, 2013 that the US government officially **acknowledged** the existence of the **restricted** area, Area 51. Nowadays, many people still doubt whether aliens and the UFO aircraft are truly placed in Area 51. However, one thing can be sure is that the mysterious site offers **military** and UFO fans a lot of topics to talk about.

☥ 51 區

　　美國著名的空軍機構，51 區，位於美國西部內華達州。根據估測，這一個巨大的軍用航空站可能主要目的是用來測試及發展實驗飛機和武器系統。然而事實上，在那裡所做的事一般是隱瞞不為大眾所知的，這樣的作法為這個區域增添了神祕的氣氛。最常聽見的謠傳之一是，在這個基地裡有墜毀的外星人太空船。此外，這裡也進行著有關於外星人太空船的製造以及活著的或死了的外星人的研究。所以，51 區一向吸引世界各地的幽浮迷，他們同時也盼望能參觀它附近的公共場所。一直到 2013 年 7 月，美國政府才正式承認 51 禁區的存在。今日來說，許多人仍懷疑 51 區內是否真的有外星人和幽浮太空船。但是，有一點可以確定的是這個神祕基地提供軍事和幽浮迷許多可以討論的話題。

⚠ 關鍵單字解密

facility *n.* 設施；場所

purpose *n.* 目的；用途

atmosphere *n.* 大氣層；氣氛

manufacture *n.* 製造；虛構

surrounding *adj.* 周圍的；附近的

acknowledge *v.* 承認；致意

restricted *adj.* 有限的；受限制的

military *adj.* 軍事的；軍隊的

 **文法分析**

例句 It is estimated that probably the main purpose of the large military airfield is to test and develop the experimental aircraft and weapons systems.

例句 It is estimated that probably the main purpose of the large military airfield is test and develop the experimental aircraft and weapons systems.

中譯

根據估測,這一個巨大的軍用航空站可能主要目的是用來測試及發展實驗飛機和武器系統。

用法解析

不定詞片語 to VR 可作主詞補語或名詞的同位語。因 be 動詞 is 後需要不定詞片語 to VR 作主詞補語,而非只是原形動詞 test 及 develop,故第 2 句屬於錯誤的句子。

分析 **2.**

例句 | Therefore, Area 51 has always attracted UFO fans all over the world and <u>they all hope to visit</u> the public areas surrounding it.

○

例句 | Therefore, Area 51 has always attracted UFO fans all over the world and <u>they all hope to visiting</u> the public areas surrounding it.

✕

中譯

所以，51 區一向吸引世界各地的幽浮迷，他們同時也盼望能參觀它附近的公共場所。

用法解析

及物動詞如 try, plan, hope, learn, decide, determine, promise, refuse, manage, pretend,…等後面常接不定詞片語 to VR 做為受詞。第 2 句中動詞 hope 後應接不定詞片語 to visit，而非動名詞 visiting，所以是錯誤的用法。

不定詞 2
The Valley of Death　死亡谷

 不定詞進一步的用法如下：

I. 不定詞的副詞片語，可用以表示「目的」。可以用 in order to, so as to（為了要……）表示肯定「目的」，表示否定「目的」則用 in order not to, so as not to（為了不要……）。

♦ Mark got up early in order to（= so as to）catch the early train.　馬克早起為了要趕上早班列車。

♦ We decided to take a taxi there so as not to be late for the seminar.　我們決定坐計程車到那裏，為了研討會不要遲到。

II. 不定詞的副詞片語用法，可用以表示「結果」。表示「結果」，可以用 as to, enough to（如此……以至於……）表肯定「結果」，否定「結果」則用 too…to…（太……以至於不能……）。

♦ Ted studied so diligently as to enter a national university.
→ Ted studied diligently enough to enter a national university.　泰德讀書如此地用功以至於進入國立大學。

♦ The father was too angry to utter a word.　這名父親生氣到說不出話。

III. 不定詞完成式的用法：

1. 不定詞的完成式（to have＋p.p.）常用於動詞 hoped, expected, planned, wanted, meant, intended, supposed, thought …… 等之後以表達過去未能實現的事情。

    ♦ I didn't mean to have kept you waiting so long. I'm terribly sorry!　我不是故意讓你等那麼久。真抱歉！

    ♦ Richard intended to have helped his roommate move, but something suddenly came up, and he failed to.　理查原來打算幫助他的室友搬家，但是臨時有事而沒有幫忙。

2. 不定詞的完成式（to have＋p.p.）也常用以表達過去曾存在的狀態，過去曾完成的動作，或過去曾經歷的事情。

    ♦ The old lady seemed to have been a beauty in her youth. 這名老婦人年輕時似乎是一名美女。

    ♦ Chris was disappointed to have missed the great circus show last night.　克里斯很失望於昨晚錯過了很棒的馬戲團表演。

    ♦ Mr. Young was proud to have won three championships in the golf game.　楊先生很驕傲於得過三次高爾夫球賽的冠軍。

IV. 下列是由不定詞組成常見的獨立不定詞片語，常置於句首，修飾整個句子：

    ♦ to tell the truth 說實話……
    ♦ to sum up / to be brief 簡言之……
    ♦ to begin / start with 首先……
    ♦ to be frank / plain（with you）坦白說……
    ♦ to do sb. justice 平心而論
    ♦ to make matters worse 更糟糕的是……
    ♦ to be on the safe side 為了安全起見

One of the most horrible **valleys** of death in the world is in Kamchatka, Russia. No **vegetation**, no birds, and no animals could ever survive there. The valley lies in the western slope of Kikhpinych Volcano in Kamchatka, **ranging** about 2,000 meters long, 100 to 300 meters wide. It has **crooked,** rough, uneven surfaces and formations, and also it has allegedly poisonous volcanic gases. In addition, the valley was rumored to have been a mystic zone like hell and was **dubbed** the "Valley of Death". It was once filled with dead bodies and skeletons of various living things, such as birds, foxes, wolves, bears, and other unknown victims. Some of the animals were witnessed to suddenly fall down in pain and die. Reports had it that over years, at least 30 **innocent** people were found dead there. Researchers held the theory that the poisonous volcanic gases consisting of carbon dioxide, hydrogen sulfide and highly **toxic** cyanides might be the causes of the death of these living things. Therefore, to be on the safe side, tourists and lovers of **extreme** trips had better be careful when planning to explore the valley, for no one knows for sure what might happen there next.

☥ 死亡谷

全世界最恐怖的死亡谷之一，是在俄羅斯的堪姆恰特卡。在那裡，從未有任何的植物、鳥類，或動物可以存活。這座山谷位於堪姆恰特卡，奇克皮查火山的西面山坡上，橫跨 2,000 公尺長，100~300 公尺寬。它有蜿蜒、粗糙，不均衡的表面及構造，而且據說含有劇毒的火山瓦斯氣體。此外，據謠傳這座山谷是地獄般的神秘區域，並有「死亡之谷」的稱號。這裡一度充滿著各式各樣生物的死屍和骷髏，譬如像鳥、狐狸、狼、熊，以及其他不知名的受害者。有些動物曾被目擊突然痛苦倒地並死亡。據報導，多年以來，至少曾有 30 名無辜民眾被發現在此喪命。研究學者認為，包含有二氧化碳、硫化氫，和有高度劇毒氰化物的毒火山氣體，可能是導致這些生物死亡的原因。因此，為了安全起見，觀光客及熱愛極限旅遊者計劃要到此山谷探險時，最好小心一點，因為沒有人確定那裡接下來會發生什麼事。

關鍵單字解密

valley *n.*	山谷；流域
vegetation *n.*	植物；草木
range *v.*	排列；分類
crooked *adj.*	彎曲的；欺詐的
dub *v.*	叫做；取綽號
innocent *adj.*	無罪的；清白的
toxic *adj.*	有毒的；毒性的
extreme *adj.*	極端的；激烈的

文法分析

分析 **1.**

例句 In addition, the valley <u>was rumored to have been</u> a mystic zone like hell and was dubbed the "Valley of Death."

例句 In addition, the valley <u>was rumored to be</u> a mystic zone like hell and was dubbed the "Valley of Death."

中譯

此外，據謠傳這座山谷是地獄般的神秘區域，並有「死亡之谷」的稱號。

用法解析

不定詞的完成式（to have＋p.p.）常用以表達過去曾存在的狀態，過去曾完成的動作，或過去曾經歷的事情。第 2 句屬於錯誤的句子，因未用不定詞的完成式 to have been 以表達過去曾存在的狀態。

分析 **2.**

例句 | Therefore, to be on the safe side, tourists and lovers of extreme trips had better be careful when planning to explore the valley, for no one knows for sure what might happen there next.

○

例句 | Therefore, being on the safe side, tourists and lovers of extreme trips had better be careful when planning to explore the valley, for no one knows for sure what might happen there next.

✕

中譯

因此，為了安全起見，觀光客及熱愛極限旅遊者計劃要到此山谷探險時，最好小心一點，因為沒有人確定那裡接下來會發生什麼事。

用法解析

不定詞組成常見的獨立不定詞片語，常置於句首，修飾整個句子。第 2 句屬於錯誤的句子，因未使用獨立不定詞片語 to be on the safe side。

UNIT
10

名詞與代名詞
Black Holes
黑洞

 名詞以及代名詞的類別及使用方法如下：

I. 可數名詞有普通名詞和集合名詞：

  1. 普通名詞單數變複數時，一般名詞字尾＋s，字尾為 s, x, z, ch, sh 者字尾＋es，字尾為 f 或 fe，則去掉 f 或 fe，加上 ves。

  2. 集合名詞如 family, class, committee ⋯⋯等，若當普通名詞用，則加複數動詞，若當集合名詞用，則加單數動詞。police, cattle, crew ⋯⋯等僅有複數名詞用法。

II. 不可數名詞有專有名詞、物質名詞及抽象名詞：

  1. 專有名詞指特有專屬的名詞，包括人、地方、國家名等。要大寫，不可數。

  2. 物質名詞，如 air, water, money, milk, time ⋯⋯等無法計數的東西或材料，不加冠詞，無單、複數之分，可用 some, a little, much 修飾。若要確切計量，可使用如 a piece of, a loaf of, a bottle of, a glass of, a box of ⋯⋯等片語。

3. 抽象名詞 love, hatred, happiness, friendship, loyalty,…等具抽象含意,不可數。

III. 由連字號連接用以修飾名詞的合併字內,如 seven-year-old 中,year 既充當形容詞作用,儘管前面有 seven 之數字,仍不可加 s,恆為單數。

- ◆ a five-day holiday
- ◆ a seven-story building

IV. 代名詞的種類及使用方法如下:

1. 人稱代名詞可充當主詞、受詞或形容詞。如 I, you, he, she, it, we, they 是主格。me, you, him, her, it, us, them 是受格。

2. 指示代名詞,如 this, that, these, those, so, such 等,常用以取代前面已敘述過者,以避免重覆。

3. 不定代名詞,如 some, any, one, ones, each, all, none, another, others, something, anything, nothing, either, neither,…等常用以取代有所指的人或事物。

4. 前面出現過兩個名詞,再次提到時,為避免重覆,可用 the former 及 the latter 來代替前面提過的名詞(the former…the latter…前者……後者……)。

5. 代名詞取代重覆名詞的用法:句子中,宜避免有重複的部份,常用不定代名詞 one 取代重複的非特定單數名詞,ones 則取代複數名詞。

Ablack hole is a region in space with **gravitational** effects so strong that nothing, including light, can escape from it. Once dying stars burn up all its energy, with nothing to counter its gravity, they begin to collapse under their own weight. Soon the stars get so small and **dense** that they form black holes. In accordance with Einstein's Theory of Relativity, a black hole, due to its massive gravitational influence, **distorts** space and time of the neighborhood. The theories of black holes were first proposed by scientists during the mid-eighteenth century. And in 1974, Professor Stephen Hawking maintained that black holes would eventually **evaporate** over time. When this theory, known as "Hawking Radiation," still needs time to **verify**, black holes create mysterious and dangerous images in ordinary people's minds. Usually the closer we get to a black hole, the slower time runs. Whatever gets pulled into a black hole can never escape. However, it is only when objects get too close to the black hole that the stronger gravitational force will become **apparent** and pull objects in. With so much mystery of black holes in our Milky Way **Galaxy**, the astronomical phenomenon leaves us endless space of **enchantment** and imagination.

☥ 黑洞

　　黑洞在太空是一個有著如此強烈重力效果的區域，以至於包括光在內，沒有任何一樣東西能夠逃離它。垂死的恆星一旦燃盡它所有的能量，沒有任何東西能和它的重力抗衡，它們就開始在自己的重量下瓦解。很快地，恆星變得如此的小，而且密度大，以至於就此形成黑洞。符合於愛因斯坦的相對論，由於它本身巨大的重力影響，黑洞扭曲在它附近的空間和時間。黑洞理論是在 18 世紀中期首度由科學家所提出來的。然後在1974 年，史蒂芬‧霍金教授主張黑洞隨著時間終將蒸發。這個所謂「霍金輻射」的理論仍需要時間來證實之餘，黑洞在一般人的心目中創造出神秘且危險的形象。一般說來，我們越接近黑洞，時間進行的越緩慢。任何被拉進黑洞中的物件便永遠無法逃脫。然而唯有當物件太靠近黑洞時，才會導致較強烈的重力變得明顯並且把物件拉進去。我們的銀河系中竟存在著如此神秘的黑洞，這種天文現象留給我們無限神往及想像的空間。

🔺 關鍵單字解密

gravitational *adj.* 萬有引力的；重力的

dense *adj.* 稠密的；濃密的

distort *v.* 扭曲；曲解

evaporate *v.* 蒸發；揮發

verify *v.* 證明；證實

apparent *adj.* 表面的；明顯的

galaxy *n.* 銀河系；銀河

enchantment *n.* 魅力；著迷

右側邊欄：

1 句型結構 CHAPTER

2 字詞文法 CHAPTER

3 常見文法錯誤、文法應用 CHAPTER

 文法分析

分析 1.

例句 | A black hole is a region in space with gravitational effects so strong that <u>nothing</u>, including light, can escape from it.

例句 | A black hole is a region in space with gravitational effects so strong that <u>nobody</u>, including light, can escape from it.

中譯

黑洞在太空是一個有著如此強烈重力效果的區域，以至於包括光在內，沒有任何一樣東西能夠逃離它。

用法解析

不定代名詞，如 some, any, one, ones, each, all, none, another, others, something, anything, nothing, either, neither ……等常用以取代有所指的人或事物。第 2 句屬於錯誤的句子，因不定代名詞 nobody 用以取代有所指的人，但此處需要的是用以取代有所指事物的 nothing。

分析 2.

例句 | With so much mystery of black holes in our Milky Way Galaxy, the astronomical phenomenon leaves us endless space of enchantment and imagination.

例句 | With so much mystery of black holes in our milky way galaxy, the astronomical phenomenon leaves us endless space of enchantments and imaginations.

中譯

我們的銀河系中竟存在著如此神秘的黑洞，這種天文現象留給我們無限神往及想像的空間。

用法解析

專有名詞指特有專屬的名詞，包括人、地方、國名等。要大寫，不可數。
Milky Way Galaxy 是專有名詞，第一個字母均應大寫，非小寫。此外，抽象名詞 love, hatred, happiness, loyalty,⋯等具抽象含意，不可數。此句後半段 enchantment 及 imagination 是抽象名詞，不可數，字尾不可加 s，故第 2 句是錯誤的句子。

UNIT 11

形容詞
The Mysterious Pluto
神秘的冥王星

 英文中，形容詞用以修飾名詞及具有名詞特質的結構。類別及使用方法如下：

I. 數量形容詞及片語 few, a few, many, a great number of,…等接可數名詞，複數動詞。little, a little, much, a great deal / amount of ……等接不可數名詞及單數動詞。

   ◆ A little time is what Jenny needs to finish the rest of the work. 珍妮只需要一點點時間來完成剩餘的工作。

II. 限定形容詞直接與它修飾的名詞連用，一般的形容詞，如 beautiful, ugly, busy, green, diligent, daily, golden, stricken,…等，直接置於它修飾的名詞前。但，形容詞，如遇 something, anything, nothing ……等不定代名詞則置於後。

   ◆ You should grasp the golden opportunity and make good use of it. 你應該把握大好時機並善用它。

III. 句子中同時出現多個形容詞修飾一個名詞時，常依照下列（1）-（7）的順序排列：

（1）限定詞（2）看法，品質 （3）大小，長度，形狀
（4）年齡，顏色（5）國籍（6）名詞，-ing 形式 （7）名詞

♦ your huge yellow Swedish swimming pool
你的那座大型黃色瑞典製的游泳池。

IV. 複合形容詞：由連字號連接用以修飾名詞的合併字，如 seven-year-old，year 充當形容詞，儘管前面有 seven 之數字，仍不可加 s，恆為單數。形容詞另可搭配現在分詞或過去分詞作形容詞用，中間加上連字號「-」。常見類別如下：

1. 數字-名詞-ed：如：one-eyed, two-headed
2. 形容詞-名詞-ed：如：pretty-faced, kind-hearted
3. 形容詞-現在分詞：如：similar-seeming, handsome-looking, odd-smelling
4. 形容詞-過去分詞：如：brown-colored, green-painted

V. 比較使用中，形容詞字尾是-or 者，如 junior, senior, superior, inferior, prior, posterior, anterior ……等，比較時不用連接詞 than，要搭配介系詞 to 後接受詞。

♦ The foreign brand cars are usually superior to the domestic ones.　外國名牌車通常優於國產汽車。

VI. 形容詞如 unique, round, horizontal, vacant, everlasting, perfect, correct, eternal, unanimous ……等，表達一種完美或完整的特色，不與其他物質做比較，故沒有比較級。但可以用副詞 almost, hardly, nearly ……等修飾。

♦ Jerry gave a nearly correct answer, and Miss White accepted it.　傑瑞給了幾近正確的答案，而懷特老師接受了這個答案。

Pluto, as the planet in the solar system that is furthest from the sun, remains mysterious all the time. In 1930, an American research **assistant**, Clyde Tombaugh, aged 24, found Pluto. Meanwhile, an eleven-year-old girl Venetia Burney named it Pluto, the Roman god of the Underworld due to the similar images of the Underworld and the planet. The previous one is far away from the earth; the latter **rotates** at the furthest **reaches** of the sun. Besides, Pluto was the smallest and the last, the ninth, planet to be discovered. Pluto is believed to have a thick **methane** atmosphere about a few kilometers deep and is covered with frost and ice. During the 1970s, astronomers discovered that both Pluto and its **satellite**, Charon completed a revolution for about six to seven days by themselves and the two have almost the same size, so sometimes astronomers refer to them as double planets. Though **deemed** as an official planet for 76 years, Pluto was renamed a "Dwarf Planet" in 2006, due to the new discovery that it is merely the brightest member of the Kuiper Belt, a mass of objects that orbit the sun **beyond** Neptune. In spite of all these, the small, dark, and distant Dwarf Planet, Pluto, arouses our curiosity and interests. Hopefully, with relatively more **sophisticated** space probes, astronomers will be able to discover more about this mysterious planet in the future.

☥ 神秘的冥王星

　　身為太陽系中離太陽最遠的行星，冥王星向來保持著神祕的形象。在 1930 年時，一名 24 歲的美國研究助理，克萊德·湯博，發現了冥王星，同時，11歲大的女孩，薇妮第·伯納以羅馬地獄神之名為其命名為冥王星。如此命名的源由在於兩者擁有同樣的形象。前者離人世間相當遠，後者則於離太陽最遙遠的地方旋轉著。此外，冥王星是最小顆，同時是最後一顆，也就是第九顆被發現的行星。據了解，冥王星擁有約幾公里深濃密的沼氣大氣層，並且被霜和冰所覆蓋著。在1970年代，天文學家發現冥王星和它的衛星，查倫，完成一趟旋轉週期需要 6~7 天左右，而且這兩顆行星有著幾乎相同的大小，所以有時候天文學家稱呼它們為雙行星。冥王星雖然被視為一顆正式的行星長達 76 年，但是在 2006 年它被重新命名為「矮行星」，因為最新發現到它只是古柏帶，也就是在海王星外環繞太陽軌道運轉的一群行星體中最亮的成員。儘管如此，冥王星這顆渺小、黑暗、而且遙遠的「矮行星」激發了我們的好奇心以及興趣。衷心期盼透過更精密的太空探測器，在未來，天文學家將能更深入探索這顆神祕的行星。

⚠ 關鍵單字解密

assistant *n.* 助手；助理

rotate *v.* 旋轉；轉動

reach *n.* 伸手可及；邊緣地區

methane *n.* 甲烷；沼氣

satellite *n.* 衛星；人造衛星

deem *v.* 認為；視作

beyond *prep.* 在~的那一邊；超過

sophisticated *adj.* 複雜的；世故的

 文法分析

分析 1.

例句 | Meanwhile, an eleven-year-old girl Venetia Burney named it Pluto, the Roman god of the Underworld due to the similar images of the Underworld and the planet. The previous one is far away from the earth; the latter rotates at the furthest reaches of the sun.

○

例句 | Meanwhile, an eleven-years-old girl Venetia Burney named it Pluto, the Roman god of the Underworld due to the similar images of the Underworld and the planet. The previous one is far away from the earth; the latter rotates at the furthest reaches of the sun.

✕

中譯

同時，11 歲大的女孩，薇妮第・伯納以羅馬地獄神之名為其命名為冥王星。如此命名的源由在於兩者擁有同樣的形象，前者離人世間相當遠，後者則於離太陽最遙遠的地方旋轉著。

用法解析

複合形容詞：由連字號連接用以修飾名詞的合併字，如 seven-year-old，year 充當形容詞，儘管前面有 seven，仍不可加 s，恆為單數。第 2 句屬於錯誤的句子，因為複合形容詞 eleven-year-old 的 year 充當形容詞，儘管 eleven 是複數，仍不可加 s。

分析 **2.** ▶

例句 In spite of all these, the small, dark, and distant Dwarf Planet, Pluto, arouses our curiosity and interests.

○

例句 In spite of all these, the dark, small, and distant Dwarf Planet, Pluto, arouses our curiosity and interests.

✕

中譯

儘管如此，冥王星這顆渺小、黑暗、而且遙遠的「矮行星」激發了我們的好奇心以及興趣。

用法解析

句子中同時出現多個形容詞修飾一個名詞時，常依照下列（1）-（7）的順序排列：（1）限定詞、（2）看法，品質、（3）大小，長度，形狀、（4）年齡，顏色、（5）國籍、（6）名詞 -ing 形式、（7）名詞。形容詞 small 應置於形容詞 dark 之前，故第 2 句是錯誤的句子。

副詞
The Oregon Vortex
奧勒岡漩渦

 英文中,副詞常用以修飾動詞、形容詞、其他副詞 或全句。種類及使用重點如下:

I. 副詞可用以表狀態、時間、地方、數量、肯定、否定、頻率、程度,…… 等。修飾一般動詞時,置於後面。修飾形容詞及其他副詞時,置於形容 詞及副詞前面。

1. 表示狀態的副詞:如 quickly, angrily, sadly, slowly, nicely, peacefully ……等。

    ◆ The boss talked to his employees angrily. 老闆生氣地對員 工說話。

2. 表示時間的副詞:如 now, yesterday, today, tonight, tomorrow ……等。置於句末。

    ◆ Never leave until tomorrow what you can do today. 今日 事今日畢。

3. 表示地方的副詞:如 here, there, home, downstairs, upstairs, outside ……等。

    ◆ Lisa was practicing playing the piano upstairs when the doorbell rang. 當門鈴響時,麗莎正在樓上練習彈鋼琴。

4. 表示肯定、否定的副詞:如 yes, no, absolutely, definitely, surely, never, little ……等。表否定的副詞常置於句首倒裝後有加 強語氣的作用。

♦ A: Are you going to the book fair tomorrow? 你明天打算去書展嗎？

B: Yes, definitely! 是，一定要去。

5. 表示頻率的副詞：如 seldom, always, often, rarely, sometimes, usually, never, frequently ……等。

♦ Rick is often late for school, for he always stays up late. 瑞克上學經常遲到，因為他總是熬夜熬得很晚。

6. 表示程度的副詞：如 very, much, so, pretty, rather, somewhat, quite ……等。

♦ Jessica was pretty upset about the gossip about her. 潔西卡對於關於她的流言感到非常沮喪。

II. 副詞或副詞片語充當全句修飾語，置於句首。

♦ Unfortunately, no one survived the car crash. 很不幸地，撞車事件中無人生還。

III. 副詞加強詞，如 too, so, rather, very, even, how, enough, a little, a great deal ……等，常置於它所修飾的形容詞或副詞前。

♦ Knowing that he hit the jackpot, Jerry was too happy to say a word. 知道自己中了頭獎，傑瑞高興到說不出話。

IV. 有些名詞字尾加-ly 後轉換為形容詞，而非副詞。但是有些表示時間的名詞，如 hour, week, month, year ……等，字尾加-ly 後可同時轉換為形容詞和副詞的用法。

♦ The pretty girl gave Sam a friendly smile. 美麗的女孩給山姆一個友善的微笑。

V. 副詞字尾加 ly 及未加 ly 者，如 near（靠得近）及 nearly（幾乎），late（很晚）及 lately（最近）……等，有時表達的實質含意不同。

♦ Sam works hard, and he hardly takes a rest. 山姆工作勤勞，幾乎不休息。

Unlike **ordinary** water vortex fast spinning and pulling things into its center, the Oregon Vortex exists on land, and is a popular roadside touring spot located in Gold Hill, Oregon. Since its opening in 1930, it has attracted huge numbers of visitors. From the outside, tourists can see a small house that is not located **horizontally** on the surface; it slightly tilts. When getting close to the house of mystery, they can feel a great force pulling them inside. Inside the house, the **floating** things, such as pieces of paper, will become spiral-shaped flying all over. What's even more interesting is that the Vortex seems to be a **spherical** field of force. When a person stands inside the house, he cannot stand erect. He is, on the contrary, always in a position that inclines toward magnetic north. And if another person goes away from him towards the south, he becomes taller. According to scientists, such situation is only an optical **illusion**. What truly happens is due to the gravity in this area so **powerful** that it turns into the electromagnetic force, and thus creates the **oddly** unusual phenomena. However, in the past, these situations were referred as paranormal phenomena. **Undoubtedly**, the unexplained mysteries caused by the Oregon Vortex still need further research.

☥ 奧勒岡漩渦

　　不同於一般快速旋轉且拉扯物件進入其中心的水底漩渦，奧勒岡漩渦存在於地面上，並且是位於奧勒岡黃金山丘的一個熱門路邊觀光景點。自從 1930 年開幕以來，它吸引了眾多的訪客。從外表，觀光客看見的不是水平地座落在地面上的小房子；它有點傾斜。當他們接近神秘之屋時，可以感受到有一股把他們拉進去的巨大力量。在屋內，飄動的東西，譬如像紙張，會形成螺旋狀四處飛揚。更有趣的是，這個漩渦近似於一個球狀的力場。當一個人站立在屋內時，他無法站直。相反地，他總是站立於傾向磁鐵北方的位置。假使另一個人，朝向南方離他遙遠地站立著，他則變得比較高。根據科學家的說法，這樣的情境只是視覺上的錯覺罷了。真正發生的原因是，這個地方的重力是如此的強大以至於形成一種電磁力，因此創造出這種古怪不尋常的現象。然而，在過去，這種現象被視為超自然現象。無疑地，由奧勒岡漩渦導致無法解釋的神秘現象仍有待進一步的研究。

 關鍵單字解密

ordinary *adj.* 普通的；平凡的

horizontally *adv.* 地平地；水平地

floating *adj.* 漂浮的；流動的

spherical *adj.* 球面的；圓的

illusion *n.* 錯覺；幻想

powerful *adj.* 強大的；有權威的

oddly *adv.* 奇特地；古怪地

undoubtedly *adv.* 毫無疑問地；肯定地

## 文法分析

分析 1.

例句 │ From the outside, tourists can see a small house that is not located horizontally on the surface; it slightly tilts.

例句 │ From the outside, tourists can see a small house that is not located horizontal on the surface; it slight tilts.

中譯

從外表，觀光客看見的不是水平地座落在地面上的小房子；它有點傾斜。

用法解析

副詞可用以表狀態、時間、地方、數量、肯定、否定、頻率、程度，……等。修飾一般動詞時，置於後面。修飾形容詞及其他副詞時，置於形容詞及副詞前面。第 2 句屬於錯誤的句子，本句子中依前後文需要副詞 horizontally 及 slightly 修飾過去分詞 located 及動詞 tilt，非形容詞 horizontal 及 slight。

分析 **2.** ▶

例句 | When a person stands inside the house, he cannot stand erect.

例句 | When a person stands inside the house, he cannot stand erectly.

中譯

當一個人站立在屋內時,他無法站直。

用法解析

動詞 **stand** 屬於「不完全不及物動詞」,後面要接形容詞 **erect** 當主格補語,說明站立者的狀態,但是第 2 句中使用副詞 **erectly** 是錯誤的用法。

連接詞 1

The Zone of Silence　沉寂之區

 英文中的連接詞用以連接兩個子句。對等連接詞連接兩個對等子句。附屬連接詞則用以連接主要子句與附屬子句。對等連接詞使用方法如下：

I. 對等連接詞連接對稱結構，如兩個對等的單字、片語，或子句。and（和；而）表示累積及同時發生的情境。but（但是；然而）表示相反語意。for（因為）則說明理由。

◆ David loves outdoor activities a lot. He loves swimming, camping, and bungee jumping.　大衛非常喜歡戶外活動。他喜愛游泳、露營，以及高空彈跳。

◆ Tom cannot speak English, but he can speak fluent Spanish.　湯姆不會說英文，但是他會說流利的西班牙文。

II. 對等連接 or（或；否則）表示選擇或否則。so（所以）表示結果及目的。nor（也不）則表示否定含意。對等連接詞連接對稱結構，如兩個對等的單字、片語，或子句。

◆ Steven has been working hard recently, so he may have the chance to get promoted.　史蒂芬最近工作很認真，所以他也許有機會升遷。

◆ Sherry cannot type, nor does the skill interest her.　雪莉不會打字，而這項技能也吸引不了她。

III. 對等式的連接詞片語用以連接對稱結構，如兩個單字、片語或子句。如 both…and…（…和…兩者；既… 而且…）。either…or…（不是… 就是…）。neither…nor…（既不…，也不…）。not only…but （also）（不僅…，而且…）。

- ◆ Both Willy and Vivian are interested in music.　威利和薇薇安兩人對音樂有興趣。
- ◆ You can either go on to graduate school or start finding a job.　你可以繼續念研究所或開始找工作。

IV. rather than 為一連接詞式的片語，用以連接兩個對稱結構（如兩個對等的名詞、動詞、形容詞、或介系詞片語等），中文解釋為「是…而非…」。此外，rather than 可和 prefer to 搭配成為「…prefer to… rather than…」的連接詞片語，連接兩個對稱的動詞，而且必須是兩個原形動詞。中文解釋為「寧可…而不願…」。

- ◆ You should put emphasis on quality rather than on quantity.　你應該重質不重量。
- ◆ According to experts, we need simple nutritious food rather than greasy meals to stay healthy.　根據專家的說法，我們需要簡易滋養的食物，而非油膩的飲食來保持健康。
- ◆ During holidays, Susan prefers to stay home and rest rather than go socializing with others.　假日時，蘇珊寧可待在家裡休息而不願意與人交際。

The Zone of **Silence** refers to a desert area near Durango, northern Mexico. Since the 1930s, the Zone has been noted for its **horrible** weather, all kinds of strange ancient **fossils**, and falling meteorites. Above all, alleged sayings have it that there must be a strong magnetic field underground which causes magnetic **disturbances**, for all the radio signals, **communications** equipment would fail to work there for some unknown reasons. The frequent malfunction of any type of communications: no television, radio, short wave, microwave, or satellite signals seem to be **prevalent** in this Zone. A perfect silence seems to prevail over this dark and silent Zone. According to scientists and investigators, there may be some unusual magnetic properties associated either with the minerals in the soil containing **chalk**, or with the contamination from the meteorites, thus a strong magnetic field is created. Another theory is that the underground magnetic field might have been the place where the aliens store their abundant energy, for there have been not only frequent reports of aliens and UFO sightings but also other unusual phenomena mainly caused by the unusual magnetic properties. With such a mysterious atmosphere, the Zone of Silence will probably remain silent and **continue** to puzzle us all the time.

☥ 沉寂之區

　　沉寂之區指的是墨西哥北部靠近都蘭哥的一個沙漠區域。自從 1930 年代以來，這個區域一直以它惡劣的天氣、各式各樣奇特的古代化石，以及掉落的隕石著名。尤其是，據傳聞這個區域必定存在有導致磁力干擾的強烈地下磁場。因為所有的收音機訊號和通訊設備在那裡會因不知明原因而無法運作。任何一種通訊常見的作用不良的情形，譬如像沒有電視、收音機、短波、微波，或是衛星訊息似乎可以盛行於這個區域。全然的死寂似乎籠罩在這黑暗且沉寂的區域。根據科學家和調查員的說法，這裡也許存在著某些不尋常的磁場特性，有可能是跟包含有白堊土壤中的礦物質有關，或是跟來自於隕石的汙染物有關，因此製造出一個強烈的磁場。另外一個理論是說，地底下的磁場可能是外星人儲存它們大量能源的地方，因為那裡不僅有目擊外星人與幽浮的報導，還有其他主要是因不尋常的磁場特質所導致不尋常的現象。有著如此極其神秘的氣氛，沉寂之區很可能將保持沉默，並且永遠持續地困惑我們。

🔺 關鍵單字解密

silence *n.* 無聲；寂靜

horrible *adj.* 可怕的；惡劣的

fossil *n.* 化石；守舊的事物

disturbance *n.* 干擾；打擾

communication *n.* 溝通；訊息

prevalent *adj.* 盛行的；普遍的

chalk *n.* 白堊；粉筆

continue *v.* 繼續；延伸

 **文法分析**

分析 **1.**

例句 | Above all, alleged sayings have it that there must be a strong magnetic field underground which causes magnetic disturbances, for all the radio signals, communications equipment would fail to work there for some unknown reasons.

例句 | Above all, alleged sayings have it that there must be a strong magnetic field underground which causes magnetic disturbances, so all the radio signals, communications equipment would fail to work there for some unknown reasons.

中譯

尤其是，據傳聞這個區域必定存在有導致磁力干擾的強烈地下磁場。因為所有的收音機訊號和通訊設備在那裡會因不知明原因而無法運作。

用法解析

對等連接詞連接對稱結構，如兩個對等的單字、片語，及子句。for（因為）說明理由，對等連接 so（所以）表示結果及目的。第 2 句屬於錯誤的句子，因此子句在說明理由，應用對等連接詞 for，非表示結果及目的的對等連接詞 so 以連接前後子句。

分析 2.

例句 | According to scientists and investigators, there may be some unusual magnetic properties associated <u>either with</u> the minerals in the soil containing chalk, <u>or with</u> the contamination from the meteorites, thus a strong magnetic field is created.

例句 | According to scientists and investigators, there may be some unusual magnetic properties associated <u>either with</u> the minerals in the soil containing chalk, <u>with or</u> the contamination from the meteorites, thus a strong magnetic field is created.

中譯

根據科學家和調查員的說法，這裡也許存在著某些不尋常的磁場特性，有可能是跟包含有白堊土壤中的礦物質有關，或是跟來自於隕石的汙染物有關，因此製造出一個強烈的磁場。

用法解析

對等式的連接詞片語用以連接對稱結構，如兩個單字、片語或子句。如 both… and…（…和…兩者；既…而且…）。either…or…（不是…就是…）。neither…nor…（既不…，也不…）。not only…but（also）（不僅…，而且…）。在此句中 either… or…（不是…就是…）連接兩個對稱結構由 with 開頭的介系詞片語。第 2 句中 with 未置於連接詞 or 後是錯誤的用法。

UNIT 14

連接詞 2

Halley's Comet

哈雷彗星

 英文中，附屬連接詞用以連接主要子句及附屬子句，依語意有下列不同類型：

I. 附屬連接詞及片語，如 when, while, as, before, after, until, since, as soon as 用以表示「時間」。

- ♦ It's been quite a long time since we saw Bill last.　自從我們上次見到比爾已經過了很長一段時間了。
- ♦ The telephone rang as soon as Jessie returned home. 潔西一回到家電話鈴聲就響了。

II. 附屬連接詞及片語 because, since, as, because of 表示「原因」或「理由」。

- ♦ Since you are here, why not have a chat with Miss Brown?　既然你在這裡，為什麼不和布朗小姐聊天？
- ♦ Because of the coming typhoon, the boat trip was canceled.　因為颱風即將來臨，乘船之旅被取消了。

III. 附屬連接詞片語，如 so that, in order that, so…that, for fear that, lest…should ……等用以表示「目的」或「結果」。

- ♦ Mira was so angry that she slammed the door shut.　米拉是如此的生氣以至於砰一聲把門關上。

♦ You should try the shoes on lest they should not fit. 你應該試穿鞋子為的是怕鞋子不合。

IV. 附屬連接詞及片語，如 though, as, although, in spite of / despite the fact that, even though / if ……等用以表示「讓步」。

   ♦ Little girl though / as Annie is, she can cook delicious food. 安妮雖然是小女孩，她能夠煮美味的食物。

   ♦ Despite the fact that she was sick, Mrs. Hill still went on the parade. 儘管生病了，希爾太太仍舊參加遊行。

V. 附屬連接詞及片語，如 if, unless, supposing（that）, provided that, on condition that ……等用以表明「條件」。

   ♦ You are going to be late for the concert unless you take a taxi. 除非你搭乘計程車，否則演唱會你會遲到。

   ♦ Provided that there is no opposition, we can hold our gathering right here. 假使無人反對的話，我們可以在此舉行我們的聚會。

VI. 下列是其他近似於用以引導「時間」副詞子句的連接詞單詞如 once （一旦）, instantly / directly（一… 就…）, immediately（即刻）……等及連接詞片語如 by the time（當…的時候）, the moment / the minute（一… 就…）, the instant（立即）, the second（瞬間）, every time（每當…）, any time（任何時刻）……等。

   ♦ Once you make a promise, you should try to fulfill it. 一旦做了承諾，你應該試著實現它。

   ♦ The moment Peter arrived at the train station, the train left. 彼得一到達火車站，火車就開走了。

 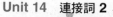

Though comets are rarely seen in the sky, they are important heavenly bodies of the **solar** system. Among them, Halley's Comet is probably the most famous. Every 75 to 76 years, this short-period comet is clearly **visible** to the naked eye from earth. The early track of it could be dated back as far as 240 BC when the ancient Chinese astronomers kept the **records** of its appearances. However, in 1705, an English astronomer, Edmund Halley, first concluded the comet's regular and periodic appearances, and it was thus named after him. In 1986, the year of its previous **perihelion** passage, through space **probes** of several different countries, Halley's Comet was **observed** in detail for the first time. The structure of its nucleus, the mechanism of coma and tail formation were further observed and **confirmed**. According to astronomers, Halley's Comet is probably composed of water, carbon dioxide, ammonia, dust, etc., like a "dirty snowball," because a small portion of it is icy. In addition, Halley's Comet has long been thought to be an omen and has been awed by the general public, for after its appearances, great disasters and **unfavorable** changes might take place. Nevertheless, we still look forward to the coming of 2016 when Halley's Comet is predicted to reappear, for we expect to appreciate this impressive old friend of ours again!

☥ 哈雷彗星

　　雖然彗星在天空中很罕見，它們卻是太陽系中重要的天體。在所有的彗星之中，哈雷彗星很可能是最著名的。每隔 75~76 年間，這顆短周期彗星可以從地球很清楚地用肉眼看見。哈雷彗星軌跡的追蹤最早可以追溯到西元前 240 年，當時古代的中國天文學者記載下它的出現。然而，在 1705年，英國天文學家，艾德蒙‧哈雷，首度推斷哈雷彗星規律且定期的出現，由此哈雷彗星因他而命名。在 1986 年，也就是上一次最靠近太陽的那一年，透過數個不同國家的太空探測器，哈雷彗星首度仔細地被觀測。哈雷彗星彗核的結構，彗髮的構造，以及彗尾的形成，進一步地被觀察並確認。根據天文學家的說法，它很可能是由水、二氧化碳、氨、塵埃…等等所組成，宛如一顆「骯髒雪球」，而且它有一小部分是冰凍的。此外，哈雷彗星長久一來被視為一種惡兆，同時被大眾所敬畏著，因為它的出現過後，重大災難以及不利的變動可能發生。然而，我們仍舊期盼 2016 年的到來，也就是預測哈雷彗星會再度出現的那一年。因為我們希望可以再度欣賞這位令我們印象深刻的老朋友！

關鍵單字解密

solar *adj.* 太陽的；源自太陽的

visible *adj.* 可看見的；清晰的

record *n.* 記錄；記載

perihelion *n.* 近日點；最高點

probe *n.* 探索；太空探測器

observe *v.* 觀察；注意到

confirm *v.* 證實；確定

unfavorable *adj.* 不利的；不吉利的

 **文法分析**

分析 **1.**

例句 | Though comets are rarely seen in the sky, they are important heavenly bodies of the solar system.

例句 | If comets are rarely seen in the sky, they are important heavenly bodies of the solar system.

中譯

雖然彗星在天空中很罕見，它們卻是太陽系中重要的天體。

用法解析

附屬連接詞及片語，如 if, unless, supposing（that）, provided that, on condition that ⋯⋯等用以表明「條件」，另外，如 though, as, although, in spite of / despite the fact that, even though / if ⋯⋯等用以表示「讓步」。本句表示「讓步」的語意，非「條件」，應用 though，非 if，故第 2 句屬於錯誤的句子。

分析 2.

例句 | Nevertheless, we still look forward to the coming of 2016, when Halley's Comet is predicted to reappear, for we expect to appreciate this impressive old friend of ours again!

例句 | Nevertheless, we still look forward to the coming of 2016, because of Halley's Comet is predicted to reappear, for we expect to appreciate this impressive old friend of ours again!

中譯

然而，我們仍舊期盼 2016 年的到來，也就是預測哈雷彗星會再度出現的那一年。因為我們希望可以再度欣賞這位令我們印象深刻的老朋友！

用法解析

附屬連接詞及片語，如 when, while, as, before, after, until, since, as soon as ……等用以表示「時間」。2016 年指「時間」，應搭配連接詞 when，非說明「理由」的片語 because of，因此第 2 句是錯誤的用法。

UNIT 15

介系詞
The Red Planet
紅色星球

 英文中,介系詞常置於名詞或代名詞前來說明位置、時間、方向或方法等。

I. 表示「位置」的介系詞:in 指「裡面」,或與大地方連用。at 指「定點」,或與 小地方連用。on 指「在表面」,或與街道合用。over 上方,under 下方。between 兩者之間。across 橫越過~。about, around 在~周圍。by, beside 在~旁邊。

♦ Mr. Hills has lived in Japan for five years.
希爾先生已在日本住了五年。

II. 表示「時間」的介系詞:in 與長時間連合,at 指時間的某一定點,on 指特定的日子。for 常與一段時間連合,during 指在~期間。before 指在~之前,after 在~之後,since 自從~,until / till 直到~。

III.表「方向」的介系詞:in 指某方向,at 朝某定點,into 進入某處,toward 朝向~,for 朝某目的地,from 從某處來,away from 從~遠離,out of~ 離開~。

♦ The professor walked away hurriedly in the opposite direction.
教授急忙地往相反方向走去。

IV. 表示「方法」的介系詞：by 指利用某種交通工具，不接冠詞 a 或 the。in 常接汽車、計程車、火車、船等，on 則先接冠詞 a 或 the 後，接巴士、飛機等。with 後接某工具，by 常接手工、機器，in 則接某語言或某種材料。

 ♦ The bag is made of leather by hand.
 這個袋子是手工皮革製品。

V. 介系詞後面接名詞或具有名詞特性的結構，如代名詞、動名詞、名詞子句等。

 ♦ Mrs. Norman has got tired of preparing meals all her life.
 諾曼太太厭倦於一輩子都在準備餐飲。

VI. 介系詞可和及物動詞連用，形成雙字動詞片語。如 call on（拜訪），deal with（處理），get to（到達），head for（前往），look after（照料），run into（偶遇），stand for（代表），wait on（服侍），carry out（實現）……等。

 ♦ Let's head for the museum now.
 咱們現在前往博物館。

VII. 上述的雙字動詞片語，受詞無論是名詞或代名詞均置於介系詞之後，不可將及物動詞及介系詞拆開。此類片語又稱為「不可分的雙字動詞片語」。

 ♦ The manger is dealing with the customer's complaints now.
 經理現在正在處理客訴。

Mars is often referred to as the "Red Planet" because of its reddish coloring, resulting from the iron oxide on its surface. The Greeks and Romans named the planet after the God of War, Mars. Astronomers have long been interested in it, and from space probes, more and more interesting discoveries were shown to the world. In 1976 and 2001 separately, photographs of a human face drew worldwide attention. People interested in extraterrestrial life maintained that aliens created the "Face." However, scientists explained that the "Face" was likely only an optical illusion. Mars is similar to the earth in several ways, such as its geological formations, rotational periods, seasonal cycles, and so on. What's more, it is the closest planet to Earth, and what intrigues scientists is the assumed presence of liquid water on the planet's surface. Evidence shows that in the past, liquid water once existed on Mars, which will be vital for the future possibility of humans' immigrating and surviving there. Till today, there are still ongoing assessments and research of the possible future living in Mars. Whether humans will carry out the wishes of building a space colony there or not still needs time and effort.

☥ 紅色星球

　　火星由於表面上的氧化鐵，使得它有著紅色的外表，常被稱為「紅色星球」。希臘羅馬人依戰神之名替它命名為火星。天文學家長久以來對它擁有高度興趣，經由太空探測，有越來越多有趣的發現呈現給世人。分別在 1976 和 2001 年，一張人臉的照片吸引全世界的矚目。對外星生物有興趣的人們主張是外星人創造了這一張人臉，然而科學家解釋這張臉很可能只是一種視覺上的錯覺罷了。火星在某些方面類似於地球，譬如它的地質構造、轉動週期、季節循環…等等。再者，它是最靠近地球的行星，而令科學家感到興奮的是，火星表面有可能存在液態水。證據顯示，在過去，液態水曾經存在於火星，而這點對未來人類移居並生存於火星的可能性是很關鍵的。直到今日，目前還有許多對未來住在火星可能性的評估和研究正在進行著。人類是否將會實現在那裡建築太空殖民地的心願仍需要時間和努力。

關鍵單字解密

reddish *adj.* 帶紅色的；淡紅的

separately *adv.* 個別地；分別地

optical *adj.* 眼睛的；光學的

rotational *adj.* 旋轉的；輪流的

intrigue *v.* 激起好奇心；使迷惑

immigrating *adj.* 遷移的；遷入的

assessment *n.* 評價；估價

colony *n.* 殖民地；聚居地

文法分析

例句：Mars is often referred to as the "Red Planet" because of its reddish coloring, resulting from the iron oxide <u>on its surface</u>.

例句：Mars is often referred to as the "Red Planet" because of its reddish coloring, resulting from the iron oxide <u>beside its surface</u>

中譯

火星由於表面上的氧化鐵，使得它有著紅色的外表，常被稱為「紅色星球」。

用法解析

表示「位置」的介系詞：in 指「裡面」，或與大地方連用。at 指「定點」，或與 小地方連用。on 指「在表面」，或與街道合用。 over 上方，under 下方。between 兩者之間。across 橫越過~。about, around 在~周圍。by, beside 在~旁邊。「表面上」on the surface 介系詞應用 on，不是 beside，故第 2 句是錯誤的句子。

分析 2.

例句：Whether humans will <u>carry out the wishes</u> of building a space colony there or not still needs time and effort.

例句：Whether humans will carry the wishes out of building a space colony there or not still needs time and effort.

中譯

人類是否將會實現在那裡建築太空殖民地的心願仍需要時間和努力。

用法解析

介系詞可和及物動詞連用，形成雙字動詞片語。雙字動詞片語，受詞無論是名詞或代名詞均置於介系詞之後，不可將及物動詞及介系詞拆開。此類片語又稱為「不可分的雙字動詞片語」。carry out 是「不可分的雙字動詞片語」，不可將及物動詞及介系詞拆開，所以第 2 句 the wishes 置於 carry 和 out 中間是錯誤的用法。

CHAPTER

3

常見文法錯誤、文法應用

搭配主題 神秘歷史事件、藝術、人文篇

UNIT 1

單字拼法

The Mahatma Gandhi
聖雄甘地

 英文單字是一切的基礎，應注意拼字方式及拼字的規則，力求正確。

I. 在原單字加上特定含意的字首，即具新的意義。如 il-, ir-, mis-, un- 指的是「否定」的含意。

♦ legal→illegal, spell→misspell, responsible→irresponsible

II. 在原單字字尾加上特定含意的字尾，即具新的意義。如 -er, -or 指的是「執行者」 的含意， -ize 有「能執行～的動作」的含意， -less，「沒有～」，-ly，「～情態」……等。

♦ teach→teacher, conduct→conductor

III. 原單字若字尾是 e，加上一字尾為母音開頭者，如-able, -ance, 或-ous 等，要把原單字字尾 e 去掉，再加上去。但字尾是 -ce 或 -ge 者則不用去掉 e。

♦ fame→famous, guide→guidance

IV. 原單字若字尾是 y，加字尾時，要把 y 改成 i，再加上字尾的部份，如 –ful，-ness ……等。

♦ beauty→beautiful   happy→happiness

V. 遇到單音節短母音字時，字尾則要重覆後再加字尾附加的部分。如 plan→planned, run→runner, 及 stun→stunning ……等。

VI. 重音若落在第二音節上，而第二音節部分是「母音＋子音」的情形時，也要重覆字尾後再加字尾附加的部分。如 refer→referred, occur→occurrence。

VII. 單數字要改成複數字則時，要注意下列拼字規則，而在字尾做變化：一般名詞字尾＋s，字尾為 s, x, z, ch, sh 者字尾＋es，字尾為 f 或 fe，則去掉 f 或 fe，加上 ves。另外，字尾為子音＋o 時，字尾＋es，若為母音＋o，則字尾＋s，字尾若為子音＋y，則要去 y，變成 ies，若為母音＋y，則直接＋s 即可。

◆ pencil→pencils	◆ church→churches	◆ leaf→leaves
◆ tomato→tomatoes	◆ city→cities	◆ toy→toys

VIII. 下列字拼法類似容易弄錯，其實兩者意義不同。這類型的字要特別注意。

◆ angel（天使）	◆ angle（角度）
◆ later（稍晚些）	◆ latter（後者）
◆ quiet（安靜的）	◆ quite（相當）
◆ through（穿越～）	◆ thorough（周密的）
◆ formerly（先前地）	◆ formally（正式地）

Mohandas Karamchand Gandhi was the spiritual leader of the Indian National Liberation Movement opposing the British rule. To fight for the rights of the Indian people in South Asia and the independence from British government, Gandhi preached the concept of nonviolent civil disobedience and non-cooperation instead of a violent protest or actual combats. His ideals and practices inspired a huge crowd of faithful followers, and he was highly honored as "Mahatma," meaning a respectable holy person. Throughout his life, he dedicated himself to eliminating poverty, promoting women's rights, building religious and ethnic harmony, and achieving autonomy. In 1947, they finally won the independence granted by Britain. However, some religious extremists have long opposed Gandhi's doctrine of nonviolence and his being too gentle and moderate to the Muslims. On 30 January 1948, Nathuram Godse, a Hindu nationalist, assassinated Gandhi by firing three bullets into his chest in a close distance, and was tried and executed in 1949. Nevertheless, prior to Gandhi's death, there had been five unsuccessful assassination attempts. The mystery lies in the doubts that the Indian police and government should have made better precautions against the possible assassination, but unfortunately, they failed to. Thus, the great Mahatma Gandhi fell and that will always sadden the world with sorrow and regrets.

♀ 聖雄甘地

　　莫罕達斯・卡蘭默肯・甘地是對抗英國統治，印度民族解放運動的精神領袖。為了爭取南亞印度人的權益和脫離英國政府而獨立，甘地倡導以非暴力的不合作運動來取代暴力的抗議或實質的戰鬥。他的理念和做法激勵了大批忠誠的追隨者，而他被高度地推崇為「聖雄」，表示是一名備受敬重的聖人。終其一生，他致力於消弭貧窮，提升婦女權益，建立宗教和種族和諧，並且努力取得自治。在 1947 年，他們終於得到英國認可的獨立。然而，某些宗教極端份子，長久以來反對甘地非暴力的論說以及他對回教徒太過於溫和容忍的態度。在 1948 年 1 月 30 日，那順拉姆・戈德塞，一名印度國家主義者，近距離對甘地的胸部射擊三發子彈，暗殺了甘地。在 1949 年，戈德塞被審判並執行死刑。但是在甘地身亡前，已有過五次未成功的暗殺意圖。人民懷疑的是印度警方和政府原先應做好預防暗殺可能性的措施，但是不幸地他們並沒有這麼做。因此，聖雄甘地殞落了。而這將會讓世人永遠感受悲傷及遺憾。

關鍵單字解密

spiritual *adj.* 精神上的；心靈的

independence *n.* 獨立；自主

combat *n.* 戰鬥；格鬥

dedicate *v.* 奉獻；獻身於

extremist *n.* 極端主義者；過激分子

doctrine *n.* 信條；教義

execute *v.* 執行；處死

precaution *n.* 警惕；預防措施

 **文法分析**

分析 **1.**

例句 | To fight for the rights of the Indian people in South Asia and the independence from British government, Gandhi preached the concept of nonviolent civil disobedience and non-cooperation instead of a violent protest or actual combats.

例句 | To fight for the rights of the Indian people in South Asia and the dependence from British government, Gandhi preached the concept of violent civil obedience and cooperation instead of a violent protest or actual combats.

中譯

為了爭取南亞印度人的權益和脫離英國政府而獨立，甘地倡導以非暴力的不合作運動來取代暴力的抗議或實質的戰鬥。

用法解析

在原單字加上特定含意的字首，即具新的意義。如 il-, ir-, mis-, un- 指的是「否定」的含意，pre- 有「預先」的含意，en-，「使能夠～」，dis-，「遠離，與～相反」，ex-，「排除～」，in- 則有「不能～」及「在～內部」兩種含意。dependence, violent, obedience, 及 cooperation 加上特定含意的字首，in-, non-, dis- 及 non- 的字首即具新的否定的意義。第 2 句屬於錯誤的句子，因為此句依上下文可知需要代表否定的字。

分析 **2.**

例句 His ideals and practices inspired a huge crowd of <u>faithful</u> <u>followers,</u> and he was highly honored as "Mahatma," meaning a <u>respectable</u> holy person.

例句 His ideals and practices inspired a huge crowd of <u>faith</u> <u>follow,</u> and he was highly honored as "Mahatma," meaning a <u>respect</u> holy person.

中譯

他的理念和做法激勵了大批忠誠的追隨者，而他被高度地推崇為「聖雄」，表示是一名備受敬重的聖人

用法解析

在原單字字尾加上特定含意的字尾，即具新的意義。第 2 句中 faith 字尾需加上-ful，變成形容詞，follow 字尾需加上-er，變成表示「人」，respect 字尾需加上-able，變成形容詞，否則是錯誤的用法。

UNIT 2

動詞形式
The Attack on Pearl Harbor
偷襲珍珠港

 英文動詞使用時，應注意動詞變化的規則、固定用字的意義及用法，力求正確。

I. 動詞基本類別分為 be 動詞與一般動詞。be 動詞包含有指現在式的 am / is / are 或過去式的 was / were。一般動詞，有現在式，過去式，未來式，過去分詞（p.p）及現在分詞（V.ing），…等等的變化。現在式中，當主詞為第三人稱單數時，一般動詞字尾要加「s」，「es」，或變化成「ies」。過去式時，動詞變化則有分規則變化，字尾加「ed」或變化成「ied」，及不規則的動詞變化。

II. 動詞 lie, lay 的正確用法：

1. lie 是不及物動詞，可解釋為「躺、臥」或「位於」，過去式，過去分詞，現在分詞，分別是 lay, lain 及 lying。lie 也可解釋為「說謊」，動詞變化是 lied, lied 及 lying。

   ♦ Michelle lay in bed reading a novel.
     蜜雪兒躺在床上閱讀小說。

2. lay 是及物動詞，可解釋為「放置」或「下蛋」，動詞變化分別是 laid laid laying。

   ♦ Birds usually lay eggs in the nest they build.

鳥經常下蛋在牠們築的鳥巢裡。

III. 動詞 spend, take, cost 的正確用法：人花時間或花錢用 spend，後接動名詞（V-ing）。it 當主詞時，花時間要用 take，花錢則要用 cost，後接不定詞（to V）。

1. 人＋spend＋時間＋（in）V-ing = It take＋人＋時間＋to V（時間的花費）

2. 人＋spend＋金錢＋on 物品 = It cost＋人＋金錢＋to V（金錢的花費）

   ◆ Ben spent one whole week（in）preparing for the final exam.
   = It took Ben one whole week to prepare for the final exam.
   Ben 花一整個星期準備期末考試。

IV. 動詞 rise, arise, rouse, arouse 的正確用法：rise（上升）及 arise（發生）是不及物動詞，後面不接受詞。rouse（叫醒）及 arouse（激起）是及物動詞，後面要接受詞。

   ◆ The sun rises in the east and sets in the west.
   日出於東，日落於西。

   ◆ A great number of financial problems arise during economic recession.
   在經濟蕭條時，發生了許多金融問題。

   ◆ The telephone roused the little baby from its sleep.
   電話把小寶寶從睡夢中吵醒。

   ◆ The hobo in shabby clothes aroused May's sympathy.
   衣衫襤褸的遊民激發梅的同情心。

★ The Attack on **Pearl Harbor**

Track 35

During World War Two, due to President Roosevelt's oil **embargo**, Japan had chosen to start a war against the US, for it was entirely dependent on imported oil. Therefore, on the 7th of December, 1941, Japanese aircraft had an attack on Pearl Harbor in Hawaii, where the American naval base lay. The severe destruction included 18 warships and 300 aircraft destroyed, and heavy **casualties**: 2,451 US **personnel** killed, 1,282 injured. Different from the previous attitude of **Isolationism** toward the War, Americans were **overwhelmed** with shock and fury; patriotism was thus aroused. With the support of most Americans, President Franklin D. Roosevelt declared war on Japan the day after the raid. America's involvement in the War brought total defeat of the Axis powers represented by Japan, Germany, and Italy, and eventually led the Allies to victory. Though Roosevelt described the date of the Raid as "a date that will live in **infamy**", it was **theorized** that the US was warned of the Japanese attack in advance. However, Roosevelt seemed to have deliberately ignored the warning and have allowed it to happen to get a **legitimate** reason for declaring a war on Japan, since before that, most public and political opinions had been against America's entry into the War. In this way, the attack on Pearl Harbor drew America into the War and changed the course of history. As for the truth behind, time will tell.

☥ 偷襲珍珠港

　　二次大戰期間，由於羅斯福總統石油禁運的政策，日本選擇對美國開戰，因為日本非常依賴進口石油。因此在 1941 年 12 月 7 日，日本飛機對美國海軍基地所在地夏威夷的珍珠港進行偷襲轟炸。嚴重的損失包含有 18 艘戰艦、300 架飛機毀損，以及 2,451 美國人員死亡，1,282 人受傷的重大傷亡。不同於先前對於二次世界大戰採取「孤立主義」的態度，美國人飽受重大的震撼及憤怒，因而激發起愛國心。有大部分美國人的支持，富蘭克林・羅斯福總統在偷襲日的第二天對日本宣戰。美國的參戰導致軸心國，日本、德國和義大利全面挫敗，最終將同盟國帶往勝利之路。雖然羅斯福總統把偷襲日描述成「蒙羞日」，人們推論美國先前已被警告日本即將來襲。但是，羅斯福總統似乎是蓄意忽視這個警告，並且默許它發生以取得一個名正言順的理由來對日本宣戰，因為在此之前，多數的美國民意和政界人士皆反對美國參戰。如此一來，偷襲珍珠港使得美國參戰，並且改變歷史軌跡。至於背後的真相，時間自會驗證一切。

⧪ 關鍵單字解密

embargo *n.* 禁運；禁止買賣

casualty *n.* 傷亡人員；受害人

personnel *n.* 人員；員工

Isolationism *n.* 孤立主義；孤立政策

overwhelm *v.* 壓倒；不知所措

infamy *n.* 惡名；醜事

theorize *v.* 建立理論；推理

legitimate *adj.* 合法的；正當的

 文法分析

分析 1. ▶

例句 | Therefore, on the 7th of December, 1941. Japanese aircraft had a surprise attack on Pearl Harbor in Hawaii, <u>where the American naval base lay.</u>

例句 | Therefore, on the 7th of December, 1941. Japanese aircraft had a surprise attack on Pearl Harbor in Hawaii, <u>where the American naval base lied.</u>

中譯

因此在 1941 年 12 月 7 日，日本飛機對美國海軍基地所在地夏威夷的珍珠港進行偷襲轟炸。

用法解析

lie 是不及物動詞，解釋為「躺、臥」或「位於」，過去式，過去分詞，現在分詞，是 lay, lain 及 lying。lie 也可解釋為「說謊」，動詞變化是 lied, lied 及 lying。第 2 句屬於錯誤的句子，因「位於」的 lie 過去式是 lay，不是 lied。

分析 **2.**

例句 | Different from the previous attitude of Isolationism toward the War, Americans were overwhelmed with shock and fury; patriotism was thus aroused.

例句 | Different from the previous attitude of Isolationism toward the War, Americans were overwhelmed with shock and fury; patriotism was thus risen.

中譯

不同於先前對於二次世界大戰採取「孤立主義」的態度，美國人飽受重大的震撼及憤怒，因而激發起愛國心。

用法解析

動詞 rise, arise, rouse, arouse 的正確用法：rise（上升）及 arise（發生）是不及物動詞，後面不接受詞。rouse（叫醒）及 arouse（激起）是及物動詞，後面要接受詞。但是第 2 句中「激發起」過去分詞應用 aroused，非 risen，所以是錯誤的用法。

UNIT 3 主動與被動

The Assassination of John F. Kennedy
約翰・甘迺迪遇刺

 主動與被動語態使用時，宜確實掌握各語態特定的用法，避免錯誤。下列是被動語態各種時式的類型以及使用時要注意的重點：

I. 被動語態各種時式的類型：

1. 現在被動： S＋am / is / are＋p.p.＋by O
2. 過去被動： S＋was / were＋p.p.＋by O
3. 未來被動： S＋will be＋p.p.＋by O
4. 現在進行被動： S＋am / is / are＋being＋p.p.＋by O
5. 過去進行被動： S＋was / were＋being＋p.p.＋by O
6. 現在完成被動： S＋have / has＋been＋p.p.＋by O
7. 過去完成被動： S＋had＋been＋p.p.＋by O
8. 未來完成被動： S＋will have＋been＋p.p.＋by O
9. 助動詞被動： S＋can / may / must / could / might / would / ⋯ ＋be＋p.p.＋by O

II. .英文中，若是陳述客觀事實、新聞報導、行為動作者不確定或不重要時，宜使用被動語態，可使文句顯得簡潔客觀。被動語態結構中「by ＋動作者」可省略不用。為使文章生動，宜多用主動語態書寫。

　　◆ Finally the broken road is being repaired（by someone）

now.

現在毀損的道路終於在修補中了。

III. 特定類別的動詞沒有被動語態：表示測量的動詞如 cost, weigh, measure ⋯⋯等，表示擁有的動詞如 have, belong to ⋯⋯等，連綴動詞如 appear, become, turn, seem, remain ⋯⋯等，和完全不及物動詞如 arrive, come, die, rise, run, sit, talk ⋯⋯等，均不用被動語態，要用主動語態。

- ♦ The big container weighs eleven tons.
  這個大的容器重達 11 公噸。

IV. 授與動詞如 give, buy, bring, show, teach, send, prepare ⋯⋯等，有兩個受詞。用事物做為直接受詞，用人做為間接受詞。主動改為被動語態時，可改成兩種各以事物或以人為主的被動語態，以人為主的被動語態較常見。

- ♦ Kevin sent Fanny a bunch of roses on Valentine's Day.
  → Fanny was sent a bunch of roses by Kevin on Valentine's Day.
  → A bunch of roses were sent to Fanny by Kevin on Valentine's Day.
  凱文在情人節送芬妮一束玫瑰花。

V. 下列類似被動語態表示「情緒」或「感情」的片語，表面上用被動形式，事實上表達的是主動的語意：be interested in（感興趣），be satisfied with（滿意），be surprised at（驚訝），be devoted to（致力於），be absorbed in（專心於）⋯⋯等。

John Fitzgerald Kennedy was **elected** the 35th president of the US in November, 1960. The **promising** young president was expected to accomplish great achievements during his presidency. However, on the 22nd of November, 1963, he was assassinated by Lee Harvey Oswald in Dallas, Texas. Oswald was **arrested** and charged with the assassination. Unexpectedly, two days later, Oswald was shot and killed by Jack Ruby, a Dallas nightclub owner. The JFK assassination was one of the world's most shocking moments, and a **majority** of Americans believed that there was a conspiracy behind. In fact, numerous conspiracy theories have been put forth since then. Conspiracy parties allegedly included the CIA, the Mafia, the KGB, the Cuban President, Castro, or even the US Vice President Lyndon Johnson, who **succeeded** Kennedy after his death. To find out the true murderer, the US government set up the Warren **Commission** on the 29th of November, 1963 to investigate the assassination. And in 1964, the Warren Report was released asserting that there was no conspiracy, and Oswald acted alone. However, the US government was believed to have **intentionally** covered up the crucial information. Besides, the complete "Warren Report" is now held back by the US government and **scheduled** to be released publicly only after 2038 when the mystery might be unraveled then.

☥ 約翰・甘迺迪遇刺

　　約翰・費茲傑羅・甘迺迪在 1960 年 11 月獲選為美國第 35 屆總統。這位前途被看好的年輕總統，原來被預期在他總統任內能夠成就偉大成就。但是，在 1963 年 11 月 22 日時，他在德州達拉斯被李・哈維・奧斯華所暗殺。奧斯華被逮捕並以暗殺罪名起訴。出乎意料地，兩天後，奧斯華被達拉斯夜總會老闆，傑克・盧比槍殺身亡。甘迺迪遇刺是令世人最震驚的時刻之一，而大多數美國人相信背後存在著一個重大的陰謀。事實上，從那時起，數種陰謀論被提出。據說陰謀集團包括有中央情報局、黑手黨、前蘇聯國安會、古巴總統卡斯楚，甚至甘迺迪死後的繼位者，副總統林登・強生。為了找出真正的兇手，美國政府在 1963 年 11 月 29 日設立「華倫委員會」來調查這起刺殺案件。在 1964 年，「華倫報告」公布並宣稱沒有陰謀，奧斯華是獨自犯案。但是人們相信美國政府蓄意掩蓋關鍵的情資。此外，完整的「華倫報告」目前被美國政府所扣留，預計在 2038 年之後才會公諸於世，屆時也許會揭曉這起神秘遇刺案。

◬ 關鍵單字解密

elect *v.* 選舉；推選

promising *adj.* 有前途的；大有可為的

arrest *v.* 逮捕；拘留

majority *n.* 大多數；過半數

succeed *v.* 成功；繼任

commission *n.* 委任；委員會

intentionally *adv.* 有意地；故意地

schedule *v.* 計劃；預定

 **文法分析**

分析 **1.**

例句 | In fact, numerous conspiracy theories <u>have been put forth</u> <u>since then</u>.

例句 | In fact, numerous conspiracy theories <u>have put forth since</u> <u>then</u>.

中譯

事實上，從那時起，數種陰謀論被提出。

用法解析

副詞片語 since then 應搭配現在完成被動： S＋have／has＋been＋ p.p.＋by O，第 2 句屬於錯誤的句子，因 have 與 put 中少了代表被動 的 been。

分析 2.

例句 | Besides, the complete "Warren Report" is now held back by the US government and scheduled to be released publicly only after 2038, when maybe the mystery will be unraveled.

例句 | Besides, the complete "Warren Report" is now holding back by the US government and scheduled to be released publicly only after 2038, when maybe the mystery will be unraveled.

中譯

此外，完整的「華倫報告」目前被美國政府所扣留，預計在 2038 年之後才會公諸於世，屆時也許會揭曉這起神秘遇刺案。

用法解析

副詞 now 應搭配現在被動語態：S＋am / is / are＋p.p.＋by O，第 2 句中，因 is 後應與代表被動的過去分詞 held 連用，非用代表主動的現在分詞 holding，所以是錯誤的用法。

名詞子句
The Derinkuyu Underground City
土耳其地下城

英文中，**名詞子句**可以是由附屬連接詞 **that** 所引導的名詞子句，或是由**wh-疑問詞** who, whom, which, what, whose, how, when, where, why, whether ……等所引導的名詞子句。使用時名詞子句時，宜確實掌握各**特定的規則及用法**，避免錯誤。

I. 名詞子句可以有充當主詞的功用，也可以當做及物動詞及介系詞的受詞。由 that 引導的名詞子句若太長時可以用 it 來取代，稱為假主詞或假受詞。

　◆ Peter hopes that he will become a lawyer in the future.
　　彼得希望未來將成為一名律師。

　◆ It is true that all men are created equal.
　　人人生而平等是真實的。

II. 名詞子句有充當主詞補語的功用，說明主詞的內容。它也可以當受詞補語，來補充說明受詞的情境。另外，名詞子句還可以作名詞的同位語，用來敘述前面名詞的內容。

　◆ His excuse for coming late was that he missed the train.
　　他遲到的理由是他沒趕上火車。

♦ The fact that global warming endangers the earth is undeniable.

全球暖化危及地球的這個事實是不可否認的。

III. 由 wh- 疑問詞所引導的名詞子句中， what 是一個結合了先行詞和關係代名詞的字，相當於 that which 或 those which。它引導的名詞子句當主詞或受詞時使用「主詞＋動詞」的形式。

♦ What matters in life is that you have fulfilled your responsibility.

人生重要的事是你盡了你的責任。

IV. 由附屬連接詞 that 所引導的名詞子句當受詞時，連接詞 that 可以省略。但如果是當主詞、主詞補語、或作名詞的同位語時，為避免語意不明確，that 不可以省略。

♦ George expects (that) he could hit the jackpot and become rich overnight.

喬治期盼中頭獎並且一夕致富。

♦ That the earth is round is known to everyone.

人人皆知地球是圓的。

V. 由 wh- 疑問詞所引導的名詞子句可以當介系詞的受詞。但是由附屬連接詞 that 所引導的名詞子句，除了 in / but / except that 等特定用法外，不可以當介系詞的受詞。

♦ You should watch out for what you're trying to do.

你應該小心你將試著要做的事。

♦ All the children were allowed to take away whichever toy they chose.

所有的兒童被允許拿走任何他們選擇的玩具。

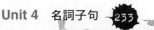

★ The Derinkuyu Underground City

In history, Turkey has been at the center of several **empires** and a bridge between the Eastern and Western cultures. Among Turkey's many **naturally** formed tourists' attractions, the Derinkuyu Underground City is an amazing mystery to the world. With caves built in the soft volcanic rock, it is located in the Cappadocia region, where the world's most **exquisite** collection of underground cities and villages were found. It was discovered in 1963 by accident when a man **renovated** his home finding a stone passageway behind a wall. It is a collection of long tunnels and lots of rooms stretching around 60 meters below the surface. Researchers speculated that with about 4,000 years of history, it might have been used for two purposes. One was to function as an **agricultural** space for storing and transporting food and produce. Furthermore, it was once capable of housing up to around 20,000 people. So, the other function was to create a hiding place. According to **historians**, in case of attacks, a great part of the Turkish population would take refuge in these underground chambers to escape **persecution**. However, just exactly by whom, how, and when the underground structures were built still need further research. And in fact it's the **aroma** of mystery hung about the Derinkuyu Underground City that can elicit even greater curiosity and interests from the worldwide tourists.

♀ 土耳其地下城

　　歷史上，土耳其一向是帝國的重鎮，並且是東西文化的橋樑。在土耳其眾多天然形成的觀光景點之中，代林庫悠地下城對全世界來說是一個神奇之謎。有著建築在柔軟火山岩中的山洞，地下城位於卡帕多西亞高原中，這座高原中有著全世界最雅緻的地下城市及村莊。它是在 1963 年無意中被發現的，當時有一個整修房子的人在一面牆後方發現一座石製的通道。它集結了往地底下延伸約 60 公尺的漫長隧道和大量的房間。研究學者推測，它具有 4000 年的歷史，很可能具有兩種作用。一個是充當儲存及輸送食物和農產品的農業處所。此外，它一度曾經能夠容納高達兩萬人。所以，另一個功用是創造一個隱藏的處所。根據歷史學家的說法，萬一遭逢攻擊，極大比例的土耳其人會在地下房間避難以遠離迫害。然而，究竟這些地下城的結構是由誰建造的，如何建造的，及何時建造的，仍須進一步研究。事實上，這些環繞在代林庫悠地下城神秘的氛圍可以引發來自於世界各地觀光客更深的好奇和興趣。

⚼ 關鍵單字解密

empire *n.* 帝國；大企業

naturally *adv.* 順理成章地；自然地

exquisite *adj.* 精緻的；製作精良的

renovate *v.* 整修；更新

agricultural *adj.* 農業的；農藝的

historian *n.* 歷史學家

persecution *n.* 迫害；困擾

aroma *n.* 香氣；風味

 **文法分析**

分析 1.

例句 | Researchers speculated that with about 4,000 years of history, it might have been used for two purposes.

例句 | Researchers speculated it with about 4,000 years of history, it might have been used for two purposes.

中譯

研究學者推測,它具有 **4000** 年的歷史,很可能具有兩種作用。

用法解析

名詞子句可以有充當主詞的功用,也可以當做及物動詞及介系詞的受詞。由 **that** 引導的名詞子句若太長時可以用 **it** 來取代,稱為假主詞或假受詞。但本句中及物動詞 **speculated** 是以 **that** 引導的名詞子句作為受詞,並非假受詞 **it** 的用法,故第 2 句屬於錯誤的句子。

分析 2. ▶

例句 | However, just exactly by whom, how, and when the underground structures were built still need further researches.

例句 | However, just exactly by whom, how, and when the underground structures were built still needs further researches.

中譯

然而，究竟這些地下城的結構是由誰建造的，如何建造的，及何時建造的，仍須進一步研究。

用法解析

名詞子句可以是由 wh- 疑問詞 who, whom, which, what, whose, how, where, when, why, whether ……等所引導的名詞子句。第 2 句中 by whom, how, and when the underground structures were built 由連接詞 and 連接 3 段 wh- 疑問詞子句當做整句的主詞，是複數主詞，動詞 need 不應該加 s。

字詞片語搭配

The Berlin Wall

柏林圍牆

英文中字詞片語搭配指的是**各個詞類的單字詞彙間固定的組合關係。常見的字詞片語搭配詞有多種組合，使用時，宜確實掌握正確搭配及用法，避免錯誤。**

I. 及物動詞搭配連用介系詞，可形成「不可分的雙字動詞片語」。受詞無論是名詞或代名詞均置於介系詞之後，不可將及物動詞及介系詞拆開。

◆ The police plan to seek for some evidence in the house.
警方計畫在屋內搜尋一些證據。

II. 1. 介系詞後面不接受詞者，另稱為「介副詞」。及物動詞亦可搭配連用介副詞，形成「可分的雙字動詞片語」。此類搭配的動詞片語可把雙字拆開，受詞是名詞時，置於介副詞前面或後面，受詞是代名詞則一定要置於及物動詞及介副詞之間。

◆ The Chinese like to set off firecrackers on Chinese New Year.
中國人在中國春節時喜歡放鞭炮。

2. 使用及物動詞搭配連用介副詞時要注意各個介副詞不同的語意，如 on 表示連接、繼續，up 表示出現、完全，down 表示記錄下、毀

壞，over 表示轉換、始終，off 表示消失、遠離，out 表示熄滅、離去，……等。

♦ Janet left the engine on while waiting for her husband.
珍妮特等丈夫時把引擎開著。

♦ It's amazing that Terry drank up the whole bottle of wine.
很驚人的是泰瑞把整瓶酒喝光了。

III. 及物動詞亦可搭配連用介副詞、介系詞，另外形成「三字動詞片語」。但受詞不可更換位置，無論名詞或代名詞必置於介系詞之後。

♦ Before you go abroad, you should brush up on English.
出國前，你應該複習英文。

♦ Don't wait up for me tonight; I will come home late.
晚上不用等我了；我很晚才會回家。

IV. 字詞的文法搭配應遵循文法規則做正確的搭配。如感官動詞及連綴動詞文法規定要搭配的主詞補語是名詞或形容詞。另外，及物動詞如 mind, practice, keep, enjoy, imagine, avoid ……等後面要接動名詞做為受詞等。

♦ The soup tastes delicious.
湯喝起來很美味。

♦ Kyle seems upset today.
凱爾今天似乎很生氣。

V. 固定的字彙搭配應符合使用規則。如動詞 unravel（解開…），常以人常主詞，字彙搭配應搭配 the difficulty（難題）, plot（陰謀）, puzzle（困惑）, mystery（謎）……等類似含意的字。

♦ Jenny is at a loss how to unravel the problem.
珍妮對於如何解決問題感到很困惑。

On 13 August 1961, the Berlin Wall was **constructed** to close the border between East and West Berlin. The Wall was used as a way of preventing East Germans from entering West Germany. Nevertheless, many East German **defectors** kept trying to escape across the Wall to West Berlin, only to be shot **relentlessly** by border guards as traitors. On 9 November 1989, the East Germans could put up with the Wall no more and it was finally brought down, allowing the crowds to rush to the other side. The fall of the Berlin Wall symbolized the end of the **tyrannical** communism and also the end of the Cold War starting from the end of World War Two. According to historians, the mystery of building the Wall lay in the **subtle** reactions of the American President John F. Kennedy. He got **increasingly** concerned about a coming war after Nikita Khrushchev, the Soviet Union leader, warned him to remove western forces. Therefore, when Kennedy heard of the construction of the Wall, to the public, he **condemned** it as a physical representation of the Communist Iron Curtain. However, he didn't take any **concrete** action. Instead, it's said that he actually felt relieved. He was reported to have said that a wall should be a lot better than a war and that ended Berlin Crisis. Whether this is true or not may need time and specific evidence to clarify.

☥ 柏林圍牆

　　在 1961 年 8 月 13 日，柏林圍牆被築起以關閉東西柏林間的邊境。這座牆被用來做為阻擋東德人進入西德的一個方式。然而，許多東德叛逃者不斷地嘗試跨越過圍牆逃到西柏林，最終是被邊境守衛視同叛徒無情地射殺。在 1989 年 11 月 9 日，東德人再也無法忍受這座圍牆而它終於被拆除，允許群眾衝向另外一端。柏林圍牆的倒塌象徵暴虐共產主義的結束，並且是從二次大戰末開始冷戰的結束。根據歷史學家的說法，柏林圍牆建築之謎在於美國總統約翰甘迺迪微妙的反應。他在前蘇聯領袖，尼克塔‧赫魯雪夫警告他要撤除西方武力後，逐漸地警戒到即將有戰爭的來臨。因此，當甘迺迪聽聞柏林圍牆的建築時，表面上，他譴責柏林圍牆是一種共產主義鐵幕實質的表徵。然而，他並沒有採取任何具體的行動。相反地，據說他事實上感覺鬆了一口氣。據報導，他曾說，一道圍牆應該比一場戰爭好太多了，而那也終止了柏林危機。無論真相如何也許都需要時間和具體的證據來澄清。

⚠ 關鍵單字解密

construct *v.* 建造；創立

defector *n.* 叛離者；背叛者

relentlessly *adv.* 無情地；殘酷地

tyrannical *adj.* 暴虐的；專制君主的

subtle *adj.* 微妙的；詭秘的

increasingly *adv.* 漸增地；越來越多地

condemn *v.* 責難；譴責

concrete *adj.* 具體的；實在的

文法分析

分析 1.

例句 Nevertheless, many East German defectors kept trying to escape across the Wall to West Berlin, only to be shot relentlessly by border guards as traitors.

例句 Nevertheless, many East German defectors kept to try to escape across the Wall to West Berlin, only to be shot relentlessly by border guards as traitors.

中譯

然而，許多東德叛逃者不斷地嘗試跨越過圍牆逃到西柏林，最終是被邊境守衛視同叛徒無情地射殺。

用法解析

字詞的文法搭配應遵循文法規則做正確的搭配。如感官動詞及連綴動詞文法規定要搭配的主詞補語是名詞或形容詞。另外，及物動詞如 mind, practice, keep, enjoy, imagine, avoid ……等後面要接動名詞做為受詞等。第 2 句屬於錯誤的句子，因及物動詞 kept 後應該要搭配動名詞 trying，並非不定詞 to try。

1
句型結構
CHAPTER

2
字詞文法
CHAPTER

3
常見文法錯誤、文法應用
CHAPTER

分析 **2.** ▶

例句 | On 9 November 1989, the East Germans could put up with the Wall no more and it was finally brought down, allowing the crowds to rush to the other side.

〇

例句 | On 9 November 1989, the East Germans could put up the Wall with no more and it was finally brought down, allowing the crowds to rush to the other side.

✕

中譯

在 1989 年 11 月 9 日，東德人再也無法忍受這座圍牆而它終於被拆除，允許群眾衝向另外一端。

用法解析

及物動詞可搭配連用介副詞、介系詞，另外形成「三字動詞片語」。但受詞不可更換位置，無論名詞或代名詞必置於介系詞之後。但是第 2 句中「三字動詞片語」 put up with 被拆開而置入 the Wall 是錯誤的用法。

主詞與動詞一致

The Easter Island
復活島

英文句子中，**動詞依主詞而定**，主詞的認定規則要熟悉確定，固定用法及句型，也要謹慎使用，主詞與動詞要能一致，以避免錯誤。下列是應注意的規則及句型：

I. 由連接詞 and 或 or 併合的主詞要依其實際的語意確定是單數或複數而決定動詞的單、複數。1）併合主詞是複數主詞，動詞要搭配複數動詞。2）併合主詞意指同一人或物，動詞則要搭配單數動詞。3）併合主詞意義上是視為同一單位，就應該使用單數動詞。4）併合主詞帶有強調個別含意的字及片語，如 every, each, many a ……等，主詞視為單數。

- ♦ Rachel and Simon were out for their Christmas shopping.
  瑞秋和賽門外出做耶誕節的採購。
- ♦ Ham and eggs is Little Johnny's favorite. 火腿蛋是小強尼最愛吃的。
- ♦ Many a boy and girl likes to surf the Internet. 許多男孩女孩喜歡上網。

II. 句子一般字序是先主詞再動詞，句型如 There is/are＋S（有 … ）及 The following is / are＋S（下列是 … ）的是先動詞再主詞，要根據動詞後的主詞決定單、複數。

- ♦ There are lots of fans waiting for their idol to show up. 有許多粉絲正在等待他們的偶像出現。

III. 類似 A, not B（是 A，不是 B）或 A rather than B（是 A，而非 B）的結構，訊息焦點在前者，非後者時，動詞要和置於前的主詞 A 一致。

- Philip's uncle, not his parents, is coming to the parent-teacher meeting.　飛利浦的叔叔，而非他的雙親，將會參加家長座談會。

IV. 特定名詞，如國名、書名、學科名、疾病名、瀑布名、公司名…等，具有複數名詞的形式，但若所指的是一個，具單數意義，亦當單數，搭配單數動詞。

- Niagara Falls is world-famous for its spectacular sights.　尼加拉瓜大瀑布以它奇特的風景而世界聞名。

V. 關係代名詞 who / which 後的動詞根據先行詞主詞是單數或複數而不同。如 Those / People / He who…（凡是…的人），關係代名詞 who 前若是複數主詞 those 或 people，用複數動詞，若是單數主詞 he，則要用單數動詞。

- He who hesitates will lose the golden opportunity.　猶豫不決的人將失去大好機會。

VI. 集合名詞如family, class, jury, committee, …等，當普通名詞用時，搭配複數動詞，當集合名詞用，搭配單數動詞。

- The committee is ready to announce the results of the investigation.　委員會準備好要宣布調查結果。

VII. 片語如not only A but also B (不僅A而且B)，either A or B (不是A就是B)，及neither A nor B (不是A，也不是B)，動詞要與靠近它的B一致。A as well as B (A以及B) 及A along / together with B (A連同B)，動詞要則要與A一致。

- Neither Debby nor her parents are coming to the ceremony tonight.　黛比和她的雙親都不會來參加晚上的典禮。

Easter Island is a tiny Polynesian island in the southeastern Pacific Ocean. It has become famous since the eighteenth century when European explorers arrived at this **remote** island and discovered Moai, the Easter Island Heads. According to archaeologists, the Heads were probably built **sometime** between 1,000 and 1,100 AD though the Island's earliest civilization might have started as early as 400 AD. Along the Pacific Ocean, the Island was lined with hundreds of god-like **statues** carved from volcanic rock. Each huge statue wore a **crown**, had very long ears, and **weighed** up to 14 tons, facing inland, away from the sea. They were believed to have **represented** the tribe's ancestors, probably the status symbols of the powerful chiefs. However, the legend had it that sometime during the late seventeenth century, the tribe that built the statues was completely destroyed in a **fatal** battle, and the tragedy brought ghostly air to the Island and the inhabitants. In fact, not only the legendary tribe's tragic doom but also the exact purpose of building the huge sculptures and how they were mounted into place till today still puzzle the world a lot. Before the puzzles are fully solved, the **majestic** Easter Island Moai will always be a great mystery.

⚲ 復活島

　　復活島是位於太平洋東南方一座小的波里尼西亞島。它從 18 世紀以來變得出名了，當時歐洲探險家到達這座遙遠的島嶼並且發現摩埃，也就是復活島頭像。根據考古學家的說法，雖然這座島最早的文化可能是從西元 400 年開始的，這些頭像可能是在西元 1,000 至 1,100 年之間某時刻建造的。沿著太平洋，復活島佈滿著數百尊由火山岩雕刻出來神一般的雕像。每一尊巨大的雕像戴著皇冠，有著非常長的耳朵，重達 14 公噸，遠遠地離海而面向島內。人們相信它們代表著部落的祖先，極可能是很大權勢酋長地位的象徵。然而，有傳聞說 17 世紀末期的某個時刻，建造這些雕像的部落，在一次致命的戰役當中全數被殲滅了，而這個悲劇帶給復活島和當地居民一股鬼魅般的氣氛。事實上，不僅是傳說中部落悲慘的命運，建造巨型雕像確切的目的，以及它們是如何被搬移定位，迄今也仍令世人十分地困惑。在謎底確實揭曉前，宏偉的復活島摩埃雕像將永遠是一個謎。

 關鍵單字解密

remote *adj.* 遙遠的；偏僻的

sometime *adv.* 某一時刻；改天

statue *n.* 雕像；塑像

crown *n.* 皇冠；王冠狀的東西

weigh *v.* 重達；重壓

represent *v.* 表示；代表

fatal *adj.* 命運的；致命的

majestic *adj.* 雄偉的；崇高的

 文法分析

分析 **1.**

例句 However, the legend had it that sometime during the late seventeenth century, the tribe that built the statues was completely destroyed in a fatal battle, and the tragedy brought ghostly air to the Island and the inhabitants.

例句 However, the legend had it that sometime during the late seventeenth century, the tribe that built the statues were completely destroyed in a fatal battle, and the tragedy brought ghostly air to the Island and the inhabitants.

中譯

然而，有傳聞説 17 世紀末期的某個時刻，建造這些雕像的部落，在一次致命的戰役當中全數被殲滅了，而這個悲劇帶給復活島和當地居民一股鬼魅般的氣氛。

用法解析

關係代名詞後的動詞根據先行詞主詞是單數或複數而不同。關係代名詞前若是複數主詞，用複數動詞，若是單數主詞，則要用單數動詞。第 2 句屬於錯誤的句子，因為關係子句 that built the statues 的先行詞 tribe 是單數，應接單數動詞 was ，非複數動詞 were 。

分析 2. ▶

例句 | In fact, not only the legendary tribe's tragic doom but also the exact purpose of building the huge sculptures and how they were mounted into place till today still puzzle the world a lot.

例句 | In fact, not only the legendary tribe's tragic doom but also the exact purpose of building the huge sculptures and how they were mounted into place till today still puzzles the world a lot.

中譯

事實上，不僅是傳說中部落悲慘的命運，建造巨型雕像確切的目的，以及它們是如何被搬移定位，迄今也仍令世人十分地困惑。

用法解析

片語如 not only A but also B（不僅 A 而且 B）， either A or B（不是 A 就是 B），及 neither A nor B（不是 A，也不是 B），動詞要與靠近它的 B 一致。第 2 句中的 B 主詞 the exact purpose of building the huge sculptures and how they were mounted into place 是複數，所以應用複數動詞 puzzle ，而非單數動詞 puzzles ，所以是錯誤的用法。

子句連接詞
The Fall of A Kungfu King
功夫之王的殞落

 英文中子句連接詞用以連接兩個子句。就文法句子結構而言，是必要且重要的。使用時，宜確實掌握特定文法規則、用法及句型，力求使用正確流暢。

I. 對等連接詞有 and（和；而），but（但是；然而），for（因為），or（或；否則），so（所以）及 nor（也不）⋯⋯等，用以連接兩個對等子句。

II. 附屬連接詞，則用以連接主要子句與附屬子句。如 when, while, as, before, after, until, since ⋯⋯等表示「時間」。because, since, as ⋯⋯等表示「原因」。though, as, although ⋯⋯等表示「讓步」。if, unless, supposing, ⋯等則表明「條件」。

◆ **Since Steven started playing golf, he has taken great interest in it.** 自從史帝芬開始打高爾夫球，他對它產生極大的興趣。

III. 連接詞式的副詞也常用以連接子句。表示「時間」的有 afterwards, meanwhile, meantime ⋯⋯等。表示「次序」的有 firstly, then, next, formerly ⋯⋯等。表示「空間」的有 before, above, around ⋯⋯等。表示「對比」的有 however, nevertheless, whereas, conversely, instead ⋯⋯等。表示「強調、附加」的有 indeed, moreover, besides, similarly, likewise ……等。表示「結果」的有 thus, hence, therefore ……等。

IV. 有連接詞功用的副詞用於連接子句時要另外加上連接詞或代表連接詞作用的分號（；），該副詞後加逗點或另起一句，否則不合文法規定。

- ♦ Jack played too much; thus, he failed the test.
- ♦ Jack played too much, and thus, he failed the test.
- ♦ Jack played too much. Thus, he failed the test.
  傑克太貪玩了；因此，他考試考不及格。

V. 下列是使用時要注意的重點：

1. 子句連接詞用以連接子句，介系詞後接具名詞特色的結構，不可用來連接子句，不可誤用。如 as 和 like 中文解釋一樣是「像」，但前者是連接詞，後者是介系詞，要區分清楚。

2. 子句連接詞要做正確的搭配。如比較級的句子中要搭配的連接詞是 than。

3. because 是附屬連接詞，用以引導表示「原因」的子句，不能像連接詞 that 可引導名詞子句做主詞、受詞、或補語等。

4. 勿錯用 neither 及 nor。neither 及 nor 中文解釋雖然一樣是「…也不」，但 neither 是副詞，不是子句連接詞，句中要另加連接詞，如 and 來連接。但 nor 本身是附屬連接詞，可直接用以連接子句。

- ♦ Jerry isn't for the plan, nor / and neither is Helen.
  傑瑞不贊成這個計畫，而海倫也不贊成。

Bruce Lee, though died young, had made great contributions to Chinese Kungfu. He is **considered** one of the most influential martial artists of all time. Skilled in Chinese martial arts, Lee taught Kungfu, wrote books, and acted in popular Chinese Kungfu movies. Through his unique Kungfu movies, Lee's self-discipline, **diligence** and excellence in martial techniques finally won him world **recognition** as a Kungfu king. In fact, not only Lee himself but the special and fantastic Chinese martial arts were seen and admired by the world. However, Lee's sudden death in 1973 shocked the world and the causes of his death have remained mysterious since then. The official reports stated that he died from brain **swelling** due to a serious **allergic** reaction to Equagesic, a painkiller for headache, and it was "a death by misadventure". Nevertheless, other speculations varied, which included the murders being Chinese Triads, martial arts followers, or Italian Mafia, and so on. Among others, the most **weird** one was about Lee's family **curse**, which **previously** took his older brother's life, and after twenty years, accidentally in a gun-shooting movie scene, took his son, Brandon's life. To Bruce's Kungfu fans, hopefully one day the mystery of Lee's death could be unraveled.

☥ 功夫之王的殞落

　　李小龍，雖然英年早逝，對中國功夫有極大的貢獻。他被視為有史以來最具有影響力的功夫大師之一。李小龍的中國武術精湛，他傳授功夫，撰寫書籍，並且在受歡迎的中國功夫電影裡演戲。透過他獨特的功夫電影，李小龍的自律、勤勉，以及功夫武術的精湛，終於為他贏得全世界公認的功夫大師的美譽。事實上，不僅李小龍本人，特殊且奇妙的中國武術也被世人看見及仰慕。然而，李小龍 1973 的驟逝震撼整個世界，而從那時起，他的死因一直是十分地神秘。正式的報告陳述說他對一種治頭疼的止痛藥—艾奎杰希克，嚴重過敏，導致腦腫脹而死亡，而且這是一樁「意外死亡」。但是，各式各樣的揣測眾說紛紜，包含有兇手可能是中國三合會、武術的追隨者，或義大利的黑手黨等等。其中，最奇特的說法是有關於李小龍的家族詛咒。這個詛咒先前奪去他哥哥的生命，而 20 年後在一個槍枝射擊的電影場景中奪去他兒子布蘭登的生命。對李小龍的功夫影迷來說，期盼有一天李小龍的死亡之謎能夠被解開。

 關鍵單字解密

consider *v.* 考慮；認為

diligence *n.* 勤勉；勤奮

recognition *n.* 確認；表彰

swell *v.* 腫起；腫脹

allergic *adj.* 過敏的

weird *adj.* 古怪的；奇特的；神秘的

curse *n.* 詛咒；咒語

previously *adv.* 事先；先前地

 文法分析

例句 | Skilled in Chinese martial arts, Lee taught Kungfu, wrote books, <u>and</u> acted in popular Chinese Kungfu movies.

例句 | Skilled in Chinese martial arts, Lee taught Kungfu, wrote books, <u>but</u> acted in popular Chinese Kungfu movies.

中譯

李小龍的中國武術精湛,他傳授功夫,撰寫書籍,並且在受歡迎的中國功夫電影裡演戲。

用法解析

對等連接詞有 and(和;而),but(但是;然而),for(因為),or（或;否則）,so（所以）及 nor（也不）……等,用以連接兩個對等子句。第 2 句屬於錯誤的句子,因為依上下文意,需要的是正面連貫語意的 and,而非相反語意的 but。

分析 2. ▶

例句 | The official reports stated that he died from brain swelling due to a serious allergic reaction to Equagesic, a painkiller for headache, and it was "a death by misadventure". Nevertheless, other speculations varied.

例句 | The official reports stated that he died from brain swelling due to a serious allergic reaction to Equagesic, a painkiller for headache, and it was "a death by misadventure". Firstly, other speculations varied.

中譯

正式的報告陳述說他對一種治頭疼的止痛藥—艾奎杰希克，嚴重過敏，導致腦腫脹而死亡，而且這是一樁「意外死亡」。但是，各式各樣的揣測眾說紛紜。

用法解析

連接詞式的副詞用以連接子句。表示「次序」的有 firstly, then, next, formerly ……等。表示「對比」的有 however, nevertheless, whereas, conversely, instead ……等。第 2 句依上下文意需要的是表示「對比」的 nevertheless，並非表示「次序」的 firstly，所以是錯誤的用法。

UNIT 8 語法常犯的錯誤
Martin Luther King, Jr.
馬丁路德‧金恩二世

 英文句子結構上而言，容易有錯誤的語法產生。造句或寫作時應注意避免寫出錯誤的句子，產生語意不明確而欠清晰的文字。下列是常見的錯誤語法：

I. 句子片段（Sentence-Fragment）：一個英文句子中一定要有主詞及動詞，缺一則形成不完整的句子，也就是片段的句子。兩個子句則應要有一個連接詞連接，但若僅有一個子句則不須要有連接詞，否則也是一個不完整片段的句子。

　　◆ Mike home watching TV.（×）
　　⇒ Mike stayed home and watched TV.（○）
　　麥克待在家裡看電視。

II. 流水句（Run-On Sentence）：句子該正確地標上逗點而使句意清楚明確，否則 就會產生「流水句」。用具連接詞功用的副詞連接子句時要加上連接詞或代表連接詞的分號（；），並在該副詞後加逗點，或另起一句，否則即是錯誤的。

　　◆ It snowed heavily outside however Richard still went camping.（×）
　　⇒ It snowed heavily outside; however, Richard still went camping.（○）
　　外面下大雪；但是，理查還是去露營了。

III. 逗點連接句（Comma Splice）：英文句子中，兩個子句應要有一個連接詞連接，或使用代表連接詞作用的分號（；）來連接，或另起一句亦可。但不可單一地以逗點來做為連接詞的作用，否則即是錯誤的「逗點連接句」。

♦ Frank didn't work hard enough, he got fired by his boss.（✕）

⇨ Frank didn't work hard enough, so he got fired by his boss.（○）

法蘭克工作不力，所以被老闆炒魷魚。

IV. 多餘連接詞（Redundant Conjunction）：英文句子中，兩個子句應要有一個連接詞連接，但若多加入一個連接詞連接兩個子句則成為錯誤的「多餘連接詞」。

♦ Though Bob wasn't admitted to the school team, but he had done his best.（✕）

⇨ Though Bob wasn't admitted to the school team, he had done his best.（○）

雖然包柏沒被選入校隊，他已經盡力了。

V. 虛懸分詞（Dangling Participle）：現在分詞或過去分詞的分詞構句功用上在說明主詞的狀況，若此分詞片語意義上未能修飾到實質上主詞的情境，就是一種錯誤的結構，稱為「虛懸分詞」。

♦ Written in great haste, Paul made a lot of mistakes in the composition.（✕）

⇨ Written in great haste, Paul's composition is full of mistakes.（◡）

由於是倉促完成的，保羅的作文充滿錯誤。

Dr. Martin Luther King, Jr. was an important **civil** rights leader fighting for the equality of the African-Americans in the 1950s. He **preached** non-violence in marches, strikes, and **demonstrations** against racial discrimination and **segregation**. Owing to his sustained endeavors, he won worldwide recognition and was awarded the prestigious Nobel Peace Prize in 1964. In his famous soul-touching speech, *I Have a Dream*, given in front of the Lincoln Memorial to huge crowds of whites and blacks, he told of a dream world where equality could be rooted in the American Dream and freed from racial **prejudice**. Nevertheless, on April 4, 1968, he was assassinated in Memphis, Tennessee. It was a racist and **opponent** of Dr. King's ideals, James Earl Ray that was responsible for the assassination. With sufficient and hard evidence, he was arrested and sentenced to 99 years in prison. However, until his death in prison on April 23, 1998, Ray had consistently maintained his **innocence**. Speculations had it that Ray could not have acted alone and should only be part of a larger conspiracy by the government, either directly or **indirectly**. The murdering was a means of silencing the active and influential Civil Rights leader. Till today, the assassination is still considered one of the greatest unsolved mysteries of all time.

☥ 馬丁路德・金恩二世

　　馬丁路德・金恩二世博士在 1950 年代是為非裔美國人爭取平等重要的人權領袖。他倡導在對抗種族歧視和隔離政策時舉行的遊行、罷工、和示威活動中使用非暴力。他堅持不懈的努力為他贏得全世界的肯定，並且在 1964 年獲頒聲譽卓越的諾貝爾和平獎。在林肯紀念堂前，他對成群的白人和黑人發表著名感人「我有一個夢想」的演說，並闡述一個根植於美國夢想並且免除種族偏見的平等美夢世界。但是，1968 年 4 月 4 日，他在田納西州曼菲斯被暗殺。這是由一名種族歧視，並且反對金恩博士理念的反對者，詹姆士・厄爾・雷所犯下的罪刑。由於有足夠且確鑿的證據，他被逮捕，並被宣判 99 年的徒刑。但是，直到 1998 年 4 月 23 日，雷在監獄死亡之前，不斷宣稱自己是無辜的。人們揣測雷不可能獨自犯案，而應該只是直接或間接地由政府所策劃大型陰謀中的一部份。這一起謀殺的目的，是要使得活耀且具影響力的民權運動領袖消音。直至今日，這一椿暗殺事件，仍被認為是有史以來最難解的神祕案件之一。

⚠ 關鍵單字解密

civil *adj.* 市民的；公民的

preach *v.* 講道；宣揚

demonstration *n.* 示範；示威（運動）

segregation *n.* 分離；種族隔離

prejudice *n.* 偏見；歧視

opponent *n.* 對手；反對者

innocence *n.* 無辜；清白

indirectly *adv.* 間接地；迂迴地

 **文法分析**

分析 1.

例句 | Owing to his sustained endeavors, he won worldwide recognition and was awarded the prestigious Nobel Peace Prize in 1964.

例句 | Owing his sustained endeavors, he won worldwide recognition, was awarded the prestigious Nobel Peace Prize in 1964.

中譯

他堅持不懈的努力為他贏得全世界的肯定，並且在 1964 年獲頒聲譽卓越的諾貝爾和平獎。

用法解析

英文句子中，兩個子句應要有一個連接詞連接，或使用代表連接詞作用的分號（；）來連接，或另起一句亦可。但不可單一地以逗點來做為連接詞的作用，否則即是錯誤的「逗點連接句」。第 2 句屬於錯誤的句子，因 **was awarded** 前所缺的連接詞 **and** 不應單一地以逗點來取代。

分析 2. ▶

例句 | Until his death in prison on April 23, 1998, Ray had consistently maintained his innocence.

○

例句 | Until his death in prison on April 23, 1998. Ray had consistently maintained his innocence.

✕

中譯

直到 1998 年 4 月 23 日，雷在監獄死亡之前，不斷宣稱自己是無辜的。

用法解析

英文句子中一定要有主詞及動詞，缺一則形成片段的句子。兩個子句則應要有一個連接詞連接，但若僅有一個子句則不須要有連接詞，否則也是一個不完整片段的句子。第 2 句是錯誤的，因連接詞 until 應用來連接上下子句，不可單獨形成一句，所以是一個錯誤不完整的「片段句」。

虛詞 it 及 there

The Great Pyramids of Giza　吉薩大金字塔

 英文中，虛詞 it 及 there 具多重用途可讓英文句子更簡潔達意。使用時，宜確實掌握各特定的用法及句型，避免錯誤，並讓文字更豐富。

I. it 可以代表時間、天氣、距離 ……等，而引介出主要的內容。

- ◆ It is raining outside now. You'd better take an umbrella with you.　現在外面正在下雨，你最好帶一把雨傘。

II. 以名詞子句、動名詞片語、或不定詞片語做句子主詞或受詞而太長時可用 it 取代，使句子更簡潔。此時被取代的名詞子句、動名詞片語、或不定詞片語是「真主詞」或「真受詞」，it 則稱為「假主詞」或「假受詞」。常見句型如下：

1. it 當「假受詞」：S＋V＋it＋名詞／形容詞＋to V。「不完全及物動詞」如 find、think、consider、believe、make、suppose 等，接受詞後語意不完整，須接名詞或形容詞做受詞補語。受詞 to V 片語太長時可使用假受詞 it 取代。

2. it 當「假主詞」：
- ◆ It take＋人＋時間＋to V / It cost＋人＋金錢＋to V。
- ◆ It seems that＋S＋V... = S＋seem＋to V…似乎…。在此句型

262

中，若以 it 當主詞，seem 後接 that 子句。若以人、事、物當主詞，seem 後面接不定詞片語。

♦ ⑴ It is＋形容詞＋for 人＋ to V。⑵ It is＋形容詞＋of 人＋ to V。句型⑴搭配形容詞如 easy、necessary、important、convenient 等，形容事物，介系詞用 for。句型 ⑵ 搭配 nice、cruel、rude、foolish、clever 等，形容人，介系詞用 of。

♦ 表示客觀說法的句型： It is believed / said / reported / rumored that＋S＋V（一般相信 / 據說 / 據報導 / 據謠傳…）

III. 為強調主詞，可將 there 置於句首加上一般動詞，後接主詞。主詞是名詞時，動詞應倒裝到主詞之前，主詞是代名詞時，動詞則不用倒裝。

♦ The bus goes there. = There goes the bus!
巴士走了！

IV. There is no＋動名詞（V-ing）…「…是不可能的」。no 後面省略 way / possibility of...。可代換成：It is impossible＋不定詞（to V）…。

♦ There is no predicting the future occurrences.
= It is impossible to predict the future occurrences.
未來的事情是無法預測的。

V. There is no use＋動名詞（V-ing）…「…沒有用」。可代換成： It is of no use / useless＋不定詞（to V）…。

♦ There is no use reasoning with that stubborn man.
= It is of no use / useless to reason with that stubborn man.
和那個固執的人是無法講道理的。

★ The Great Pyramids of Giza

The Great Pyramids of Giza from ancient Egypt are the most **impressive** spectacles of human civilization and important Egyptian **heritage**. Guarded by the statue of the Sphinx, they were built as royal tombs for Pharaohs between 2,575 BC and 2,465 BC. Also, they probably served **ritualistic** purposes and astronomical functions as well. The largest of them held the record for the world's tallest structure for its height of 481 feet, with a base area around 570,000 square feet. Inside the pyramids, there were elaborate **corridors** and huge chambers, with jewelry, stone blocks, and cutting tools found. Till today, amazing things about the Great Pyramids of Giza still puzzle the world a lot. It is estimated that it took at least 20 years to complete the construction of pyramids, and it **required** the labor of a hundred thousand workers moving 2.6 million blocks of stone into the site. People used to think that only the highly intelligent aliens from the outer space could have possibly created the huge and perfect pyramids. Otherwise, it would be impossible for the ancient Egyptians, supposedly with limited **mathematical** and astronomical knowledge, to have achieved the difficult task of making the exact measurements. And also, without the help of modern **technology**, it was deemed unlikely for the ancient Egyptians to get those huge stones into the right position. At present, the Great Pyramids with so many unexplained and unanswerable mysteries keep **perplexing** the world.

☥ 吉薩大金字塔

　　起源於古埃及的吉薩大金塔是人類文明最令人印象深刻的奇觀，並且是一項重要的埃及文化遺產。由人面獅身像所看守著，它們在西元前 2,575 年到西元前 2,465 年間被建為法老的皇室陵墓。它們同時可能有儀式上的目的以及天文上的作用。最大的一座金字塔以它 481 英尺的高度，以及 57 萬平方英尺的底座面積，具有全世界最高建築物的紀錄。在金字塔內，有複雜的通道以及巨大的房間，連同珠寶、石塊以及切割工具。直至今日，有關於吉薩大金字塔驚人的狀況仍極度地困惑世人。據估計，完成這項建築至少花費 20 年，同時它需要十萬工人的勞力搬動 260 萬塊石塊到達建築地點。人們過去認為只有來自於外太空具有高度智慧的外星人才有可能創造出如此巨大而且完美的金字塔。否則，對於具有有限的數學和天文知識的古埃及人來說，是不可能去完成如此精準的測量。同樣地，沒有現代科技的幫助，古埃及人也不可能把巨大石塊搬到正確的位置。目前，有如此多無法說明且無法解答的神秘大金字塔仍持續地困惑世人。

⚠ 關鍵單字解密

impressive *adj.* 令人印象深刻的；令人欽佩的

heritage *n.* 遺產；繼承物

ritualistic *adj.* 儀式的；慣例的

corridor *n.* 走廊；通道

require *v.* 需要；要求

mathematical *adj.* 數學上的；精確的

technology *n.* 工藝；技術

perplex *v.* 困惑；難解

 **文法分析**

分析 **1.**

例句 | Inside the pyramids, <u>there were</u> elaborate corridors and huge chambers, with jewelry, stone blocks, and cutting tools found.

例句 | Inside the pyramids, <u>there had</u> elaborate corridors and huge chambers, with jewelry, stone blocks, and cutting tools found.

中譯

在金字塔內,有複雜的通道以及巨大的房間,連同珠寶、石塊以及切割工具。

用法解析

There be V+S（有…）是常用到的句型。第 2 句屬於錯誤的句子,因 there had 是中文式的英文,「有…」的正確英文應用 there were。

分析 2. ▶

例句 | It is estimated that it took at least 20 years to complete the construction of pyramids and it required the labor of a hundred thousand workers moving 2.6 million blocks of stone into the site.

例句 | It is estimated that it cost at least 20 years to complete the construction of pyramids and it required the labor of a hundred thousand workers moving 2.6 million blocks of stone into the site.

中譯

據估計，完成這項建築至少花費 20 年，同時它需要十萬工人的勞力搬動 260 萬塊石塊到達建築地點。

用法解析

人花時間或花錢用 it 當主詞時，花時間要用 take ，花錢則要用 cost，後接不定詞（to V）。但是第 2 句中時間花費用 cost 是錯誤的用法，應用 took 才對。

關係子句

The Mysterious Death of Princess Diana
黛安娜王妃死亡之謎

 關係子句的應用：**關係代名詞可引導形容詞作用或名詞作用的關係子句。**

I. 關係代名詞 who 主格，whom 受格，代替人（who 可取代 whom），which（主格或受格）代替物，that（主格或受格）可代替人或物。先行詞「人」時所有格用 whose，「事物」用 of which 或 whose。what 結合了先行詞和關係代名詞，相當於 that / those which。引導的名詞子句當主詞時用「主詞＋動詞」的形式。

- ◆ The man who / that spoke to my father was Mr. Blake.
  跟我父親說話的那個人是布雷克先生。

II. 關係代名詞先行詞是複數時，用複數動詞，主詞單數，則用單數動詞。受格的關係代名詞常被省略，但前面有介系詞或逗點時，則不可以省略。

- ◆ Heaven helps those who help themselves.
  天助自助者。

III. 介系詞＋關係代名詞的用法：在此用法中，介系詞是由後面動詞片語中的介系詞往前移所產生的，此時此關係代名詞雖然是受詞作用，仍不可省略。

- ◆ This is the apartment in which I live with my best friend.
  這就是我跟我最要好的朋友住的公寓。

IV.複合關係代名詞用法（1）：關係代名詞後加上 -ever 即形成複合關係代名詞。相當於先行詞加上關係代名詞，如 who（m）ever 相當於 anyone who（m），whatever 相當於 anything that，whichever 則相當於 anything of them that。

 ♦ Whatever Albert does will be supported by his family.
   無論艾伯特做什麼都會得到家人的支持。

V. 複合關係代名詞用法（2）：who（m）ever, whichever, whatever 具名詞性質，引導名詞子句，可做主詞或受詞。whichever, whatever 可當形容詞，修飾名詞。

 ♦ Whichever they choose, we should respect their decision.
   無論他們選擇哪一項，我們應該尊重他們的決定。

VI.關係代名詞的限定用法：關係子句的先行詞用形容詞子句去界定它的性質，前面不加逗點，即為限定用法的關係子句。

 ♦ Kate has a pony which has a long tail.
   凱特有一匹有長尾巴的小馬。

VII.關係代名詞的非限定用法：非限定（補述）用法的關係子句，用以形容補充說明前述「唯一或專有名詞」的先行詞，前面加逗點。此關係代名詞不可省略，也不可用 that 取代 who 或 which，以避免語意不清。先行詞若是前面整個子句，用以說明前述整個子句情境的後續狀況，關係詞後的動詞要用單數動詞。

 ♦ Ann's mom is a career woman, who is devoted to all her duties.
   安的媽媽是一名職業婦女，她全心奉獻於她的職責。

In 1997, Princess Diana was killed in a tunnel car crash, and the world **mourned** her death. Originally a nameless **kindergarten** teacher, Diana's fairy-tale encounter and marriage with Prince Charles were envied and blessed. With her charm and **elegance**, she successfully caught the world's eye, which helped her a lot in her devotion to the good **cause** of charity. However, though Diana left the royal family after the divorce, her private life was still constantly the focus of the paparazzi, whose chasing of her car allegedly resulted in the tragedy. In fact, Diana's mysterious death has been the center of **whispers** for years. It was speculated that Diana and her Egyptian boyfriend, Dodi Fayed, whom she was about to get **engaged** to as a mother-to-be, were murdered by agents sent by the British Royal Family. There was no chance that a Muslim could be the stepfather to the future British King, who might also have a possible half-Egyptian and half-Muslim **sibling**. Furthermore, Diana's death was so unacceptable to her fans that she was even said to have staged her own death for some **privacy** she wanted so much, only to go terribly wrong in the end. Hopefully, the mystery of the Princess's death could one day be clarified.

♀ 黛安娜王妃死亡之謎

　　在 1997 年，黛安娜王妃喪命於隧道車禍中，世人均哀悼她的死亡。她原來是默默無名的幼稚園老師，而她與查爾斯王子童話般的邂逅與婚姻令眾人稱羨及祝福。藉由她的魅力和優雅，她成功地受到世人矚目，而大大有助於她奉獻於慈善工作的努力。但是，雖然離婚後離開了皇室家族，黛安娜王妃的私生活仍是狗仔隊追逐的焦點，據傳言是由於狗仔隊的追逐，才導致悲劇的發生。事實上，黛安娜王妃神秘的死亡，多年以來一直是人們耳語的焦點。據推測，黛安娜與她的埃及籍男友，道迪‧菲德，懷有身孕並即將訂婚，卻雙雙被英國皇室特派員所謀殺。因為一名回教徒不可能是未來英國國王的繼父，而英國國王也不被允許有埃及和回教徒血統的手足。再者，黛安娜的死亡對她的支持者是如此地無法接受，以至於被謠傳說她為了取得渴望已久的隱私權自導自演車禍，沒想到最後釀成大禍。儘管如此，仍期盼未來黛安娜王妃死亡之謎終得以澄清。

⚠ 關鍵單字解密

mourn *v.* 哀痛；哀悼

kindergarten *n.* 幼稚園

elegance *n.* 優雅；雅緻

cause *n.* 目標；理想

whisper *n.* 耳語；傳聞

engaged *adj.* 訂婚的

sibling *n.* 兄弟姊妹

privacy *n.* 隱私；隱退

文法分析

例句 | However, though leaving the royal family after the divorce, Diana's private life was still constantly the focus of the paparazzi, whose chasing of her car allegedly resulted in the tragedy. ◯

例句 | However, though leaving the royal family after the divorce, Diana's private life was still constantly the focus of the paparazzi, who chasing of her car allegedly resulted in the tragedy. ✕

中譯

但是，雖然離婚後離開了皇室家族，黛安娜王妃的私生活仍是狗仔隊追逐的焦點，據傳言是由於狗仔隊的追逐，才導致悲劇的發生。

用法解析

關係代名詞 who 主格， whom 受格，代替人（who 可取代 whom），which 主格或受格，代替物。先行詞「人」時所有格用 whose。第 2 句屬於錯誤的句子，因此處需要的是所有格 whose，而非主格代替人的 who。

分析 2.

例句 | It was speculated that Diana and her Egyptian boyfriend, Dodi Fayed, whom she was about to get engaged to as a mother-to-be, were murdered by agents sent by the British Royal Family.

例句 | It was speculated that Diana and her Egyptian boyfriend, Dodi Fayed whom she was about to get engaged to as a mother-to-be, were murdered by agents sent by the British Royal Family.

中譯

據推測,黛安娜與她的埃及籍男友,道迪‧菲德,懷有身孕並即將訂婚,卻雙雙被英國皇室特派員所謀殺。

用法解析

關係子句的先行詞用形容詞子句去界定它的性質,前面不加逗點,即為限定用法。非限定(補述)用法的關係子句,則用以形容補充說明前述「唯一或專有名詞」的先行詞,前面加逗點。**Dodi Fayed** 是「唯一」,有指定的人,應用非限定(補述)用法的關係子句修飾,要加上逗點才對,所以第 2 句是錯誤的句子。

對等與平行結構
The Mysterious Stonehenge
神秘的巨石陣

 英文中就文法句子結構或語意修辭而言，對等連接及平行句構都是十分必要且重要的。

I. 對等連接詞的類別：連接詞如 and, but, or, for …等是單一式對等連接詞。both …and …, not only… but also …, either … or …, neither … nor …, not … but …等是相關式對等連接詞。instead of（是…，而非…），rather than（…而非…）…等是片語式對等連接詞。

II. 名詞單、複數在用對等連接詞句構連接，平行使用時要正確地對等。

◆ Nancy planned to write three letters and read two novels this week.
南西計畫這個星期要寫三封信並且閱讀兩本小說。

III. 等連接詞句構要連接兩個對稱結構，如兩個對等的名詞、動詞、形容詞、副詞、代名詞、現在與過去分詞、不定詞、與動名詞或片語等，不可隨意搭配。

◆ Victor cared not the service but the food in the restaurant.
維特在乎的是餐廳裡的食物而非服務品質。

IV. 對等連接詞句構連接時要對等地連接兩個對等的時態，使有平行結構的時態，如對等的現在式、過去式、未來式、進行式、完成式等。

 ♦ **The atmosphere wasn't good. Most of the guests neither sang nor danced.**
 當時的氣氛不好。大部分的賓客不唱歌也不跳舞。

V. 對等連接詞句構，如 not only A but also B（不僅 A 而且 B），either A or B（不是 A 就是 B），neither A nor B（不是 A，也不是 B）…等，A 與 B 對稱結構的位置應固定，要保持平行結構的排列位置，不可任意變更。

VI. 對等與平行結構常見的句型：

1. not because …, but because … 意指「不是因…，而是因為…」，用來說明並列對等的理由。

2. some…, others…, and still others…意指「一些…，另一些…，還有一些…」，用來描述並列對等的三種類型眾多的人或事物。

3. on the one hand, …, but on the other hand, …意指「一方面…，另一方面…」，用來描述一種類型的人或事物兩方面並列對等的情境。

Stonehenge is a prehistoric monument located in Salisbury Plain, Southern England. For centuries, archaeologists have been puzzled about the mysteries of how and why it was constructed. Built from around 3,100 BC to 1,100 BC, Stonehenge was composed of nearly 100 massive upright stones placed as an enclosure in a specific circular arrangement with each weighing up to 20 to 50 tons. It remains a mystery how the ancient Neolithic builders, without modern technology, could have moved the huge stones from different faraway places in Western Wales to the site. On the one hand, the theory of the last ice-age glaciers' carrying them there was once raised. On the other hand, the stories of King Arthur were once associated with it. Legend had it that it was the wizard Merlin who flew the mighty stones into place with his magic powers. As for the purposes it served, opinions and theories varied. Some suggest that it was used as an observatory and an astronomical calendar to predict lunar and solar eclipses. Others believe that the ceremonial site held certain religious significance and was a memorial erected to honor their ancestors, and still others claim that it was constructed for burial rituals of royalty buried there. Since Stonehenge became one of the UNESCO World Heritage Sites in 1986, more and more tourists have come to visit the sacred place when it remains to be one of the greatest mysteries of the world.

☥ 神秘的巨石陣

　　巨石陣是位於英國南方，塞里斯貝瑞平原的史前遺跡。許多世紀以來，考古學家對於它如何並且為何被建造之謎感到困惑。巨石陣建築於約西元前 3,100 年到西元前 1,100 之間，是由將近 100 塊巨大直立的石塊以封閉且特別的圓形排列，每一個石塊重達 20 到 50 公噸。古代新石器時代的建築者，如何在沒有現代科技之下，可以把巨大石塊從西威爾斯各個不同的地方搬到建築地點，仍舊是個謎。一方面來說，上一個冰河時期的冰河把它們帶到那裏的理論曾經被提出，但是從未被證實。在另一方面，亞瑟王的故事曾經與它有關聯。據傳說，是梅林巫師用他的魔法將它們搬移到那裏的。至於它的功用，各方的意見和理論不一。有些人認為，它被用作天文觀測台以及天文曆法來預測月全蝕以及日全蝕，有些人相信，這個儀式的地點具有特定的宗教意義，並且此地是一個為了要推崇祖先所設立的紀念碑，而又有一些人宣稱，它是為了替埋葬於那裏的貴族舉行葬禮的儀式而被建造的。自從 1986 年，巨石陣成為聯合國教科文組織世界文化遺址之一後，有越來越多的觀光客前來參觀這一座聖地，巨石陣至今仍是全世界最神秘事件之一。

⚠ 關鍵單字解密

monument *n.* 紀念碑；歷史遺跡

compose *v.* 組成；構成

enclosure *n.* 圈用地；圍場

Neolithic *adj.* 新石器時代的

glacier *n.* 冰河

associate *v.* 聯想；有關聯

erect *v.* 豎立；建立

royalty *n.*（總稱）皇族（成員）

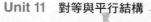
Unit 11　對等與平行結構

# 文法分析

分析 1.

例句 | On the one hand, the theory of the last ice-age glaciers' carrying them there was once raised. On the other hand, the stories of King Arthur were once associated with it.

○

例句 | On the one hand, the theory of the last ice-age glaciers' carrying them there was once raised. For that reason, the stories of King Arthur were once associated with it.

✕

中譯

一方面來說，上一個冰河時期的冰河把它們帶到那裏的理論曾經被提出，但是從未被證實。在另一方面，亞瑟王的故事曾經與它有關聯。

用法解析

on the one hand, …, but on the other hand, …意指「一方面…，另一方面…」，用來描述一種類型的人或事務兩方面並列對等的情境。平行結構所用固定的句型片語，不可任意變更，故第 2 句屬於錯誤的句子。

分析 2.

例句 | <u>Some</u> suggest that it was used as ... <u>Others</u> believe that the ceremonial site held certain religious significance and was a memorial erected to honor their ancestors, <u>and still others</u> claim that it was constructed for burial rituals of royalty buried there.

例句 | <u>Some</u> suggest that it was used as ... <u>the others</u> believe that the ceremonial site held certain religious significance and was a memorial erected to honor their ancestors, <u>and still another</u> claim that it was constructed for burial rituals of royalty buried there.

中譯

有些人認為，它被用作…，有些人相信，這個儀式的地點具有特定的宗教意義，並且此地是一個為了要推崇祖先所設立的紀念碑，而又有一些人宣稱，它是為了替埋葬於那裏的貴族舉行葬禮的儀式而被建造的。

用法解析

some…, others…, and still others…意指「一些…，另一些…，還有一些…」，用來描述並列對等的三種類型眾多的人或事務。平行結構所用固定的句型片語，不可任意變更，故第 2 句屬於錯誤的句子。

UNIT 12 比較與對比
The Unsinkable Titanic
永不沉沒的鐵達尼號

英文句子或段落文章中，可根據兩件事物的相似或相異處，利用「比較」或「對比」來使文字清晰達意。強調兩者的相似情形用「比較」的方式，強調兩者的相異情境則使用「對比」。下列是比較與對比常用到的用字、片語、及句型：

I. 表示「比較」的用字及片語：as, like, resemble, alike, similarly, likewise, identical, equivalent, correspondingly, as well, equally important, vice versa, in the same way, no less than, in comparison with ……等。

　　◆ Likewise, Henry hopes to enter an ideal college.
　　同樣地，亨利希望能夠進入一所理想的大學。

II. 表示「比較」的句型：

　　1. 表示倍數的比較句型：…倍數詞＋形容詞比較級＋than… 或 …倍數詞＋as＋形容詞原級＋as…。此句型用以做倍數的比較。使用倍數詞如 half、twice、three times、four times 等，倍數詞後面所接的形容詞常見的則如 old、large、many、much、heavy、tall、high、wide、deep 等。

　　◆ This mansion is five times larger than / as large as that

house.

這座豪宅是那棟房子的五倍大。

2. Like / Unlike N …, S＋V … （如同 / 不同於…，…）As S＋V …, so S＋V … （如同…，… 亦如是）

◆ Just as rust eats iron, so care eats the heart.

憂慮會損耗心神，就像銹會蝕鐵一樣。

3. A is to B as C is to D （A 之於 B 正如 C 之於 D）

◆ The hands are to humans as the wings are to birds.

手之於人類宛如翅膀之於鳥一樣的重要。

III. 「對比」常用到的用字、片語、及句型：

1. 表示「相反、對照」的用字及片語： unlike, but, still, despite, however, nevertheless, while, whereas, conversely, instead, rather than, far from, contrast with, contrary / opposite to, regardless of, stand in contrast to, as opposed to, on the contrary……等。

2. 表示「相反、對照」的句型：

● It may be true as assumed by others, but S don't / doesn't. S＋believe（s）＋that 子句 （別人可能認為這是事實，但 … 不是。… 認為…）

● On the contrary, …＝ By contrast, … （相反地，…）

● However, it is a pity＋that 子句 （然而，很可惜的是…）

● On the one hand, … On the other hand, …（一方面，…。另一方面，…。）

The Titanic, dubbed "Unsinkable," was the largest, the fastest, and the most **luxurious** ship ever built. Unfortunately, on the contrary, she **submerged** on her maiden voyage of sailing glory on April 14, 1912. In order to match up to the good fame of perfection, she sailed in the Atlantic Ocean at high speed, even during the dark midnight. Thus, only two days at sea and more than half way between England and the New York **destination**, she **collided** with a ghostly-looking iceberg. Panic, fires on ship, and not providing enough lifeboats resulted in the heavy casualties of 1,500 deaths out of around 2,500 passengers. Over the years, legends surrounding the tragic happening prevailed. After careful examination and analysis, experts concluded that both the constructing materials and the **compartment** designing went wrong. Besides, the owners of the Titanic were too sure to **equip** enough lifeboats on board, being only one–fourth of her total passengers. In addition, the **superstition** of Titanic **Mummy**'s Curse was the most prevalent cause of the tragedy. When the ship plunged, on board was a stone case with an Egyptian mummy inside, which allegedly would drown whoever made contact with it. It's a pity that the truth with supernatural and mystic touch might forever be buried deep down the ocean with the Titanic.

♀ 永不沉沒的鐵達尼號

　　號稱「永不沉沒」的鐵達尼號是有史以來最巨大、最快速,且最豪華的輪船。很不幸,相反地,她在1912年4月14日光榮的首航中沉沒了。為了要符合她完美的美名,她甚至在光線昏暗的夜半時分裡以高速疾馳於大西洋中。因此,在海上僅航行兩天,同時是從英國航行到目的地紐約的半途中,她與鬼魅般的冰山相撞。驚慌、船上的大火,以及救生艇提供不足導致大約2,500名乘客中,有1,500名死亡的重大死傷。多年來,環繞這個悲劇的傳說盛行。經過仔細的檢閱和分析,專家作結論說是建築材料和艙房的設計出了差錯。再者,鐵達尼號的船主,太有把握而沒有在船上配給足夠的救生艇,僅配備所有旅客四分之一的數量。此外,鐵達尼號木乃伊詛咒的迷信傳說是最盛行的沉船主因。當輪船下沉的時候,在船上有一個木乃伊石棺,據說凡是跟它接觸過的人都會溺斃。令人惋惜的是,帶有超自然和神祕色彩的真相,可能將與鐵達尼號永遠被深埋在大海之中。

 關鍵單字解密

luxurious *adj.* 奢侈的;豪華的

submerge *v.* 淹沒;沉沒

destination *n.* 目的地;目標

collide *v.* 碰撞;相撞

compartment *n.* 劃分;隔間

equip *v.* 裝備;配備

superstition *n.* 迷信;盲目恐懼

mummy *n.* 木乃伊;不腐屍體

文法分析

分析 1.

例句│The Titanic, dubbed "Unsinkable," was the largest, the fastest, and the most luxurious ship ever built. Unfortunately, on the contrary, she submerged on her maiden voyage of sailing glory on April 14, 1912.

例句│The Titanic, dubbed "Unsinkable," was the largest, the fastest, and the most luxurious ship ever built. Unfortunately, in comparison with, she submerged on her maiden voyage of sailing glory on April 14, 1912.

中譯

號稱「永不沉沒」的鐵達尼號是有史以來最巨大、最快速，且最豪華的輪船。很不幸，相反地，她在 1912 年 4 月 14 日光榮的首航中沉沒了。

用法解析

on the contrary 是表示「相反、對照」的片語，in comparison with 則是表示「比較」的片語。第 2 句屬於錯誤的句子，因根據上下語意，應用表示「相反」的 on the contrary，而非表示「比較」的 in comparison with。

分析 2.

例句 | It's a pity that the truth with supernatural and mystic touch might forever be buried deep down the ocean with the Titanic.

例句 | In the same way, the truth with supernatural and mystic touch might forever be buried deep down the ocean with the Titanic.

中譯

令人惋惜的是，帶有超自然和神祕色彩的真相，可能將與鐵達尼號永遠被深埋在大海之中。

用法解析

However, it is a pity＋that 子句（然而，很可惜的是…）是表示「相反、對照」的句型，是此處依上下文意需要的句型。但是第 2 句中 In the same way 則是表示「比較」的片語，非表示「相反」的語意。所以第 2 句是錯誤的用法。

UNIT 13

倒裝強調與焦點

The Ancient Machu Picchu

馬丘比丘古城

英文中為了要加強文字語意，常使用倒裝、強調、與焦點的句構。下列是常見的用法及句型，可多應用。

I. 倒裝句常見的用法及句型：

1. Only＋副詞片語…, be V／助動詞＋S V 2）Only＋副詞子句＋be V／助動詞＋S V 。only 置於句首，後接副詞片語或副詞子句時，主要子句必須要倒裝。

2. no sooner… than …（一 … 就…）的句型中，no sooner 固定後接過去完成式的子句，than 後則接過去式的子句，no sooner 置於句首時，過去完成式的子句必須要倒裝。

3. S＋… not＋V until…（直到 …才…）= Not until…＋助動詞＋S ＋V= It is not until…that S＋V。not 常與 until 連用。not 置於句首時，後面的子句要倒裝，用以加強語氣。另外亦可用 It is not until…＋that 子句來強調。

   ◆ One doesn't realize the importance of health until he loses it.

   = Until one loses health does he realize the importance of it.

   = It is not until one loses health that he realizes the importance of it. 一個人直到失去健康後才體會到它的重要。

II. 強調句常見的用法及句型：

1. no / not / never…＋without＋N / V-ing（沒有…不…；每…必…）。這是用雙重否定來表示強調的句型，否定字 no、not、或 never 後接 without 即形成雙重否定，是一種加強語氣的用法，介系詞 without 後面要接名詞或動名詞。

   ♦ No one can live without friends.　人人都應該要有朋友。

2. cannot…too much / enough…（再 / 無論…也不為過；越…越好…）。也可用 It is impossible to over-V… 或 It is not too much to V…來加強語氣。

   ♦ One cannot emphasize the importance of honesty too much / enough.
   = It is impossible to overemphasize the importance of honesty.
   = It is not too much to emphasize the importance of honesty.　誠實的重要性再怎麼強調也不為過。

III. 訊息焦點由分裂句表達常見的用法及句型：

1. It is / was＋加強的主詞 / 受詞 / 副詞＋that＋句子其餘的部份。分裂句句型 It is / was … that …用以強調訊息焦點主詞、受詞、時間副詞、地方副詞等。關係詞除了用 that 以外也可以根據加強的主詞、受詞、副詞，使用不同的關係詞，如代名詞 who、which，或關係副詞 when、where 等。

   ♦ It was Max that / who got grounded by his mom yesterday.　是麥克斯昨天被他的媽媽所禁足。

2. wh- 疑問詞引導的子句可形成分裂句以強調句中主詞或補語訊的訊息焦 點。

   ♦ What Andy needs is more persistence.
   = More persistence is what Andy needs. 安迪需要的是更多的恆心。

Machu Picchu lies on an **inaccessible** ridge high above the Urubamba Valley in the Peruvian Andes. Used as a summer resort for Incan emperors, it was once discovered by the Spanish **conquerors** in the mid-15th century. And then, in 1911, it was the American explorer Hiram Bingham that discovered it accidentally and revealed the secrets of the ancient lost city to the world. It was built in the ancient Incan style, with three **primary** structures constructed with **interlocking** walls of smooth and polished stones by the ancient Incans, precisely fitting the stones together **seamlessly**. One mystery about Machu Picchu is how Incans could possibly move the heavy and huge stones, and place them in the site. Another mystery is the function of a peculiar giant rock situated on a raised platform towering above the plaza. It was believed to have been used for the astronomical observation. Nowadays, Machu Picchu's superb preservation, excellent quality and its original **architecture**, and the breathtaking mountain scenery surrounding it have made itself Peru's most **iconic** sightseeing spot. Tourists' trips to Peru won't be complete without visiting it. With its rich Incan cultural characteristics, the ancient Machu Picchu inspired the world in its **unique** way.

☥ 馬丘比丘古城

馬丘比丘位於祕魯安地斯山脈，很難到達的烏魯班巴山谷山脊上。它最早是印加國王的避暑勝地，一度曾經在 15 世紀中葉被西班牙征服者發現。然後在 1911 年，是美國探險家，海拉默·班漢姆，在無意中發現它，並且把這一座失落古城的秘密公諸於世。馬丘比丘是以古印加風格所建立的，它具有三個主要的建築物，由古印加人利用平滑且拋光的石塊精準無縫地連結鑲嵌在牆面上而建造的。有關於馬丘比丘的一個謎是，印加人如何移動巨大沉重的石塊並且放置於建築的地點。另一個謎是，有一塊在廣場上端一塊突起的平台上奇特巨大石塊的用途。人們相信它有天文觀測的作用。今日來說，馬丘比丘絕佳的保存，原始建築的卓越品質，以及令人屏息的山景使它成為秘魯最具有代表性的觀光景點。它是觀光客來秘魯旅遊的必遊之處。馬丘比丘古城有它豐富的印加文化特色，並且以它獨特的方式啟發世人。

 關鍵單字解密

inaccessible *adj.* 難接近的；達不到的

conqueror *n.* 征服者；勝利者

primary *adj.* 首要的；主要的

interlock *v.* 連結；連扣

seamlessly *adv.* 無縫地

architecture *n.* 建築物；建築風格

iconic *adj.* 圖像的；偶像的

unique *adj.* 獨特的；唯一的

 **文法分析**

分析 1. ▶

例句 | And then, in 1911, it was the American explorer Hiram Bingham that discovered it accidentally and revealed the secrets of the ancient lost city to the world.　　○

例句 | And then, in 1911, this was the American explorer Hiram Bingham that discovered it accidentally and revealed the secrets of the ancient lost city to the world.　　✕

中譯

然後在 1911 年，是美國探險家，海拉默·班漢姆，在無意中發現它，並且把這一座失落古城的秘密公諸於世。

用法解析

分裂句句型 It is／was＋加強的主詞／受詞／副詞＋that＋句子其餘的部份用以強調訊息焦點主詞、受詞、時間副詞、地方副詞等。第 2 句屬於錯誤的句子，因分裂句句型所用固定的 it 不可任意變更為 this。

分析 2.

例句 | Tourists' trips to Peru won't be complete without visiting it.

〇

例句 | Tourists' trips to Peru won't be complete with visiting it

✕

中譯

它是觀光客來秘魯旅遊的必遊之處。

用法解析

no / not / never…＋without＋N / V-ing（沒有…不…；每…必…）是用雙重否定來表示強調的句型，否定字 no、not、或 never 後接 without 即形成雙重否定，是一種加強語氣的用法。此固定的句型中，不可將 without 變更為 with，否則不具有雙重否定的語意，故第 2 句屬於錯誤的句子。

連貫與統一

The Mysterious Stone Spheres

神祕石球

 英文段落文章應要能達「連貫」（Coherence）與「統一」（Unity）的原則。要使段落書寫能達到「連貫」與「統一」原則的基本要點如下：

I. 段落文章一般主要分三個部分：主題句（Topic Sentence）、段落發展（Paragraph Development）、及結論句（Concluding Sentence）。

　1. 主題句是整段的摘要，說明整段文章的主旨，應力求完整精簡、具體清晰。

　2. 段落發展是整個段落的論述部份。這個部份所有的句子用以支持主題句，要能提出支持主題句的論點，再依各點分別解釋或舉例。

　3. 結論句通常是用來總結段落，回到主題句中的主旨。

II. 達到「連貫」（Coherence）原則的基本要點如下：

　1. 分別使用代名詞如 he, she, it, their, her, them ……等或指示詞如 this, that, these, those ……等來敘述前面已提及的內容，以避免重覆，並可緊密連結上下文。

2. 使用省略、代換、同義詞彙重述的方式，及對等平行結構等達到同樣的功效。

3. 利用「轉承語」（Transitional Words）來使文章論點間的連接，保持流暢。如表示「時間」的有 afterwards, meanwhile, at first, for the time being,…等。「次序」：firstly, next, in the first place, to begin with,…等。「空間」：above, around, in the distance, at the bottom,…等。

III. 達到「統一」（Unity）原則的基本要點如下：

1. 一篇文章應只有一個中心思想（Controlling Idea），敘事觀點與內容須一致。應避免寫出與主題不相干的句子（Irrelevant Sentences）或具有同樣語意的冗贅句子（Redundant Sentences）。

2. 可利用不同的句子來使文章具一致性，如簡單句可有語意簡單清晰的功效，兩個對等子句可表達緊密的相關性，或者是利用具起承轉合作用的複句或複合句來使文章前後段落富變化，而且統整有組織，不至雜亂離題。

3. 搭配各種不同段落寫作的技巧，也可達到文章統一，有條不紊的效用。如描寫文中先寫一般情境，再描述特殊性。敘事文可依時間先後順序或空間遠近書寫。論說文及說明文則可依重要性的順序，由最不重要延伸到最重要等。

The stone spheres of Costa Rica, first discovered in the Diquis Delta of Costa Rica during the 1930s, are a **collection** of over 300 almost perfect spherical balls. Ranging in size from a basketball to a compact car, most of them are sculpted from an igneous rock similar to granite. Probably created sometime between 200 BC and 1,600 BC, the mysterious balls, always pointing to the magnetic north, were arranged together in at least 20 stone balls in regular **geometric** patterns. The mysteriously smooth and **perfectly** spherical stones have long been regarded as symbols of tradition and ancient **wisdom**. However, the exact significance of the handmade stone balls and the amazing skills employed to create such refined stone balls remain unsolved mysteries. According to **archaeologists**, probably they were created so as to serve certain ritualistic purposes, or simply to show status differences. Nevertheless, the tools the ancient Costa Ricans used and how some of the huge stone spheres could ever be moved around still remain unknown. Besides, the stones seemed to have been **arranged** and made into certain large patterns, which might have some **astronomical** significance connected with aliens' spacecraft landing. To sum up, all these unexplained mysteries will still need further research to work on and **clarify**.

☥ 神祕石球

　　哥斯大黎加的石球，於 1930 年代在哥斯大黎加迪奎斯三角洲首度被發現，是一群超過三百顆幾近完美的球體。它們大多數有從一顆籃球到一部小車的大小，是由類似花崗岩的火成岩所雕刻而成的。這些神秘石球可能是在西元前 200 年到西元前 1,600 年之間被創造，它們經常指向磁鐵的北方，並以至少 20 顆球一起排列成規律的幾何圖案。這些神秘、光滑，而且幾近完美的石球長久以來被視為是傳統和古代智慧的象徵。但是，這些手工製石球的確切意義以及被用來創造如此優質石球的驚人技術，一直是難解之謎。根據考古學家的說法，它們被創造的目的是為了某些宗教目的，或只是為了表現不同的階級。然而，古代哥斯大黎加人使用的工具以及某些巨大石球如何被四處搬動，仍舊是無從知曉。此外，這些石球似乎被排列製作成特定大型的圖案，具有可能是與外星人駕駛的太空船降落有所連結的特殊含意。總而言之，所有這些無法說明的謎題，仍將需要進一步的研究並澄清。

 關鍵單字解密

collection *n.* 收集；積聚

geometric *adj.* 幾何的；幾何圖形的

perfectly *adv.* 完美地；完全地

wisdom *n.* 智慧；才智

archaeologist *n.* 考古學家

arrange *v.* 排列；安排

astronomical *adj.* 天文的；天文學的

clarify *v.* 澄清；闡明

文法分析

分析 1.

例句 | Ranging in size from a basketball to a compact car, <u>most of them</u> are sculpted from an igneous rock similar to granite.

例句 | Ranging in size from a basketball to a compact car, <u>most of the stone spheres of Costa Rica</u> are sculpted from an igneous rock similar to granite.

中譯

它們大多數有從一顆籃球到一部小車的大小，是由類似花崗岩的火成岩所雕刻而成的。

用法解析

為了達到「連貫」原則可使用代名詞如 he, she, it, their, her, them ……等或指示詞如 this, that, these, those ……等來敘述前面已提及的內容，以避免重覆，並可緊密連結上下文。第 2 句屬於錯誤的句子，因未使用受詞代名詞 them 取代前句的 the stone spheres of Costa Rica，以達到「連貫」原則。

分析 2.

例句 | Besides, the stones seemed to … have some astronomical significance connected with aliens' spacecraft landing. To sum up, all these unexplained mysteries will still need further researches to work on and clarify.

例句 | Besides, the stones seemed to … have some astronomical significance connected with aliens' spacecraft landing. Aliens are ugly and horrible creatures. To sum up, all these unexplained mysteries will still need further researches to work on and clarify.

中譯

此外，這些石球似乎被安排成特定大型的圖案，具有可能是與外星人駕駛的太空船降落有所連結的特殊含意。總而言之，所有這些無法說明的謎題，仍將需要進一步的研究並澄清。

用法解析

為達到「統一」原則，文章中應只有一個中心思想，敘事觀點與內容須一致。應避免寫出與主題不相干的句子。但是第 2 句中，加進一句與上下文不相干的 **Alien are ugly and horrible creatures.** 有違「統一」原則，所以是錯誤的用法。

UNIT 15 簡潔明確與邏輯

The Mausoleum of the Emperor Qin Shi Huang　秦始皇陵墓

 英文段落文章除了要能達「連貫」（Coherence）與「統一」（Unity）的原則外，**簡潔**（Concise）、**明確**（Precise）、**邏輯**（Logic）的原則也是同樣地重要。要使段落書寫能達到「簡潔」、「明確」、與「邏輯」原則的基本要點如下：

I. 達到「簡潔」（Concise）原則的基本要點如下：

1. 可利用省略、對照、替代、均衡、逐項列舉等符合「效用」（Effectiveness）的方法使文字達到簡明扼要的功用。

2. 避免使用複雜且過分冗長的句子，善用易懂常用但精確、合乎習慣用法的字彙、片語、及句型。

3. 要把握主題，多使用簡單句並活用精簡合併的句子，如分詞構句、it 虛主詞及虛受詞等，可使文字簡潔易懂，生動活躍。

II. 達到「明確」（Precise）原則的基本要點如下：

1. 用字遣詞時需確知單字、詞類、片語、及句子的含意、用法、字詞搭配、及正確的文法規則。句子結構上而言，容易有錯誤的語法產生，應注意避免寫出錯誤百出、語意模稜兩可、欠清晰的文字。

2. 勿使用中式的英文，多使用主動語態及肯定語氣陳述，避免不必要的重覆達成文章的確切易懂。多強調重點，可利用倒裝句、分裂句、或雙重否定結構 等使文字精簡深刻，具説服力。

3. 段落寫作時，要有明確的主題。段落開頭要使用主題句，中間段落發展要能連貫一致，切合主題，結尾則要呼應主題句，提升層級境界。並要使用正確的標點符號及寫作格式，避免混淆。

III. 達到「邏輯」（Logic）原則的基本要點如下：

1. 文章邏輯要合宜清楚，段落敘述應有條理、有組織，符合起承轉合的原則。前後文內容觀點與主題切合，並要能達到合理邏輯的安排，而不至於不夠具體，過於籠統廣泛。

2. 文字字序（**Word Order**）要符合句構章法的邏輯，並應避免語意過於主觀武斷，要客觀合理，善用表示可能性的副詞及句型等。此外，要善用連貫詞彙，使前後文銜接合乎邏輯。

3. 文章寫作要以符合邏輯原則的結構書寫，如因果關係、空間結構、時間順序、類比的使用等，敘述內容由次重要的推進至最重要的，説理要根據條列的事實推論，結論應由事實推論中取得，不可驟下結論，而寫出似是而非、不合邏輯原則的文字。

The **Mausoleum** of Qin Shi Huang is a 76-meter-tall tomb **complex** located in Xi'an in northwest China's Shaanxi Province. Since its accidental discovery in 1974, archaeologists have tried to unravel the mysteries not only of the overall planning and construction, but of the three tomb vaults where about 7,500 **terracotta** warriors and horses were **excavated**. Amazingly, each of them had unique outlooks and the real size of a soldier, around 2 meters in height. Originally, the Mausoleum was made for Qin Shi Huang, who was the first emperor of the Qin Dynasty（221 BC-207 BC）and also of China. He **unified** the warring China, the systems of laws and weights, and the Chinese written language. However, the **dictatorial** Emperor, to suppress opposition, ordered the burning of the books written by philosophers and the execution of the intellectual scholars. Besides, he had hundreds of thousands of slave laborers construct the Great Wall. Believing in immortality, he was obsessed with finding an **elixir** of life to stay alive forever and forced 700,000 laborers to build the Mausoleum. Furthermore, the 7,500 terracotta warriors were made and buried there for guarding and protecting him in the afterlife. After the excavation of the spectacular Mausoleum, it has drawn worldwide attention, and has been at present a popular tourist attraction in China. As archaeological technology **advances**, hopefully one day we can fully reveal the entire ground palace to the public and unravel all the unsolved mysteries.

♀ 秦始皇陵墓

　　秦始皇陵墓是位於中國北方陝西省西安 76 公尺高的陵墓建築。自從 1974 年，它意外地被發現後，考古學家試圖揭開它整體規畫建築的謎，以及從陵墓挖掘出 3 穴坑共約 7500 尊兵馬俑的謎。令人驚訝的是，每一尊兵馬俑都具有獨特的外貌，而且具有士兵真人的大小，大約 2 公尺的高度。原先這座陵墓是為中國秦朝（西元前 221~西元前 207 年）第一位皇帝，秦始皇所建造的。他統一戰亂的中國，法律和度量衡的制度，以及中國文字。但是，這位獨裁的皇帝為了要鎮壓反對勢力，下令焚燒哲學家所著的書籍以及處死知識淵博的學者。此外，他命令數十萬的奴工建築萬里長城。他本身相信永生，所以著迷於尋找長生不老藥以獲得永生，並且強迫 70 萬勞工建立陵墓。再者，7500 尊兵馬俑被建造且埋葬於陵墓中，在來生時守衛並保護他。壯觀的陵墓被挖掘出來之後，引起全世界的矚目，並且目前在中國是十分受歡迎的觀光景點。隨著考古科技的進步，期盼有一天我們可以將完整的地底皇宮公諸於世，並且揭開所有的未解之謎。

 ## 關鍵單字解密

mausoleum *n.* 陵墓

complex *n.* 綜合物；建築群

terracotta *n.* 赤陶；赤土

excavate *v.* 開鑿；發掘（古物）

unify *v.* 統一；使一致

dictatorial *adj.* 獨裁的；獨裁者的

elixir *n.* 長生不老藥；萬能藥

advance *v.* 前進；進步

文法分析

例句 Amazingly, each of them had unique outlooks and the real size of a soldier, around 2 meters in height.

例句 Amazingly, each of the three vaults of about 7,500 terracotta warriors and horses excavated from the tomb had unique outlooks and had around 2 meters height the real soldier size.

中譯

令人驚訝的是,每一尊兵馬俑都具有獨特的外貌,而且具有士兵真人的大小,大約 2 公尺的高度。

用法解析

要達到「明確」原則應不可使用中式的英文,多使用主動語態及肯定語氣陳述,避免不必要的重覆等。第 2 句屬於錯誤的句子,因前半段有不必要的重覆,後半段有中式的英文,欠缺明確清楚,造成閱讀上的困擾。

分析 2.

例句 │ However, the dictatorial Emperor, to suppress opposition, ordered the burning of the books written by philosophers and the execution of the intellectual scholars.

例句 │ Likewise, the dictatorial Emperor, to suppress opposition, ordered the burning philosophers written by books and of the intellectual scholars the execution .

中譯

但是，這位獨裁的皇帝為了要鎮壓反對勢力，下令焚燒哲學家所著的書籍以及處死知識淵博的學者。

用法解析

要達到「邏輯」原則，文字字序要符合句構章法，並且要善用連貫詞彙，使前後文銜接合乎邏輯。否則文字將似是而非、含糊難懂。第 2 句中因前半段使用錯誤的連貫詞，後半段文字字序未符合句構章法的邏輯，因此是錯誤的用法。

Leader 042

英文文法的奧秘（附 MP3）

探索世界神秘事件，同步學習英文文法

作　　者	孟瑞秋
發 行 人	周瑞德
執行總監	齊心瑀
企劃編輯	饒美君
校　　對	編輯部
封面構成	高鍾琪

內頁構成	菩薩蠻數位文化有限公司
印　　製	大亞彩色印刷製版股份有限公司
初　　版	2016 年 04 月
定　　價	新台幣 380 元
出　　版	力得文化
電　　話	(02) 2351-2007
傳　　真	(02) 2351-0887
地　　址	100 台北市中正區福州街 1 號 10 樓之 2
E - m a i l	best.books.service@gmail.com
網　　址	www.bestbookstw.com

港澳地區總經銷	泛華發行代理有限公司
地　　　　址	香港新界將軍澳工業邨駿昌街 7 號 2 樓
電　　　　話	(852) 2798-2323
傳　　　　真	(852) 2796-5471

國家圖書館出版品預行編目資料

英文文法的奧秘 / 孟瑞秋作. -- 初版. -
臺北市 : 力得文化, 2016.04
　　面 ; 　公分. -- (Leader ; 42)
ISBN 978-986-92856-1-2(平裝附光碟片)
1.英語 2.語法

805.16　　　　　　　　　　105003627